PRAISE FOR

THE BOY WHO SHOOTS CROWS

"Randall Silvis . . . presents a mystery so beautifully written and with characters so alive that the mystery itself becomes immaterial. Read it just for the prose."

—Thomas Lipinski, author of Shamus Award–winner *Death in the Steel City*

"*The Boy Who Shoots Crows* is a real stunner. I lost an entire afternoon rushing through the final half, because I had to know—had to know—how it ended. From the opening lines, every sentence is infused with an uncanny sense of dread. With each page turn, Randall Silvis peels away yet another layer of his characters' hidden hearts, and as he does, that sense of dread grows overwhelming. Because you become certain that you know what's going to happen next. And pray that you're wrong."

—Grant Jerkins, author of *A Very Simple Crime*

"In *The Boy Who Shoots Crows*, Randall Silvis populates a small Pennsylvania town with richly drawn characters, chief among them Marcus Gatesman, a sheriff searching for a missing twelve-year-old boy, and Charlotte Dunleavy, a painter haunted by the boy's disappearance and by her own dark history. Silvis writes with an artist's eye for detail, and his story is expertly plotted, traveling along unexpected paths on the way to its devastating conclusion."

—Harry Dolan, author of *Bad Things Happen* and *Very Bad Men*

PRAISE FOR RANDALL SILVIS AND HIS NOVELS

"Randall Silvis has a well-deserved reputation as a writer of stylish crime fiction . . . [In *Disquiet Heart*], Silvis's sly symbolism, intellectual play, and literary allusions make this novel an appropriate portrait of the twin-souled, enigmatic man whose detective stories have shown us both the dark motives of the soul and the power of reason to penetrate its mysteries."

—*Pittsburgh Post-Gazette*

"Silvis gives readers a page-turning story." —*New York Post*

continued . . .

"[A] wordsmith extraordinaire." —*Booklist*

"Randall Silvis is such a good writer, both for his prose and for what he doesn't do—turn relationships into predictable scenarios."

—*The Philadelphia Inquirer*

"The story line is riveting—complex, convoluted, and compelling; Silvis engages the reader from first word to last. I couldn't put this novel down."

—*Los Angeles Reader*

"There's genius in this book. The writing is like a melding of J. P. Donleavy and Lawrence Durrell. Silvis is reaching way out there . . . more innovative than ever, and expressing a depth of thought way beyond the reach of most modern writers. He may be the last of a dying species, the creative genius."

—William Allen, author of *Starkweather* and *The Fire in the Birdbath and Other Disturbances*

"This beautiful, melancholy novella from Silvis unfolds as a timeless Central American seaside fable . . . A masterful storyteller, Silvis doesn't waste a word in this tale about 'the tart nectar of memory's flower.'"

—*Publishers Weekly*

"My first encounter with Randall Silvis . . . left me literally spellbound . . . Silvis has a voice of his own, and what a wonderful voice! . . . I can't recommend this book enough, an exceptional reading experience for anyone who loves solid and seductive storytelling, elegant but profound writing style, and most of all the ability to disclose the lyricism hidden behind the apparent triviality of human existence." —*The New Review*

THE BOY WHO SHOOTS CROWS

Randall Silvis

BERKLEY PRIME CRIME, NEW YORK

THE BERKLEY PUBLISHING GROUP
Published by the Penguin Group
Penguin Group (USA) Inc.
375 Hudson Street, New York, New York 10014, USA
Penguin Group (Canada), 90 Eglinton Avenue East, Suite 700, Toronto, Ontario M4P 2Y3, Canada
(a division of Pearson Penguin Canada Inc.)
Penguin Books Ltd., 80 Strand, London WC2R 0RL, England
Penguin Group Ireland, 25 St. Stephen's Green, Dublin 2, Ireland (a division of Penguin Books Ltd.)
Penguin Group (Australia), 250 Camberwell Road, Camberwell, Victoria 3124, Australia
(a division of Pearson Australia Group Pty. Ltd.)
Penguin Books India Pvt. Ltd., 11 Community Centre, Panchsheel Park, New Delhi—110 017, India
Penguin Group (NZ), 67 Apollo Drive, Rosedale, Auckland 0632, New Zealand
(a division of Pearson New Zealand Ltd.)
Penguin Books (South Africa) (Pty.) Ltd., 24 Sturdee Avenue, Rosebank, Johannesburg 2196,
South Africa

Penguin Books Ltd., Registered Offices: 80 Strand, London WC2R 0RL, England

This book is an original publication of The Berkley Publishing Group.

Cover photography by Shutterstock. Cover design by George Long.
Interior text design by Tiffany Estreicher.

PRINTING HISTORY
Berkley Prime Crime trade paperback edition / December 2011

Library of Congress Cataloging-in-Publication Data

Silvis, Randall, 1950–
The boy who shoots crows / Randall Silvis.—1st ed.
p. cm.
ISBN 978-0-425-24346-6
1. Missing persons—Fiction. 2. Pennsylvania—Fiction. I. Title.
PS3569.I47235B69 2011
813'.54—dc22

2011011691

PRINTED IN THE UNITED STATES OF AMERICA

10 9 8 7 6 5 4 3 2 1

For my sons,
Bret and Nathan

With gratitude to Emily Rapoport and Peter Rubie for their insights and patience. A special thank-you to Jonathan Westover, whose early enthusiasm for this story sustained my own faith in it and in my ability to tell it.

1

THE knock on her front door was startling despite its relative softness—three muffled thumps coming from at least thirty-six feet away, into the small foyer, around the corner and through the dining room, and finally all the way through the kitchen to the northern bay window where she sat at the pine table, occasionally jotting a word or two onto a notepad but mostly just gazing out at the pond off the far edge of her property. Just a moment before the knock, as she studied the way the mist hung over the water and diffused the shadows cast by the first slant of morning sun, she had whispered aloud, "Sfumato," imagining the scene as her own painting, rendered with da Vinci's famous technique applied to soften the tangerine glow and blur all edges. Other than that word, she could recall no human voice in her house for a full day or more, and even then it would have been her own. But now, at not quite seven in the morning, there was somebody standing on her front porch, waiting at the door. The sound that person had made, the knock, seemed heavy and dark and swaddled in mist, the kind of sound a lead weight would make if dropped three times onto a pillow. She wondered if she should sit very still and make no sound, or rise and go to the door. How could a visitor at this hour be a welcome interruption?

2

SHERIFF Marcus Gatesman wondered if he should knock a second time, louder, or if he should assume that the woman who lived here was still asleep. But who slept with the front door standing open these days—with only a flimsy screen door, unlatched, between her and a violent world—especially on a cool morning so early in April? Even here in the softly folded hills of Pennsylvania, in the small towns and mostly Amish farmlands, there was no shortage of cruelty and violence. From the porch he could gaze in any direction and name a violence that had been perpetrated there. Some of it, the worst of it, he had experienced firsthand.

The morning was still chilly, though the day promised to be unseasonably warm. In the distance beyond the highway, a line of blue hills was rising to the sky, seeming to grow minute by minute out of the evanescing fog. "The Tuscarora Mountains," he said aloud. It was comforting to be able to name things.

Off to his right, just a hundred yards or so across the stubbly cornfield, crows were cawing from the trees, a tentative chorus of four or five. They would sit in the treetops awhile longer, he knew, drying their wings, then they would fly off to scavenge the countryside. It would not take them long to find a small animal or two along the highway, a road-killed rabbit or raccoon or opossum or squirrel. Dead things were always plentiful here, the detritus of every night—groundhogs and stray cats, somebody's dog, sometimes a white-tailed deer or two. Even in winter there was never any shortage of carrion to keep the crows fed.

He faced the door again. This unpleasant business of the morning as well as half of yesterday had engendered in him a deliberateness of movement even greater than usual. It was at times such as this that he felt unsuited for his job. He had not anticipated so much sadness.

He knocked a second time, only slightly louder, and followed it by calling through the screen, into the foyer not yet illuminated by southern light, "Hello? Mrs. Dunleavy? Anybody home this morning?"

3

HEARING her name spoken aloud, misspoken in the usual way with the long *e* sound of the second syllable, and with the objectionable *Mrs.* as prefix, would have startled Charlotte even more had the unfamiliar voice been more demanding. But it conveyed a warmth and gentleness that sounded like an apology. She felt, for some reason this morning, particularly receptive to gentleness. Yesterday had struck her like one long migraine, her first since moving to Pennsylvania, and in its aftermath her spirit felt restless, unfocused, as if, like a small ship after a daylong storm, she had been torn from her moorings and was uncertain of the waters through which she now drifted.

She stood and walked back through the kitchen and into the relative dimness of the foyer. A man she had never seen before was standing on her porch, hands cupped around his eyes and pressed to the screen door as he peered inside. The yard behind him was filled with light, and for just a moment she paused with the sudden recognition of the scene's possibilities. Its impact would depend on how she painted the figure of the stranger. The light behind him could either contrast or accompany his intentions.

"There you are," he said, and lowered his hands. He smiled. "I hope I'm not disturbing you."

She saw the uniform only peripherally, the beige jacket and trousers. His face filled the foreground, such a shockingly familiar face that she experienced a second soft jolt of disorientation.

He kept smiling, though he was caught more than a little off guard by the sight of her, the nicely tight blue jeans, the loose yellow shirt hanging over the jeans. She was barefoot and wore no makeup, and her eyes held a startled, almost frightened look that made him immediately want to calm her.

"I caught you in the middle of something, didn't I?" He concentrated on keeping his voice soft. "I apologize for interrupting you like this."

"No, no I just . . . You're the spitting image of James Dickey," she said.

"Ma'am?"

"James Dickey. The writer. You look just like him."

"I guess I don't know who that is," he said.

She moved a step closer and stared at him through the screen. St. Mark's Cathedral, she thought. *To the White Sea*. She and June sitting near the center of the first row, enraptured by the man's stillness and the slow melodic flow of words that bespoke a greater sorrow than the words alone. Behind him the soft yellow lights of the sanctuary. The scents of incense and candle wax. The hovering darkness in the faraway ceiling.

And now here outside her door stood a police officer looking like Dickey's twin. The same broad forehead and soft face, the same thin strands of hair combed over a prominent skull. The same extra twenty pounds around his belly. All this man lacked was the vague Southern accent.

"I'm ashamed to say that I don't do much reading," Gatesman said.

She could only nod. It all felt just too strange to her, and on a day so new, yet already ripe with an odd imbalance.

"Imagine that," he said, and smiled again. "Me looking like a writer."

There was such a total lack of menace in his smile, not the slightest hint of threat, that Charlotte smiled too.

"The thing is," he continued, the note of apology still in his voice, "we've got a little boy who didn't show up at his house last night. So I'm just driving around and asking if anybody's seen him lately. He's about this tall," the man said, and held his hand level with his chest. "Twelve years old. He's got a thick mop of black hair, brown eyes, probably wearing jeans and boots."

"Jesse," Charlotte said. The name came out before she knew she was going to say it.

"You know the boy?"

"Well it's . . ." And then it happened again—the vague, almost distant nausea, the aura of scintillating light. She saw Gatesman as if he wore a softly burning veil of sunlight—the scotoma, June had called it, the aura that sometimes precedes a migraine and sometimes occurs independently of one.

"I can't really say that I know him," she said.

Gatesman waited, still smiling that patient, understanding smile.

The aura was fascinating but it hurt her eyes, so she took a step backward and averted her gaze, looked into the corner of the foyer. A spindly ficus in a ceramic planter. Stillness and shade.

She concentrated on breathing evenly, eyes half closed. With luck she could will the aura away.

"I've only seen him from a distance," she said. "A few times this past winter I saw him cutting across the field out there and going into the woods. Every time I've seen him he's been carrying a gun that looks bigger than he is."

A pause. She imagined that Gatesman nodded and continued to smile. He said, "Any chance we could get this screen door out from between us?"

When the screen door swung open, she turned away at the waist, raised a hand to block the sunlight. She kept her eyes on the stairway, third step from the bottom.

"I'm sorry," she said, because she had felt his reaction, the sudden pause when she turned away. She released a slow breath. "I had a monster of a migraine all day yesterday. I thought it was over but . . . apparently I'm still sensitive to light."

"I'm sorry, I didn't mean to—"

"No, no it's okay, I . . ." She lowered her hand. "How about if you come inside? The kitchen faces north. Very soft light. I'll be fine there."

"Let me get my shoes off," he said.

The screen door closed with the dullest of thuds. She thought any other man would have let it bang shut. She retreated another step before looking toward the door again. Gatesman was bent double just outside the screen, untying his shoes. The aura had all but dissipated, leaving only a few sparkles scattered over the yard.

"You really needn't do that," she told him.

"I don't want to track mud into your house. I feel bad enough getting it on your porch like I did."

Only then did she realize that the sparkles in the yard were real. "It rained last night, didn't it?" she said.

"All night. You didn't hear it?"

She did not answer. She had ceased trying to explain the altered reality brought on by a migraine, then the lingering sense of displacement, of being both inside and outside the body. The feeling lasted for days sometimes, was sometimes accompanied by a trembling sense of euphoria, a feeling of transcendence. She had created two of her favorite paintings in such a state.

For now she hazarded another look beyond Gatesman and saw that it was indeed a glistening morning. The grass and tree trunks shone with dampness, the light was soft and golden. A brown sedan sat directly under the big tulip poplar, the car's fenders and tires splashed with mud.

Unfortunately she felt no buoyancy of spirit this morning. Sometimes the migraine left in its wake a deep, unnameable sadness, a profound sense of loss made evident wherever she looked. Once, not long before the divorce, she had taken a jar of capers from the refrigerator, unscrewed the cap and found a layer of gray mold, and wept uncontrollably for most of the afternoon. Today she saw loss in the quality of the light. She saw tragedy in Gatesman's smile as again he swung open the screen door and this time stepped inside. His socks were either dark blue or black. She stared at them for a moment, trying to discern the color, then finally realized, as he brought his feet together and waited there for her to move, that he wore one of each, one sock dark blue, the other faded black, and instead of smiling, amused, she turned away, led him toward the kitchen, and asked, as her throat thickened with sadness, "How do you take your coffee?"

4

OVER the years Gatesman had learned that, as an interviewer, observation and silence were his most effective tools. Both activities suited his temperament.

Atop the small table by the window, on the eastern side, lay a notepad and pen and an empty mug with the white tab of tea bag stuck to the rim. He took the western seat and faced the rising sun. He could see a portion of the woods a hundred or so yards away, across the field that last year had been planted in feed corn for Mike Verner's Angus cattle. The sun was rising behind the woods, bleeding through the trees with a broken light, leaving some of the field in shadow, some of it streaked golden. In places, the low stubble looked as black as old sticks; in others, like bleached bone. The field, still wet, showed only smeared traces of the white lime that had been spread over the ground the previous afternoon. From within the trees, crows cawed.

Gatesman looked at the notepad, saw a list of upside-down

words. *Chorizo* was the first word, *andouille* the second. Some other language, he told himself, because neither word was familiar to him.

He turned a few degrees to the right. Charlotte was pouring water from a kettle into a blue enamel mug. A small white tab attached to a string hung alongside the handle. Gatesman thought, *I thought she said coffee.*

When she set the mug in front of him, he smelled the coffee and understood. She said, "If that's too weak, I can make a full pot instead. I have a French press, but it's quite a production."

He dunked the bag several times, waited for the brew to darken. Then said, "Maybe another bag?" He looked up at her and smiled. "I prefer mine the color of motor oil."

"Of course," she said, and turned away. A few moments later she lowered another coffee single into the cup.

He waited for her to sit, but she stood with her right hand resting on the edge of the table. Her nails were manicured but painted with a clear lacquer, her fingers long and, though no longer slender, as lovely a hand as he had seen in a while. Across the webbing of skin between finger and thumb was a small Band-Aid. She wore an identical one on the other hand. He felt a subtle weakness in his chest at the sight of those injuries, an unprofessional awkwardness he hurried to suppress. "You're a tea drinker?" he asked.

She nodded but he did not see it. When he looked up at her again he saw that she was staring at his upper arm, squinting slightly. She said, "I thought you were with the state police."

The patch sewn onto his sleeve said *Cumberland County* at the top, *Sheriff* at the bottom.

"You know what," he said, "I never introduced myself, did I? I'm sorry about that. I'm Mark Gatesman, the county sheriff."

She took a step away from him, stared into his face, blinked. "Your name is Mark?"

"Is that not okay?"

"That was my ex-husband's name."

"Whoops," he said. He nodded toward the vacant chair. "Any chance you'd care to sit down before you start swinging at me?"

She moved with the slowness of a much older woman, someone brittle, afraid of a fall. "You're going to have to forgive me," she said. "I'm more than a little out of it this morning. Are you familiar with migraines?"

"Only in theory."

"They always leave me feeling so spacey and . . . logy, you know? You know that word?"

He nodded. "My dad used to use it."

"That's where I got it too. It seems to have died out with their generation, though."

He sipped his coffee. It was black now and exuded a strong, rich scent, but the deep, acrid bite was missing. "So me having your ex-husband's name, on a day when you're already feeling not so good . . ."

She smiled now. She liked his unhurried way, the soft, gentle sadness in his eyes. "Quite a shock to the system," she said.

"Actually my name is Marcus. The last person to call me that, though, was my mother. And she's been gone a good while now."

"I'm sorry," she said.

"You're not going to hold it against me, are you? My name being the same, I mean."

"We'll see how it goes."

He grinned, then looked away from her face. Looked down at her hand again. He said, "You hurt both hands in the same place."

She looked down at her hands, one and then the other. "Blisters," she said. "Working in my garden a couple days ago. Anxious to start planting."

He said, "You turned the soil over by hand? Is it a big garden?"

"Not huge," she said. "Maybe ten by fifteen."

"That's a lot of dirt to turn by hand."

She nodded. "Sometimes I start things and then . . . don't know when to stop."

Again, that flutter of weakness in his chest. He slid his gaze to the notepad. The third word was *feta*. The fourth was *Nutella*.

He said, "It looks like I interrupted you in the middle of your grocery list."

"More of a wish list, actually. Things I can't buy around here."

"May I?" he said, and held out his hand. She shoved the pad toward him. He turned it right-side up and read through the list of eleven items.

He chuckled. "Half this stuff, I don't even know what it is. The sushi, though . . . I happen to love sushi."

"You don't."

"There's this place in Harrisburg. A couple of places, actually, but the best one is a block or two off the main drag. The best spicy tuna rolls I've ever had."

"God, how I miss spicy tuna rolls."

"It's not that far, you know. Forty-five, fifty minutes. An hour if you don't break the speed limit."

He smiled softly and slid the notepad back to her.

"In any case," he said. "I didn't mean to take up so much of your time. You said you've seen Jesse sometimes on his way into the woods? But you've never talked to him, is that right?"

"That's right," she said.

"Because I was just wondering," he said, "how is it then that you know his name?"

"Oh. Sure. Well . . . I've seen him out there on school days, you know. I mean at times when he should have been in school. So I asked about him once at the post office. Cindy told me . . . No, I think it might have been Rex. Yes, it was Rex who told me Jesse's name."

The sheriff nodded. "From what I hear, the boy plays hooky a lot. According to his mother, he spends a lot of time in those woods. You know why, don't you?"

"I've heard the gunshots. And I've seen the crows come flying out."

"As long as he sticks to crows and not people," he said. Then, a few moments later: "You didn't hear any gunshots yesterday, by any chance? Or this morning, even? Or see Jesse at all in the last, what, twenty-six hours or so?"

She sat very still, forehead wrinkled, eyes in a partial squint. Finally she said, "I could answer with more certainty about last week, or even last month. But yesterday . . ."

"Because of the migraine?"

"It just wipes things out. Most of the day is just a thick, black fog."

"I had a friend in high school, his mother used to get them. He said she'd lock herself in the bedroom with all the blinds drawn tight. The whole family had to whisper and tiptoe around until she came out of it."

"A sound, a touch, a single ray of light. Any movement whatsoever. It's like an explosion inside the head. It's excruciating."

"Do you get them frequently?"

"This was the first one in close to a year."

"What time did it hit you yesterday? First thing?"

"I think I remember . . . starting to work. Getting ready, I mean."

"Painting?" He knew that much about her, what everybody knew. Even before she had moved into the farmhouse last July, the news had spread, not only throughout Belinda, the small town just three miles west of the farmhouse, but all the way to Carlisle, the county seat approximately fifteen miles distant. A rich lady from New York City, not much over forty probably, not at all hard on the eyes. She had purchased the house and two acres with its garage and garden shed. Old Bert Simmons, now living with his middle son in Kansas City, had leased the barn and fields and all the rest of the three hundred acres to Mike Verner, owner of the neighboring farm.

It had been Mike who, at the Fourth of July Volunteer Firemen's Picnic in Belinda's oak grove, had announced the newest citizen's arrival to Gatesman. "I suggest you buy yourself a treadmill," Verner had said. "Maybe get some hair plugs while you're at it."

"Who says I'm on the market?" Gatesman answered.

Verner, who had run interference for Gatesman during Belinda's three-year hold on the conference championship in the early eighties, jabbed him in the ribs and said, "You will be."

Less than a week later, Gatesman's secretary had shown up at their office in the Carlisle courthouse with an old copy of *New York Art Scene*. Tina, a former cheerleader for Belinda's conference rival, now a mother of five and as round as a pom-pom, tossed the magazine onto Gatesman's desk, the magazine folded open to a full-page photo of Charlotte Dunleavy. "She was married when that was taken," Tina informed him, "but she's a free agent now. From the looks of those legs, I'd say you've got about twenty minutes to stake your claim."

Gatesman had intended to answer with the same thing he said to her at least twice a week: How about you quit interfering in my personal life and pretend to get some work done for a change? Instead he found himself made mute by the photograph.

Tina said, "You know what you look like right now? You look like one of those hundred-and-fifty-pound linebackers trying to climb up outta the dirt after you knocked him for a loop."

"She's a good-looking woman," he had finally said. But it was more than that. It was that inexpressible something. That out-of-nowhere, for-no-reason-whatsoever fierce tug of longing. That indefinable hunger he had not felt since tenth grade, when the new girl, Patrice Moore, had walked into his homeroom. After Patrice's and little Chelsea's deaths, he had never expected to feel that need again, never wanted to. Then Tina showed him a photo in a magazine. And he resented the way it made him feel. He wanted nothing to do with such a feeling.

"So don't you think you oughta pay the lady a visit?" Tina had asked. "Welcome her to town and all that?"

He told her, "I don't get paid to be the welcome wagon."

Over the next nine months, the matchmaking attempts subsided to a halfhearted remark or two now and then—much less frequent than the number of times he remembered that photograph and the feeling it engendered. Such thoughts always came unbidden. But he had no desire to entertain a fantasy that, if indulged, could only end in grief, so whenever the airbrushed image of Charlotte Dunleavy came to mind, he immediately pushed it away by remembering that wonderful, aching fullness of Chelsea asleep on his chest, her tiny hands against the sides of his neck, or of Patrice curled against him, one leg thrown over his.

But now the woman who had been only a photograph, unreal and untouchable, sat across from him at a small pine table in a farmhouse kitchen. She suffered from migraines and had lovely, wounded hands. He could see in her eyes that her divorce or some other injury had left its mark on her too. She sat with her bare feet crossed at the ankle and tucked underneath the chair. Her chestnut hair was slightly mussed and looked as if she had not brushed it yet that day. She looked smaller and less perfect than the woman in the photograph, but unfortunately for him, Gatesman had become a man who was most touched by imperfection, most moved by the bruises and scars life left behind.

He said, "So you remember getting ready to start painting. And what time of day would this have been?"

"Well," she said, "by habit I'm an early riser. So it all depends on when I wake up. If it's still dark outside, I might run the vacuum for a while. The noise helps me to . . . I don't know how to explain it."

"To push everything else away," he said, "so that you can do what you have to do."

"Exactly," she said. "It helps me get my head empty, I guess. Get myself ready to paint."

The sheriff sipped his coffee. Then he said, "I fish."

She smiled and nodded but offered no other response.

"So you remember doing that yesterday morning?" he asked. "Vacuuming?"

"I do, yes. Then, when it started getting light out, I went into the study . . ." She nodded over her left shoulder toward a set of closed French doors. "It's the dining room, actually. Used to be. But it has the best light."

"I drove by last summer and saw the Hagan brothers doing some remodeling. They put in a punch-out and installed a bay window?"

"Not so much a bay window as a window bay. My light catcher."

"You mind if I have a look?"

"You'll have to open the curtains," she said. "I'll wait here."

The room was long and narrow, adjacent to the foyer but with the former access door walled off now. He felt for a light switch on the wall, found it, and turned on the recessed lighting. The hardwood floor was bare, as were the white walls. An eight-foot-long folding table stood against the right-hand wall. On it were jars containing brushes and water, tubes of paint, several photographs of people in Amish garb, a page torn from a magazine showing a customized Harley with extended forks, plus an assortment of painter's knives, sponges, a couple of magnifying glasses, and other tools. In the western corner stood an easel covered with a sheet. In the nearest corner, a Windsor chair and footstool, both covered in an oatmeal-colored fabric, and, beside them, atop a small bookcase holding several oversize books, a Bose CD player, and a CD holder.

He crossed to the punch-out, found the drawstring, and opened the curtains. The bay window was composed almost entirely of glass, a wide, tall center panel, and two narrower side panels. With the curtains open, the room was filled with morning light. He could see all of her front yard outside the window, plus that part of the cornfield and woods that bordered on Metcalf Road, the two-lane macadam in front of the house.

He said, "Would you mind if I take a peek at what you're working on?"

He waited a few moments, heard her slide out of her chair. Then she was at the threshold. She stood off to the side, one hand raised against the sunlight. "I haven't gotten very far with it," she said.

"If you'd rather I didn't . . ."

"It's all right," she said. "There's just not much to see."

He lifted the sheet away very carefully, took a few steps back, and considered the painting. Most of the scene was only sketched in, but the background of sky and the corner of a white Amish house were already roughed in. In the yard was a little girl in full Amish dress, the bonnet and blouse and long skirt, and she was pushing an old-fashioned rotary mower with its cylinder of whirring blades. She was just a tiny thing and had to bend forward as if walking into a heavy wind, putting all her weight against the mower. Her little brother stood a few steps behind her, whipping a sassafras stick through the air. In the foreground, coming down the highway in front of the yard, was an Amish buggy. A boy barely old enough to grow whiskers was at the reins, a young girl beside him, a toddler in her lap. Coming from the opposite direction, in the lower right foreground, was a grizzled old biker, scruffy-bearded and all leathered-up, astride his gleaming chopper. The Amish boy with the sassafras stick stood goggle-eyed in fascination of the biker, his free hand rising in a friendly wave, and the toddler was leaning out of his mother's lap so as to get a better look at the chromed-up roaring Harley. The painting wasn't even half-finished yet, but in the lines, Gatesman could see the fullness of a finished work, could see the colors and brushstrokes, could see one world greeting another in passing, the young couple bound to their time and place, the children spellbound, the grinning old biker with a continent of freedom between his sunburned hands.

He turned to the threshold to speak, but Charlotte was no longer there, so he looked at the painting a few moments longer, then carefully replaced the sheet, drew the curtains closed, and returned to the kitchen, where he found her seated at the table again.

He pulled the French doors closed and stood with his back to them. "It's amazing," he said.

"The Hagan brothers do good work."

"You know what I'm talking about," he said.

She smiled. "Thank you."

He returned to the table but did not sit. He picked up his coffee mug but only held it. "Did you actually see a scene like that? Or is it from your imagination?"

"I almost saw it. I drove past the house where the little girl was mowing and her little brother was whipping a stick through the air. Then later, closer to town, I passed the buggy. Later that night I was sitting on the porch swing, just thinking about how I might paint the scene, when a lone biker came roaring past the house. And all of a sudden the pieces just fit together perfectly for me."

"Amazing," he said again. "My wife was very creative. Music, poetry, everything. The whole process has always been a mystery to me."

Charlotte said, "Cindy at the post office told me about your family. I'm very, very sorry."

He gazed out the window. Two small, black shadows sat side by side on a tree's highest branch. Then one of them shot up and out of the bare branches, became a pair of black wings. The other crow soon followed.

He said, "I like how the trees look this time of year, don't you? Just before the leaf buds burst open. You can always tell then that spring is here because the treetops all look red."

"You sound a little bit like an artist yourself."

"Not me," he said. "I'm about as imaginative as a stone." Before she could reply, he said, "Listen, I just need a little more information. I'm sorry. You probably want to get in there and get to work."

"Not this morning," she said. "My head's not where it needs to be."

He nodded. "So, anyway. Do you recall seeing anybody else

around in the last day or so? Anybody who doesn't come around normally? A strange vehicle? Anything like that?"

She thought for a few moments. "The mailman usually comes by around noon every day. But what you're asking is . . . somebody unfamiliar. So, no. Nobody."

"Do you know what Jesse's father looks like? Denny Rankin?"

"As far as I know, I've never seen him. Nor the boy's mother, for that matter."

"Denny's maybe five-nine, fairly thin. Wiry, I guess you'd call it. He's got black hair like Jesse's, but he keeps it cut short most times. You didn't happen to see him out in the woods, or in the field, or just walking by, or anything like that?"

"I saw a man and a boy out at the pond late last summer. They were on the far side, fishing. That might have been them?"

"Probably not. Denny's more of the jittery type, not good for fishing. Anyway, I meant like yesterday or today. You didn't see him around here then?"

"No. Not a soul."

"How about Dylan Hayes?" he asked. "Have you seen him around?"

"The boy who works for Mike Verner?"

Gatesman smiled, said nothing, and waited. Having already spoken to Verner, he knew where Dylan Hayes had been yesterday, knew that Dylan and Charlotte Dunleavy were acquainted.

Perhaps ten seconds later, she said, "You know what? I think I did see him."

She thought for a moment, then told him, "I think he was out there on the tractor for a while yesterday. Most of the afternoon, in fact."

The sheriff nodded. "That's what Mike said too. Said the boy put in three hours spreading lime."

"That sounds about right."

"And as far as you know, he was out in the field that whole time? On the tractor, I mean?"

She became aware then of a subtle anxiety building inside her, a vague heaviness in her chest. Coming out of a migraine episode had always seemed to her similar to coming out of a period of intense fever marked by intermittent flashes of pain. She had no desire to dig around inside those dark hours for moments of lucidity, pieces to the sheriff's puzzle. In New York, during the settlement period with the lawyers, when the migraines were at their worst, she had talked about migraines with a female pharmacist, a mother of two who equated her own migraines with childbirth. "All I remember about being in labor was how unpleasant it was and how it seemed like it was never going to end. I have no desire to watch a video of it. You do it, you get through it, you forget it and get on with the good things again."

Charlotte wanted this conversation with the sheriff to be over. She did not dislike him; in fact, he seemed an easy man to like. She liked that he resembled James Dickey, that he seemed trustworthy and sincere. Still, she wanted him to leave. Every breath made her chest ache.

"I think he got off the tractor once and went into the woods," she said.

"And when would that have been?"

"I was inside at the kitchen window, I think. Washing a few dishes. Teacup . . . spoon . . . the saucer I had my muffin on that morning."

"So it was still morning?"

"No . . . later. Early or midafternoon, I think."

"So you were up and around by then? It wasn't the kind of migraine that kept you in bed all day?"

She sat there thinking, trying to see into the darkness. "I'm sorry, it's . . ."

"Take your time."

"What happens is . . . during a migraine and afterward, everything gets broken up and splintered. Time does, I mean. I have these little splinters of memory, but for all I know, they could be days, even weeks old. There's no . . . continuity? I'm sorry, I'm probably making no sense at all."

"Of course you are," he said. "And I apologize for putting you through this now. If it weren't for the little boy . . ."

"No, of course," she said. "I want to help." She turned her gaze out the window then, appeared to be staring at the pond more than a hundred yards away. Then her eyes closed, and she sat very still. Half a minute later she opened them.

"I was upstairs," she said. "In the spare bedroom on the eastern side of the house. The room was nicely dim, so the sun must have been at least overhead if not farther along. Otherwise I wouldn't have been able to look out the window."

"But you did?"

"I had been sleeping, I think. It's the darkest room in the house in the afternoon. And the rumbling of the tractor intruded, I guess, and woke me. I went to the window and peeked out. Dylan was out there on the tractor. The lime was spraying out in an arc behind that machine he pulled . . ."

"The spreader."

She nodded. "And the way it looked in the sun . . . that lime flying out. It was like white fire." She looked up at the sheriff and smiled. "I remember thinking it all looked like a dragon walking backward and spraying fire over the field. It was beautiful."

"You're right on the money about the time," he said. "Dylan was in school until noon. By the time he got the tractor out and over here, it would have been nearly one. It was maybe a quarter to four when he got the tractor back to Mike's. So you're doing fine here, Charlotte. Is that okay, if I call you Charlotte?"

"Of course," she said.

He was having trouble keeping his eyes off her face or even her hands. Her mouth was lovely and soft, and her eyes, when they looked at him, seemed to be asking for help of some kind, asking for kindness. The fingers of her right hand rubbed lightly over the nails of her left hand, and he caught himself wondering how it would feel to enclose those hands in his.

He realized that he was still holding the coffee mug, so he set it atop the table and took a half step toward her but turned his body so that he was looking straight out the window. He focused his gaze on the wide space between the barn to the right and, much nearer, the garden shed to the left. Her property ended just thirty yards or so beyond the clotheslines, and there the L-shaped cornfield continued all the way over to Mike Verner's soybeans, not even sprouts yet, just an expanse of flat brown soil soaking up the sunlight.

Gatesman said, "And you think Dylan got off the tractor once and went into the woods?"

Several moments passed before she answered. "Yes," she said, remembering. "He was driving right alongside the woods then. Then he stopped . . . he got off . . . and he went into the woods."

"How did . . ." Gatesman searched for the right words. "Did he jump off the tractor and go running into the woods like maybe he'd seen something surprising? Or did he just go strolling in? Or what?"

"He just climbed down and . . . jogged, I think. It was sort of a jog."

"How long would you guess he was in there?"

She continued to stare at the pond. A clump of cattails along the shore. A flash of red. "Red-winged blackbird," she said aloud.

Gatesman said, "Excuse me?"

"No, nothing, I was . . ." She looked down at the notepad, tapped her finger against the edge. She said, "Forty minutes or so?"

"Really? He was in the woods that long?"

"You said 'guess.' And that's my guess."

"And you're basing that on . . . ?"

"Just how it feels now when I think back on it. It feels like a half hour or so before I heard the tractor start up again."

"So he shut the tractor off before he went into the woods?"

"I . . . guess he must have, if I remember hearing it start up again."

"And you were at the window all this time?"

"I was back on the bed."

"When you heard it start up again, did you happen to look at a clock or anything like that?"

"No. I was just lying there on the bed, had my eyes closed, everything was very quiet. And then that growl again."

Twenty seconds passed. "Well, I guess that's all, then," he said. "I'm sorry I took up so much of your time."

She looked up at him. "I haven't been of any help at all, have I?"

Her eyes . . . He knew how dangerous it was to look at them. Doe eyes, he thought. A soft, dark brown. There seemed to be a plaintiveness in those eyes, but he wondered if he was misreading them, misinterpreting because of the weakness in his chest. He said, "You did just fine. I'll go have a talk with Dylan, see what he has to say for himself, and we'll take it from there."

"I can't imagine that Dylan would have done anything to hurt the boy."

"I'm sure he didn't. Still . . . it's my job to cover all the bases."

"Of course," she said.

The sheriff stretched out his hand to her. "I'm glad to finally meet you. I've heard a lot about you."

"I bet you have."

"Nothing like that," he said. "The painter lady from New York City, that kind of thing."

"Your eyes get narrow when you lie," she told him.

He grinned and self-consciously withdrew his hand. "It's just people talking, is all. Trying to figure out why a woman like you would want to live all alone in the middle of nowhere."

"Cindy at the post office said she heard I was in the witness protection program."

"The one I like is that you're hiding from the Russian mafia. What for, nobody knows."

"Running from a bad marriage is more like it."

"Yes, well, I guess that's too common a thing to get anybody's interest up."

"I guess so."

He offered another smile. She thought this one appeared even shier than the others. She asked, "So what are your thoughts on where Jesse is? You think he's still, you know . . . out there in the woods?"

"His mother went all through there yesterday afternoon, about five, five-thirty, she said. I'm surprised you didn't hear her calling out to him."

"You know," said Charlotte, "I thought it was just a dream I had. I heard crows and . . . a woman's voice . . . sort of all mixed together. But it was raining by then, wasn't it? I seem to remember the rain."

"It rained hard for a while in the late afternoon. Then we got a break until close to midnight. I went through the woods myself, after Livvie called me."

"There was no sign of him?" she asked.

"It was already dark by the time I went through. Dark and wet. My flashlight didn't do a lot of good."

"What about old wells of some kind?"

"I called Old Man Simmons out in Kansas about that. He says no. There was a gas well once, but it got capped with concrete long ago. Wouldn't have been big enough to fall into anyway."

Charlotte said, "Poor child. I hope he's not still out there."

"My gut tells me he's not."

"Is your gut usually right?"

He shrugged. "All we know for sure is that he didn't go to school yesterday, wasn't home when his mother got back in the afternoon, and he still hasn't come home. The shotgun and an old coat he likes to wear are missing too. We're still trying to track down his father, who's been known to show up unannounced from time to time. My guess is the two of them are off somewhere together."

"And what if they're not?"

"In that case I suspect the boy will show up on his own as soon as he gets hungry enough. Meantime, I'm just trying to cover all the bases."

Charlotte let a few moments pass. "I'll pray you find him soon."

"Me too," he said.

He stood there smiling as if he wanted to say something more but couldn't remember what it was. Then he reached inside his jacket, pulled out some business cards, peeled one off, and put the rest away again. Then he dug into three other pockets before coming up with a pen.

As he wrote on the card, he said, "This number on here is my direct line at the office. You call me if you think of anything else, anybody you might have seen hanging around, an unfamiliar vehicle, anything like that. I usually head home at six or so, so after that . . ." Now he held the card out to her, laid a fingertip beneath the fresh ink. "This is my cell phone. If you call the office after I've gone home for the day, the message will tell you to press one to talk to the officer on duty. But if you stay on the line, you'll get my voice mail, and I won't get the message till next morning. So if it's something I need to know right away, call me on my cell. I live just on the other side of Belinda, so I can easily be here in ten minutes or so."

She sat there staring at the card. An awkwardness had come between them in the last few moments. She wanted him to leave, but only because she wanted him to stay.

He said, "If you happen to see the boy, though—even if you just think it's him—you call 9-1-1 first thing, and they'll alert the officer on duty to send out a car. Do that first. We always have a car down in this area, and I might be somewhere without any cell phone service and, well, you know. I wouldn't want any opportunities to be missed."

She kept staring at his business card. For some reason she was finding it impossible to lift her eyes to him.

"Okay, then," he finally said. "You have a good day now."

She raised her head just in time to see him reach up to touch the brim of his cap. But he felt nothing there, then patted his thinning hair. He looked toward the table.

She said, "You weren't wearing a hat when you came in."

A blush rose into his cheeks. "Left it in the car, I guess."

He turned and walked away quickly, not looking back. She knew she should get up and walk him to the door, but she did not have the strength for it. Then suddenly he was at the threshold again, looking in at her.

"As long as I'm here," he said, "you mind if I take a look around a bit? See if maybe he got into your shed or barn or something?"

He had startled her again, and when she heard her own voice now she thought it sounded small and tight. "That's a good idea."

"Any of the buildings locked?"

"No. Just pull open the doors."

He smiled. "I promise not to disturb anything."

"There's nothing to disturb," she said. "By the way, the barn isn't mine. Just the garage and shed."

Again he smiled, then he turned and was gone.

She remained at the table, waiting, feeling strangely breathless. She listened but heard almost nothing of his departure. She told herself, *He's putting his shoes on now.* Then, *He's going down off the porch.*

It seemed a long time before he appeared in the backyard. He must have looked in the garage, she told herself. Nothing in there but the Jeep.

Eventually, he came around the far side of the house, looked back toward the kitchen window and, smiling sheepishly, reached up to give the brim of his cap a little tug. Then he turned and crossed quickly to the garden shed. He pulled the door open and stood there, looking inside. After a minute or so, he stepped back and shut the door and headed for the barn. Along the way, he glanced down into the rusty metal barrel where Charlotte burned her trash. She inhaled a sudden scent, or imagined she did, of smoke and ash. Then the sheriff continued up the slope to the barn's wide front door. The door slid open, he stepped inside, and he disappeared into the darkness.

She remained a long time at the window, waiting for him to emerge. She was aware of a bruised feeling deep in her chest, the weight of every breath, and she hoped the feeling did not signal a return of the old fearfulness, that paralyzing anxiety that, after she had walked out on her husband, had kept her secluded in a hotel room for most of two weeks, dangling between hysteria and numbness. She thought about calling June, the therapist who had eventually brought Charlotte back to herself, got her painting again, helped her to fashion a new determination. But it was too early in the day to call June, even though she had ceased to be Charlotte's therapist and was now a trusted friend. June would be at her breakfast table now, the twin girls off to their private school, June and Elliot enjoying an unhurried hour before their workdays began. Charlotte was determined to not intrude upon that hour.

She stood by the table, felt herself sway unsteadily, held to the rounded edge. There was too much brightness coming off the window now, a glare off the notepad. She turned and pushed herself away and, with four long strides, made her way into the studio.

The curtains over the window glowed softly with the southern light, but otherwise the room was soothingly dim. She closed the door behind her and went to the chair in the corner and sat. She concentrated on regulating her breaths—slowly in, slowly out.

The sheet draped over the easel seemed to be capturing all of the filtered sunlight that entered the room. And the longer Charlotte stared at it, the more there seemed an ominous quality to the shape the sheet held, its headless triangularity, the motionless folds. It seemed to Charlotte like a kind of dead smoke, unhealthy and cold. It was at that moment that she lost all desire to finish the painting underneath the sheet, saw all of her previous work, her decades of obsession with color and light, as trivial and selfish. It was at that moment that she started to be afraid of the unfinished painting. It was at that moment, she would tell herself later, that she started to be afraid of almost everything.

5

GATESMAN wanted to keep his mind on the morning's duties, but his thoughts kept returning to Charlotte Dunleavy. Even as he stood gazing into the cobwebby emptiness of her garden shed, he was remembering his first glimpse of her. She had emerged silently from the shadows of the little foyer, and the moment her face came into the light, he had felt a kind of soft blow inside his chest, as if somebody or something had rapped its knuckles on his heart. And it was all because of her eyes and her hands. She was pretty, yes, and in a way few women in his county remained after their teens. Local women, even the beautiful ones, usually developed a veneer of hardness by the age of thirty or so, a cynicism that brittled their femininity. But Charlotte's beauty was still soft and womanly, and her eyes were the evidence of this. The eyes of someone who could still be startled, impressed, have her breath stolen by a sudden flash of beauty.

And the delicacy of her hands. When the sunlight fell on them, the fine golden hairs at her wrist . . .

He pulled away from the thought. Closed the shed door and strode purposefully toward the barn. A glance into the burn barrel along the way. It was a third full of ashes, just like his own, just like everybody else's. *Keep your eyes open*, he told himself. *Focus.*

The barn door swung open easily, so well balanced that the considerable weight of the left-hand panel, eight feet wide and twelve high, felt negligible in his hand. A metal stake stopped its swing not quite parallel to the exterior wall. Not far from the stake lay a cement block, which he slid in front of the door to hold it open.

He paused on the threshold. A flutter of wings in the rafters. The warm scent of hay, a thick scent of dust and enclosure, a cavernous space. Thin shafts of light thick with dancing motes, tiny planets rising and falling in brief, unpredictable orbits.

A few farming implements hung from hooks along the front wall, probably left over from Old Bert's days. The plank floor was empty all the way back to the loft, though scarred and scored with the movements of eighty-odd years, dotted with a few splatters of pigeon droppings. Gatesman leaned down close to the floor, turned his head this way and that in search of footprints but saw none, only a few stray straws of hay here and there. He knew from previous conversations with Mike Verner that Mike sometimes had to make work for Dylan, find simple tasks, like sweeping out a barn, to keep the boy busy. Mike was known throughout the county for the tidiness of his farm, the impeccable state in which he maintained all of his equipment, a fastidiousness Mike was always quick to blame on Claudia, his wife.

"She makes me wash up and brush my teeth before I'm allowed to open the refrigerator," he liked to joke.

Gatesman brought himself back to the matter at hand. No dusty footprints crossing the floor. So much for the theory that Jesse fell down the feed shoot into the stalls, he told himself. It had happened to Gatesman when he was a boy, ten years old and playing barn basketball with a couple of friends, running around heedlessly. Straight down through the feed shoot he had dropped, whacking his head on the edge. He had lain unconscious on the mucked-up floor until awakened by his friend's mother flicking water in his face.

But not here, not Jesse. Even so, Gatesman told himself, you're here so just keep looking, don't be sloppy about it.

He crossed to the ladder and hauled himself up into the loft. Warm currents of air rose off the hay. The dust made his eyes itch. He gazed from wall to wall across the stacked rows of rectangular bales. Nearest the loft window, bales were missing from three of the rows, those bales nearest the window and easiest for Dylan to reach the last time he had tossed bales down to Mike's wagon. But there was no sign that Jesse had climbed into the loft, no sign that he had built himself a little cave of hay to keep himself warm through the night.

Anyway, you had to look, Gatesman thought. There had been the Rose boy, what, maybe ten or eleven years ago come summer? Built himself a little cubbyhole in the loft while his daddy and two brothers were stacking hay in the barn, then climbed in, dragged a bale close to seal himself inside, and fell asleep. His daddy and brothers went off to eat lunch.

"Where's Ronnie?" Mrs. Rose had asked.

The oldest boy said, "Last I seen him he was pestering me

about taking him to a movie. I told him to shut up and get out of my way."

"Why do you always have to be so mean to him?" his mother asked. "Now he's gone off somewhere to pout."

"Let him pout," the boy said. "At least I won't be tripping over him all afternoon."

After lunch, the work resumed. Bales were stacked eight deep on top of the sleeping child. Impossible to believe that a boy could sleep through that, except that it had happened. They never would have found him till the next summer but for the mother's dream three days after the boy disappeared. She shook her husband, Walter, awake and told him, "He's in the hay." Walt Rose was a serious man who knew not to doubt his wife. He left his other sons to sleep, then single-handedly tossed two hundred bales of hay down onto the barn floor. By dawn, when he pulled the last one aside, the coroner was waiting in the kitchen.

But not this time, not for Jesse. Besides, the heat in the loft was getting to Gatesman. The air was both heavy and dry, sitting like sand in Gatesman's chest. He let himself down the ladder, returned outside, swung the door shut, and latched it. The exterior air was cool in comparison and soothing to his eyes. *You never could've made it as a farmer,* he told himself. He walked along the side of the barn, following the rutted wagon path to where it ended at the gate to a fenced-in pasture.

Everywhere he went, Gatesman carried with him the tragedies of his county. He was in his sixteenth year as sheriff, and ever since Patrice's and Chelsea's deaths in the September of his third year, he seemed to retain the miseries too vividly. People got married and had babies and won lotteries and fishing tournaments and got their grinning faces in the paper, but it was the car wrecks and house fires and bar knifings that stuck with him, the suicides and beatings, the pregnant young wife who fell over dead in her yard from an aneurysm, the Amish carpenter who raped his twelve-year-old daughter. Life's happy moments, he imagined, were of a lighter nature and tended to float away from him, pretty but momentary butterflies that soon caught an updraft and sailed away. The pain of life, on the other hand, clung to him ounce by ounce, incident by incident. When his wife and daughter rolled over an embankment on that wet, foggy night, he had weighed one hundred ninety-two pounds. Since then, he had gained an average of four pounds per year. Exercise didn't help and neither did diet, mainly because he practiced neither of them. By his calculations, he could hold his job another five years, another twenty pounds of accumulated misery, then retire to a mountain cabin with a moderate pension and a fighting chance of avoiding a heart attack before AARP started sending him recruitment letters.

At the rear of the barn, the lower level opened onto a fenced-in pasture of approximately fifteen acres. Gatesman stood against the plank fence and gazed across the high weeds to the other side and to the row of trees beyond. No cows had grazed in that pasture for several years, not since the auction a year before Old Bert packed up for Kansas City. Scattered among the weeds were spindly, top-heavy umbrellas of Queen Anne's lace and yellow splashes of wild mustard. Running through these weeds was a skinny, sinuous path, still fresh enough that the weeds, heavy from last night's rain, had not sprung back up to conceal it; but the path was so arbitrary and directionless, no clear aim to its weaving, circling convolutions, that it certainly had not been cut by a boy who, coming out of the trees, bored with waiting for something to shoot at, had wandered across the corn stubble to the fence, then had slipped between the flat boards to make his way to the open entrance at the back of the barn. More like a stray dog chasing a rabbit, Gatesman surmised, because of the quick darting and zigzagging movements a terrified rabbit would make. *And that's where the dog lost him and lay down to catch his breath,* Gatesman thought, *that trampled down spot up against the fence.*

Sometimes Gatesman could stand very still and listen to something he had never identified by name, a wordless intuition that told him, yes, there's something here, or no, look somewhere else. He tried it here, eyes half closed and losing focus, blurring the world. But in the warmth of the sun on his face, he smelled the warmth of Charlotte's kitchen, remembered the tiny canary of sunlight that rested on the top of her hand as it lay motionless atop the table.

Man, you better get your fucking head straight, he told himself, but he softly laughed because the feeling that warmed his chest was so pleasant and so rare. Through no intention of his own, he had always been very particular when it came to females. He could name only three in his life with whom he had felt a sudden, unexplainable connection. Two of them were gone, and since their departure, he had expected to feel such a pull on his soul never again. He did not really want the feeling now and wished he could postpone it until nightfall, but he had to admit that the vague breathlessness he felt, the quickening of his pulse, made him think of himself as a bear coming out of hibernation, dragged out of a long numbness by the first scent of spring.

Still, he had a job to do. *Look for the boy,* he told himself. *Even though you know he's not here, you need to at least have a thorough look.*

Gatesman lifted the latch to step inside the fence, took his time approaching the barn. No harm in allowing himself a moment to admire the last jewels of moisture clinging to the weeds like tiny glass balls, the scent of greenery still damp with morning.

Then he stood under the overhang, the cantilevered barn floor two feet above his head. He surveyed the cobwebs hanging from the beams and posts. *Too bad we can't send those off to some lab,* he thought. Have the memories extracted from them. Splice them all together into a little movie of what they saw.

Then he looked through the wide doorway framed in heavy beams, wide enough for the cows to come lumbering out two abreast. The floor was bare earth trampled hard, the air cooler, dimmer, but not as pleasantly scented as the pasture, the sour leathery smell of cowhide, the years of urine and dung. From the doorway, an open corridor ran to the front edge of the barn. On each side of that corridor were three rows of stalls lined up lengthwise to the barn, the rows separated by perpendicular corridors. Gatesman had never been inside this barn before, but he had seen enough of cow barns to know the basic setup, even though all of the milking equipment had been removed and sold off. The milking machines would have taken up the now-empty space at the front of the barn, the lines and hoses secured to the ceiling so that the octopus-armed suction rigs could be pulled down from their swivels into the stalls. A relatively small operation that, even had the Simmons boys wanted to keep it going, would not have survived much longer.

Gatesman walked through the door to the end of the central corridor, then slowly back and forth across the length of the barn, up and down the aisles. He glanced into each stall as he passed it, his head turning left to right and back again, eyes squinting in the meager light that bled in through the cracked and broken boards. Bare, dusty bulbs hung overhead, but the power for the barn had long ago been turned off because every stall but one was empty but for an occasional bit of windblown leaf or papery wasp's nest. In the stall in the northwestern corner were twelve bags of garden manure in a rectangular stack, four rows of three bags each. One of the bags on top had split open and spilled half its contents onto the floor. But no boy. No sign of a boy anywhere, no sign he had ever been here.

Back in the driveway again, hand on his car door, Gatesman wondered about going back up onto the porch and finally decided no. *No, you need to get your breath back first,* he thought, and climbed into the car and pulled the door shut. *You need to be smarter than that dog chasing a rabbit it couldn't catch.*

He started the car and backed out of the driveway, turned and drove toward Metcalf Road. At the end of her driveway, he sat staring straight ahead through the windshield. *You got to figure out if you even want to catch that rabbit,* he told himself.

The bushes were thick along the side of the road, tense and tangled but budding with new leaves, but the sunlight made the field of low scrub grass behind the bushes seem to glow, a backdrop of soft radiance, and miles beyond the scrub grass the Tuscarora Mountains, blue and rounded against a cobalt sky.

Christ, it's a beautiful morning, he thought. But then he remembered why he had come there that morning, and he turned left onto the macadam and drove away down the road.

6

WHEN Charlotte heard the car engine's low rumble, she stood and went to the window and pulled the blinds to the side. She stood there and watched the sheriff's car stop at the end of her driveway. It did not move for what seemed to her a very long time. Only when it finally swung left and disappeared down Metcalf Road did the heaviness in her chest begin to lift a little. Afterward she stood a long time at the window. Finally, she went out onto the porch and sat on the porch swing. She could not look straight into the sun-filled yard without squinting, though her headache was not as debilitating as she had implied. Because she did not want to think about the younger boy, she thought about Dylan Hayes and wondered what he would say when the sheriff questioned him. She wished she had not had to tell the sheriff about Dylan going into the woods yesterday. She liked the teenager but had sensed at their very first meeting that he was certainly capable of violence, that there was a tautness to him, the tension of a steel string pulled nearly tight enough to snap.

It had happened the previous summer, just weeks after she had moved in.

Dylan was out there with the harvester, she was sitting at the edge of her garden, pulling a few weeds probably, enjoying the sunshine. Out in the field, the old red Farmall belched black smoke and stalled. Dylan hammered and cursed at it for ten minutes or so, then came trudging across the field and introduced himself and asked to use her phone. Afterward, he and Charlotte sat on the front porch and drank lemonade until Mike Verner arrived. During that time, Dylan told her, at first a bit shyly in answer to her questions, then with increasing volubility, that he really wanted to be a studio musician, a guitar player in Muscle Shoals. But he was dating a girl named Reenie . . .

"Short for Irene?" Charlotte asked.

He thought about it for a few seconds, then said, "I don't think so."

Reenie, in his words, was "high maintenance." Besides the movies and fast-food dinners every Friday and Saturday night, she was insisting that she and Dylan get each other's names tattooed on their shoulders—at his expense, of course—as evidence of their abiding love until he could afford an engagement ring.

"But damn if I can get it through her head," he complained, "that two tattoos will cost me near as much as a diamond ring at Sears."

An hour later, after Mike Verner had arrived and got the old beast huffing and puffing out in the field again, with Dylan once again jouncing along at the wheel, Mike came over to the house to thank Charlotte for the use of her phone.

"The boy didn't cause you any problems, did he?" Mike asked.

"None whatsoever. What kind of problems were you anticipating?"

"I just wanted to make sure he was polite and all. Respectful. You know how kids can be."

"He was a perfect gentleman."

At that, Mike smiled. "Yes, well . . . as much as can be expected, I suppose."

She invited Mike to sit and have some lemonade, and soon, without much coaxing, she pulled a fuller explanation out of him. According to Mike, Dylan had a well-documented history of antiauthoritarian behavior. A handful of arrests as a minor for vandalism and destruction of private property, a regular routine of smart-mouthing and defying his teachers, of fistfights in the school corridors with other students—he harbored a particular animosity for the athletes—and a general attitude of contempt for the world at large.

"His father has just about wore himself out trying to beat some sense into the boy," Mike said. "And I mean that literally. He was at the end of his rope when he came and asked if maybe I could find something to keep Dylan busy. So last year we got him enrolled in the co-op program. To this day there are teachers who want to shake my hand every time they see me. In fact there's one who's even offered to sleep with me. A female teacher, mind you."

"You take her up on it yet?" Charlotte asked.

He grinned. "I left it up to my wife. She's still thinking it over." He finished off his lemonade then, thanked her for her hospitality, and headed on back to his own place.

Charlotte remembered that afternoon, remembered it all quite clearly, so much clearer and more real than even the past twenty-four hours. *Dylan has a history,* she told herself. *So you shouldn't feel bad about what you said. You told it the way you remember it, didn't you?*

She winced then, a cold shiver out of nowhere.

You should get a sweater, she told herself, but did not get up from the porch swing.

You should get yourself a cup of tea.

She thought of the younger boy then. Jesse. Did not want to think of him because it made her heart ache. All the sorrow in the world, all the tears. *If you stop too long to think about all the pain in the world, it will be too much,* she told herself. *It could turn a soul to stone.*

She tried instead to pull up a mental image of the painting under the sheet in her studio, but instead of the face of the little Amish boy, she saw Jesse's face. She saw Jesse sitting in the woods on a fallen log.

The previous winter she had seen Jesse close up, had stood within a foot or so of him. Why hadn't she told the sheriff that? Because it was months ago, she told herself, and counted back—April, March, February, January. Four months ago. Ancient history.

The trees had been bare then, the sky gray. A chilly morning, she remembered. It sent a chill through her even now.

Several times before that morning she had seen the boy going into or coming out of the woods. To her eyes he appeared the size of a ten-year-old, maybe four-and-a-half-feet tall, though it was difficult to be sure at that distance, but too young, she thought, to be out there alone, trudging across the far edge of the field, following the tree line before disappearing into the darkness of trunks and limbs. Too young to be carrying a shotgun that seemed as long as he was tall. It would be just after dawn, usually, while she was repositioning the easel so as to catch the coming light from the dining room's bay window. On a few other occasions she had spotted him at dusk, when she was busy with something or other outside, sweeping leaves off the back porch or splitting wood for the fireplace, or she would be washing dishes at the sink, or just standing by the window and sipping a glass of pinot grigio. Maybe a dozen times between the fall and the spring she had watched him entering or coming out of the woods.

But it was that very first time—that first jarring volley of gunshots, three blasts in rapid succession echoing across the field while the crows squawked and burst from the treetops—that made her begin to bristle at the sight of the boy, to always associate him with that thunderclap of violence, to birds in panicked flight.

She had put up with those jarring interruptions for a while, though each time they sounded she reacted as if her own house had been dynamited. Went rigid with the very first decibel to reach her, stood frozen while the paint dripped off her brush or down over a wrist. It always took her a while to get her breath back and to calm the thump of her heart, but even then when she tried to work it was as if her eyes had become unfocused, and she could not capture again the clarity of the vision of the image she intended to paint. The echo of the shotgun blasts seemed to lodge just behind her forehead in a tight, heavy cloud of darkness. It would be impossible to paint for the rest of the day, impossible to lose herself in the world she was coaxing from the canvas. The next morning and several thereafter would begin with a residue of that cloud inside her head, but when dawn came and then full sunlight, and the crows did not shriek in terror, only then would her body relax and the cloud dissipate. Only then could she work for a few hours without the outside world intruding.

Until one day something snapped in her. It was late January, she told herself. Maybe four in the afternoon. Overcast. Frigid. The sun had been nothing more than a dull ember barely showing through the gray.

She had been standing at the sink, washing a handful of baby carrots under a stream of cool water. The last of the ahi tuna steaks, a box of eight June had sent at Thanksgiving, had been thawed out and crusted with coarsely ground black pepper. Charlotte planned to braise the baby carrots and a few brussels sprouts in olive oil, then add a tablespoon of butter and caramelize them slightly. At the last minute, she would lay the tuna steak in a very hot skillet, sear each side for less than a minute, then enjoy her dinner in front of the TV while watching Gerard Butler as the Phantom of the Opera. But the sudden jolt of booms startled her so that she dropped the carrots into the sink. Half of them went down the garbage disposal. She felt the shotgun blasts coming off the window, three icy slaps out of nowhere, as if they had exploded only inches away and not a hundred yards distant in the woods. "Goddamn it!" she screamed at the window. Then she spun away from the sink without drying her hands or shutting off the water spewing from the tap and strode into the mudroom. She grabbed her heavy Woolrich jacket off the coatrack nailed to the wall, rammed her feet into her still-new Timberlands, and with the laces flapping and dragging, she marched outside and across the snowy field. She found the boy's footsteps at the far edge of the field and followed them into the trees, stomped on them, obliterated his boot marks with her own.

Twenty yards into the woods, he was standing over a bird whose feathers lay scattered across the white ground, a black splash, crooked winged. Like a Pollack painting, she told herself. The snow around the bird was speckled with blood.

"I suppose you're going to have that crow for supper now?" she said. Her voice was louder in the woods than she intended, as if her anger, coming out, suddenly expanded in the thin light.

He jerked his head around to look at her. "People don't eat crows," he said.

His voice was not loud, but she could hear the disdain in it. She had hoped to frighten and startle him as his gunshots had startled her, but his face showed no sign of fear. He knew who she was, she could see the recognition in his dark eyes. She was the rich city lady who had bought the old Simmons farm, the woman who did nothing all day but paint pictures and walk the narrow lanes and take photographs of crumbling foundations and wind-gnarled trees. She thought it obvious from the way the boy looked at her that he considered her the intruder here, the interloper. Those woods were his domain, not hers.

"If you don't eat them, why shoot them?" Charlotte demanded, her voice softer now, the anger slowly leaking away in the chill. "What are they hurting?"

He regarded her boots, the laces hanging loose and crusted with snow. Only then did she become aware that her socks were soaked through, the open boots filled with snow. Her toes burned with cold. And she had rushed out of the house without mittens or a cap. She cupped her hands together and blew on them.

The boy looked at her with sleepy eyes. His hooded gaze and small crooked smile made her aware of how ridiculous she looked, and with this recognition, she almost smiled too, almost conceded the foolishness of her actions. She had never thought of herself as an impulsive woman, had always thought things through, considered all the angles and probabilities. Now she could scarcely remember having exited the house or the brisk stiff march across the field. She felt more than a little embarrassed by this confrontation with a child. He was, she now had to admit, a strikingly handsome boy. Had he been thirty years older and a foot or so taller, he would have disarmed her utterly with those dark, sleepy eyes, the head full of lush, black hair, and a soft, full mouth with the hint of a sneer. Later that evening, in the notebook in which she gathered quick pencil sketches, half-formed ideas, and stray bits of description that might someday be rendered in strokes and dabs of color, she wrote, "Dermot Mulroney as a boy but with a glint of menace in his eyes instead of Dermot's sparkle of mischief."

The boy looked at her for a full ten seconds. Then he simply turned and walked away, retracing her footsteps out to the field.

"You're just going to leave it lying here like this?" she called.

He didn't answer.

"You're going to kill it and then just leave it out here to rot?"

"The other crows will eat it," he said without looking back. "Or you can."

Charlotte stood motionless, watching him go. She felt the anger still inside her but now in a deep and distant place. Closer to the surface was weariness and sorrow. *What makes a little boy want to kill things?* she wondered. *Where does such an urge come from? And then to just walk away as if the death of a living thing doesn't matter.* The thought saddened her, made her feel tired and old.

With the side of an unlaced boot, she scraped a pile of snow over the shiny black feathers. Then she regarded the mound of snow. She knew that it would accomplish nothing. A fox or raccoon or a stray dog or cat would sniff out the crow sooner or later, drag it home to its burrow, grind up the frozen muscle and hollow shattered bones. Yet what more could she do? She turned away and trudged back home.

A few minutes later, barefoot, fingers and toes and ears and the tip of her nose all burning, she came into the kitchen and saw the water still flowing from the tap. She shut it off, then leaned against the sink. Slipped her hands under her armpits, hugged herself tightly, rubbed one foot atop the other. She gazed out the window, stared across the no-longer-lovely emptiness outside. "Desecrated," she said aloud.

When she thought about that afternoon now, some four months later, she could not remember any more of that day. What had she done with the remaining hours? *What did I do with the tuna?* she wondered. *It was the last one. Did I eat it or not?*

7

AFTER leaving Charlotte Dunleavy's driveway, Gatesman turned west on Metcalf Road. As he drove, he telephoned the high school, informed Karen in the front office that he was on his way. Could she pull Dylan Hayes out of class and have him waiting in the conference room, please?

Karen said, "Hold on just a second, Mark. Let me check something."

Fifteen seconds later she spoke again. "Dylan's off on a field trip with Mr. Lewis's class. Science center in Harrisburg."

"All day?" Gatesman asked.

"I wouldn't expect them till way after dark. They're doing the science center, then, let's see, a nature film at the IMAX. Then dinner at a place called Nala's."

"Middle Eastern food," Gatesman told her.

"Sour grape leaves and crackery bread? Yeah, that's going to be a big hit with the kids."

"Might expand their horizons a little."

"What do you bet they stop at McDonald's after dinner?"

"I'd give it a fifty-fifty chance."

"I'd say it's a certainty." Then she asked, "Were you wanting to talk to Dylan about Jesse Rankin being gone?"

"Thanks for your help," he told her, and snapped his cell phone shut.

He slowed the vehicle to forty miles an hour. *All right, now what?* he asked himself. He had passed the Rankins' trailer less than a quarter-mile back, and though he could not think of anything concrete to be gained from speaking with Livvie again so soon, he felt compelled to do so. Whether for his own sake or hers, he did not know. At the next driveway, he pulled in and made the turn.

Except for the single-wides in the Sunset Springs retirement village out by the interstate, or the even older ones recycled to hunting and fishing camps throughout the county, Livvie and Denny Rankin's trailer was one of the last of its kind. He could think of no other family that actually lived in one of the long, narrow boxes. Even the unemployed dopers throughout the county had HUD double-wides. Denny and Livvie could have had one, too, if Denny weren't so stubborn and prideful. Livvie, too, Gatesman thought. She'd never take anything from anybody.

He pulled into the driveway and parked behind Livvie's battered Datsun. Still no sign of Denny's pickup truck.

Within seconds, Livvie had the door open and was standing on the threshold, looking out at him with red eyes as he approached. Eyes, he thought, both hopeful and fearful.

"Nothing yet," he told her. "I just came to talk a bit."

She stood aside, then closed the door behind him. "Nobody's seen him?" she asked.

"Not a soul."

"Where in the world can he be?"

There was such plaintiveness to her voice, such frailty to the way she carried herself, as if even the slightest movement ached, that Gatesman could not help himself; he took her hand and led her to the sofa, sat down next to her, patted the back of her hand twice, wanted to hold it longer but then finally let it go.

"How about if we go through it again," he said. "Everything you saw and did when you got home yesterday morning."

She sat hunched forward slightly, hands locked together atop her lap, fingers dovetailed. He noticed that she was wearing the same jeans and plain gray sweatshirt she had had on yesterday. Probably slept in it, he thought. Not enough energy to look after herself.

Her head made little jerking movements back and forth. She blinked, squinted at the floor with its pattern of green and red tiles, then looked up at him as if he had spoken in a forgotten language.

"Take your time," he told her. And he thought, *I know what you're feeling now. You can't breathe, can't get any air into your lungs. You can't keep a straight thought in your head. You haven't eaten anything all day, can't stomach the thought of food. You'd rather just die than feel this misery.*

"It must've been about a quarter after eight or close to it," she finally said. "That's when I always get home. Denny's truck was gone and I just figured . . . he put Jesse on the bus and then went off somewhere."

"And that's fairly typical?"

"It is," she said.

"But Denny didn't mention anything to you the night before?

He had a job somewhere or . . . whatever he had planned for the day?"

Her head moved back and forth, a barely perceptible answer.

"Has he had any work lately?"

"Three days last week. A big warehouse of some kind over in Carlisle. Fifty-two hundred square feet, he said."

"Must be well heated to seal concrete at this time of year."

She made no movement, offered no reply.

"And you have no idea where he is today? No phone call yet?"

"I haven't seen or heard from him since the day before yesterday."

Gatesman nodded. He looked into the little kitchen area. Everything was spick-and-span, not so much as a dirty coffee cup. He wondered how many dozens of times in the past twenty-four hours she had wiped off the counter and tabletop. How many times she had rearranged the soup cans in the cupboard. She could clean the place a hundred times but not remember to change her clothes or brush her hair.

Of course there was another reason for it too, he remembered that as well. You blame yourself for what has happened. You want nothing to do with yourself. Maybe you intend to punish yourself by showing your own body disrespect, by not feeding it or keeping it clean, not brushing your teeth. What you want is for your self and its goddamn consciousness to disappear.

Gatesman remembered it all. He had done laundry. Day after day after day. Patrice's and Chelsea's underclothes. First the whites, then the bright colors. Patrice's and Chelsea's socks. The shorts. The jeans. The cotton items. The synthetics. He ironed everything whether it was wrinkled or not. Folded the items and put them in the drawers. Everything done, he started again.

"So you came home from the generating plant," he said,

"about a quarter after eight that morning. And then what? What's the place look like when you get here? I'm sure it wasn't as clean and neat as it is now."

"Jesse's cereal bowl is all," she said. "On the kitchen table there. The bowl and the spoon. I washed things up and put them away. Then I went to bed to get a few hours' sleep."

"You didn't happen to take a quick look in Jesse's bedroom first, see if anything was out of place or, I don't know . . ."

"Not then," she said. "Why would I?"

"You wouldn't. There'd be no reason to. You thought he was at school."

"He keeps his door closed usually. I always told him it's his space and only his."

"That's something kids need, I think. Something everybody needs."

"Even after I got up," she told him, "it never occurred to me that something was wrong. I made myself a sandwich, drank a glass of milk. I was at Mrs. Shaner's place by 12:30. Finished up there and got back here in time to meet the bus."

"Which is usually around 3:10 or so."

"Give or take a few minutes either way."

"I know you already told me all this, Livvie. I just need to hear it all again."

"The bus didn't stop," she said. "Never even slowed down when it went by."

"Which has happened before, though."

"A few times, yes. She gets distracted or something, you know. Misses the stop."

"So you're thinking she'll let Jesse off down at the Conners'."

"And I go out and get in the car and drive on down, so he doesn't have to walk the whole way back. And that Nolan Conner, he's in the same homeroom as Jesse, when the bus starts pulling away I call out to Nolan before he gets into the house. And he tells me that Jesse wasn't at school all day. Lori stopped the bus out front, beeped the horn. Jesse never came out, so she just drove on by without him. So now I'm thinking, okay, he's playing some kind of game with me. He's back home hiding under the bed or something like that. Plus, he knows he's not supposed to be playing hooky anymore. He and I were both told that if he misses any more classes, he'll either have to go to summer school or they're going to hold him back."

"But when you get back to the house, that's when you find his backpack down between the bed and the wall in his room."

"And his lunch bag is inside it. Inside the backpack. So obviously he took it out of the fridge in the morning and put it in his backpack the way he always does. But then, I don't know. He must've just decided he wasn't going to school that day."

"And that's when you discover his father's old hunting jacket and the shotgun missing."

"That's the first thing I think, that he must be out in those woods again."

"Because nothing else of Denny's is missing, right? Nothing to indicate he's been here and gotten a few things and left with the boy?"

She said, "When Denny's been here and gone, I can always tell."

"How can you tell?"

"Because the place either smells like sealant or old beer. And if it's sealant, then his dirty clothes are piled up on top of the washer. And if it's beer, Jesse's lunch money is all gone from the cupboard where I keep it."

"But that wasn't the case yesterday."

"Denny wasn't here," she said.

"Maybe he just didn't come inside the house," Gatesman suggested. "Maybe he just pulled up out front and beeped the horn."

"I guess," she said.

"Because you walked those woods yesterday. And then so did I."

"But then why would Jesse take his hunting coat and the gun and those old clodhoppers he wears out there? That's the only other thing I can't find, those old cowboy boots he picked out at Walmart last year. The only place he wears those is out into the woods. Because when he wore them to school a couple of times, he just got made fun of."

Gatesman sat silent for a few moments. Then he asked, "But this wouldn't be the first time he and Denny took off together for a couple of days."

"No, but Jesse always leaves me a note if I'm not here. He always makes sure I know what's going on."

"And they've gone crow hunting in other places before, you said."

"All over," she said. "But I only ever find out exactly where they've been when Jesse comes home and tells me. And in those cases they're only gone for a couple or three hours. Not overnight like this."

"Okay," Gatesman said. "So it's not like this is something entirely new for them. The only difference here is that you didn't get a note this time."

"It feels different," she said.

"I'm sure it does." He patted her hand again, let his own hand linger for a moment, one finger tracing the ridge of her knuckles. He told her, "So what I'm thinking happened is this. Some time early yesterday morning, after Jesse had had his breakfast and packed his backpack, but before the bus came by, Denny showed up. Then he and Jesse just decided to go off somewhere and shoot themselves a few crows. Jesse got excited and forgot to write a note. And I'm betting they're going to show up in a day or two with a couple of big grins on their faces."

"The only problem with that," Livvie said, "is that every last stitch of Denny's clothes is still here. Everything except what he was wearing when I went off to the generating plant two nights ago. He was sitting right there, watching the TV, and I asked him why, after he got his shower, did he put his jeans and a clean shirt back on. Usually he just walks around in his underwear until he goes to bed. And I told him, you better not be going out anywhere after I leave for work. You better not go and leave that little boy here alone."

"And what did Denny say?"

"He said all he was doing was he was going to run over to Glenn Paulsen's and pick up an old barbecue grill Glenn was letting us have. Glenn's working the afternoon shift this week and wouldn't get home till a little after midnight."

"And you've spoken to Glenn about this?"

"Did you see a barbecue grill outside anywhere?"

Gatesman forced a smile. "That still doesn't rule out the probability that Jesse is off with his dad somewhere."

She shook her head. "Denny waited until I went to work, and then he took off for who knows where, and he hasn't been back here since. Jesse woke up in the morning, ate a bowl of cereal, packed his backpack, and then for some reason decided he was going to ditch school again. He put on his hunting coat and his boots and he at least started out for those woods up the road there. Whether he made it that far or not is another question."

"Maybe his dad came along at just the right time. Let's say

Jesse's still walking up along Metcalf, hasn't cut into the woods yet. Along comes his dad, says, 'Hey, buddy, hop in.' And off they go together. That's what I think happened."

Livvie sat huddled into herself, slowly rocking back and forth now. After a while she nodded her head. "I don't know. Maybe that is what happened."

Gatesman offered a smile. And thought to himself, *I need to talk to Dylan Hayes the minute he gets home.*

8

THERE were eight bars within a ten-mile radius of Belinda, exactly twice as many as there were churches. Gatesman's suspicion that the boy was with his father had been weakened by Livvie's logic, and he wasn't able to dismiss the unquantifiable veracity of a mother's intuition. Unfortunately it would be nightfall before Dylan Hayes could be questioned, so the sheriff thought it might be worthwhile to spend an hour or two piecing together a clearer picture of Denny Rankin's movements at the time of his son's disappearance. He knew little of Rankin's history prior to his and Livvie's arrival in Belinda some fourteen years ago, but during that time, twice as a deputy and once as sheriff, Gatesman's office had received paperwork from the magistrate's office—arrest orders bearing the name of Dennis Rankin. All three incidents in which Rankin had been charged with assault had involved alcohol, in Gatesman's opinion the world's most common lubricant to violence, especially when mixed with an equal measure of testosterone. In the first incident, Rankin had allegedly been "staring and grinning" at a college girl for a half hour or more at the Wayside Grill one Saturday night. When Rankin allegedly cupped "his groin area," the girl's boyfriend, who was half a foot taller than Rankin, suggested that Rankin "turn around and mind his own fucking business." Rankin turned on his bar stool and faced the mirror, but several minutes later, when the boyfriend left his table to visit the men's room, Rankin followed. What happened inside the men's room became a matter of dispute, since there were no other occupants at the time. Rankin denied the use of a hunting knife, and none was found on his person at the time of his arrest, nor could the one in his trailer be identified conclusively as the one allegedly pressed against the boy's anus as he stood at the urinal. So the magistrate had had no choice but to warn both participants of the future consequences of rutting behavior in public and to send them on their way.

The second incident had cost Rankin four hundred and eighty dollars, this time for slamming a Weber charcoal grill loaded with burgers and brats against a tree trunk in response to losing a game of horseshoes at the town's annual Labor Day picnic held in the oak grove. Rankin had been found guilty of public drunkenness and destruction of private property.

The third incident, the most serious of the three, involved the alleged attempt to steal an air compressor from a construction site just off Exit 201 of the Pennsylvania Turnpike. The night watchman, sixty-seven-year-old William Ladebu of Porters Sideling, just north of Hanover, had been awakened at three A.M. by the sounds of "scraping and banging" just outside the foreman's little trailer. Ladebu emerged with a baseball bat to see Rankin with the coil of rubber hose already looped over a shoulder and the four-hundred-pound compressor already pushed up against the padlocked cyclone fence where Rankin's pickup truck waited on the other side. Ladebu had the good sense to step back inside the construction trailer, lock the door, hit the switch to the floodlights, and call the police with a description of Rankin's truck. Ladebu later told the magistrate, "As far as I can figure, he must've thought he was going to hoist that compressor up over that fence all by hisself. But then when the lights hit him, he had a change of plans." Rankin's plea of not guilty was refuted by the fact that the twenty-five-foot length of compressor hose was located in the weeds only fifteen yards from where the state police came upon Rankin's pickup truck saddlebagged in a drainage ditch alongside Pennsylvania Route 419. During Rankin's twenty days of incarceration at the county jail in Carlisle, Sheriff Gatesman had made a point of visiting Rankin on four separate occasions, each time to remind him of his duties as a father and husband and to impress upon him the ephemeral nature of youth and the lasting effects of bad choices. In each case, Rankin had accepted the advice with a meek and sober contrition.

Through this experience Gatesman had come to know Rankin as a contradiction. He was, by all accounts, a very hard worker, whenever he worked. He claimed to love Livvie and little Jesse more than life itself, but Gatesman doubted that the man had ever displayed this tenderness or voiced the same sentiments to his wife and son. He was, according to those who knew him best, domineering with his family, but generous and forgiving toward his friends. When sober, he tended to respond to life's tribulations with a crooked smile. At all other times, he could be counted on to behave with belligerence, furtiveness, guile, malice, sabotage, explosive violence, or any combination thereof.

All this, and not much more, Gatesman knew about Denny Rankin. From this knowledge he had deduced that if Denny was not currently employed or with his family, he was in all probability in or near a beer-dispensing establishment. Gatesman gave some thought to the eight bars within a ten-mile radius of Belinda. He could not picture Denny Rankin paying five dollars for a microbrewed glass of beer, nor could he picture him bellied up to either the old Colonial Hotel's polished mahogany bar flecked with light from golden wall sconces or in the sanitized, too-bright, mojito-dispensing lounge at the Ramada. Any of the others, however, all shot-and-beer facilities where a man could quench his thirst without having to change out of his work clothes first, were likely candidates.

The bartenders in the first three, two females and a male, all knew Denny Rankin but claimed to have seen nothing of him in the past seventy-two hours. The fourth place, the one Gatesman had been hoping he wouldn't have to visit, was a squat cement-block building called the Mustang Bar, but known locally as the Harley Hilton because the wide dirt lot behind the building filled with hundreds of motorcycles every Wednesday night from late spring through September. A cardboard sign in the window read "Open 11:30 Daily," but now, at not quite nine in the morning, there was a silver Nissan Altima parked close against the side of the building, and when Gatesman tried the front door, it swung open onto a spacious, dimly lit room.

Gatesman stood in the doorway, surrounded by morning light as he surveyed the room. He finally located the owner, a thin, once-pretty woman named Bonnie, alone at one of the two booths overlooking the three pool tables. A newspaper lay spread out before her on the table, a mug of coffee near her right hand.

A push broom leaned against the corner of the nearest pool table, the blue plastic dustpan balanced on the edge of the table.

She had looked up from the newspaper but said nothing when the front door swung open and Gatesman stepped inside. Now she watched him find her in the empty room, watched a smile form on his mouth when he saw her smiling across the room at him. He crossed to her and sat facing her and clasped his hands atop the small table. She continued to look at him and smile. Finally he nodded toward the paper spread open before her and asked, "Any interesting news this morning?"

"There is," she told him. "Apparently hell has frozen over."

He reached out and put a hand atop hers and squeezed her fingers. Her hand was rough but warm. "How have you been, Bonnie?"

She turned her hand against his and returned the squeeze. "Older by a decade," she said. "And you?"

"Pretty much the same. But it hasn't been that long since I've seen you."

"Oh, you've seen me," she said, "and I've seen you seeing me. But this is the first time in ten years you've come close enough to say hello."

After a few seconds he withdrew his hand. His gaze shifted away from her momentarily, and when it returned, she saw that something had shifted in his eyes and that his smile had become tired at one corner.

"So this is a business call," she said. She sipped her coffee and watched him.

He asked, "Has Denny Rankin been in here lately?"

"What do you mean by lately? Past week or so?"

"Last night or the night before."

"Not to my knowledge," she said. "But I only spend my days

here now. Judy and Joanne will show up in about an hour. You want some coffee?"

"I'd love some, but no. I've got this little hypertension thing I need to watch out for. Who are Judy and Joanne?"

"My bartenders. Twins. Judy's a redhead and Joanne's a bottle-blonde."

"That should be good for business," he said.

"And I'll tell you what else. Those two can defuse an argument faster and with far less blood than a SWAT team. They've been working here not quite a year, and what a godsend they've been."

"I've always heard that women make the best bartenders."

"The best everything," she said. "Now about that blood pressure of yours. I was just reading in here about how important it is for men your age to have a good love life."

"Show me that," he said. "I'd like to read it."

She smiled. The steadiness of her gaze made him look away for a moment. "Ten years," she said. "I can still remember it like yesterday. Do you?"

He leaned away from the table and looked at the ceiling. "Tell you what," he said. "How about we don't go there right now, okay?"

"Not now or not ever?"

"Bonnie, please."

"So you're still not over it yet," she said.

"Are you?"

"I mean the guilt. That's the one thing I never felt. You still dragging that little red wagon around with you everywhere you go?"

"I've got a child turned up missing yesterday. That's what I need to concentrate on right now."

"Denny Rankin's little boy?"

"That's the one."

"Missing how?" she asked. "Like abducted?"

"Just not at home, that's all we know. I'm betting he's off with his dad somewhere. But Livvie's worried sick."

"How could she not be?" She slid to the edge of the booth, stood and looked down at him. "I'm going to throw some eggs and hash browns on the flat top." She collected the broom and dustpan and started toward the kitchen. "Judy and Joanne will know if he's been here or not. You want a glass of juice while you're waiting for the eggs? I've got orange and I think pineapple."

"All I need is some information, Bonnie."

She turned, came back to him, stood so close that the tip of the broomstick hovered only inches from his head. "What you need is to start taking care of yourself. You look like roadkill, you know that? It's been twelve years, Mark."

"I don't need anybody to remind me how long it's been." He heard the resentment in his voice then and pulled it back. "All I need to know is if Denny Rankin's been in here the last couple of nights or not."

"You *think* that's all you need to know." She turned and walked away then. "Scrambled wet with Swiss cheese and hot sauce, as I recall."

"Bonnie, for God's sake."

She turned hard and glared at him across a pool table. "Take a fucking breath once in a while, why don't you? I'm making scrambled eggs and hash browns and you're going to eat them, or else I'm going to hunt you down and cram them down your throat."

Only after she had disappeared into the kitchen did he allow his smile to return. He called out, "Eggs are bad for my cholesterol."

"Bullshit," she said. A refrigerator door banged shut. "Eggs are incredible, they're edible, and they're nature's perfect food."

"That's just advertising," he said.

"What isn't?"

9

FOR most of the morning that January, the morning following the day she had first approached and spoken to Jesse Rankin, Charlotte seethed. The previous afternoon, she had returned to her farmhouse, kicked off her boots in the mudroom, and peeled off the sodden socks, then sat in the kitchen by the window and tried to warm and calm herself with a cup of tea. She was still tense when she climbed into bed that night, and the hours of restless sleep did nothing to relax or refresh her. The next morning, she went into her studio and stood in front of the painting and tried to see the scene come alive again, tried to imagine it filling with color and the tension of movement. But she could not shake from her mind the image of a dead crow splayed across a field of blood-specked white. When she stared at the canvas, she imagined that scene showing through from underneath the other one. *Those woods,* she told herself. *Those beautiful woods*—as if they were forever gone now, her cathedral woods blasted asunder. All the preceding summer and fall and the first weeks of winter, she had enjoyed gazing out a window and imagining some quiet woodsy scene: the young Hemingway fresh from the Italian front, camping within earshot of the Big Two-Hearted River; Thomas Moran's dark tunnel of autumnal woods with their portal into blue splendor; hoary old Robert Frost out there astride his plow horse, watching the slow flutter of snowflakes and pondering all the miles yet to travel. She had imagined that those woods and fields and distant mountains would become her Abiquiu, that here she would discover her own Black Place, her own White Place, and in the intersection of the two, she would relocate her soul. But how could she sustain that romance now, when all she could see in her mind's eye was a dead black bird on blood-speckled snow?

Maybe in the spring, she had told herself. Maybe when all the snow is gone. The sunlight would come slanting down in long narrow shafts then, spears of green poking up pale and eager through leaf-matted earth, the canopy a whispering sky of new leaves. Maybe then she would be able to stroll through those woods again, again sit with her back to rough bark, her legs splayed out across soft ground. Maybe in summer when the woods and their coolness became a world of its own, sibilant with the breeze, lush and all-enveloping.

But then the anger surged in her again, the sorrow. She stared out the window and said aloud, "You might as well have come in and taken a shit on my carpet."

What kept coming back to her that morning was the look on the boy's face. Unafraid. Disdainful. Contemptuous. And so, so familiar.

All of the hard work of the previous two years seemed suddenly for naught. All of the sobbing and sniffling in June's office, the sisyphean struggle to find herself again, to resuscitate everything Mark had crushed with his smug, disdainful smirk. Suddenly she was that woman again, untethered by a look.

Neck stiff, shoulders aching, all she had wanted to do that morning after her first meeting with Jesse Rankin was to fling paint at the canvas. Any other possibility seemed lost to her. The long, deliberate strokes, all lost. The sensuality, the organic curves of nature, the graceful sweeps of the palette knife, her muscles could not execute them now, her hands would betray her. She wanted the music again, but there was only percussion now.

Bam.

Bam.

Bam.

How did they do it, she wondered? How did they sustain the music? Those long violin moans of Van Gogh, his pizzicatos. And Turner's wonderful oboe breezes that pushed the clouds and drove the waves. Hopper's plaintive trumpet blasts of light. Magritte's teasing whispers, Klee's dreamlike harmonies . . . My God, how did they do it?

It was only by thinking of those others, those troubled, beleaguered, but resolute others, that she was finally able to push herself from the window and her anger. *Write to June,* she told herself. She sat on the sofa with a tablet and pen. *What to tell her?* she wondered. *How little I learned from her? How quickly I regress?*

In the end she made up a little fiction about a stroll she had taken "back in August, I think. Did I already tell you about this?" A story about finding a new covered bridge with an unmanned tollhouse beside it. The lavish description continued for a full page, and when Charlotte read it over to herself she was amused to see the possibility of dreamlike symbolism in those dreamed-up structures, and so she decided to accentuate the symbolism for

June's sake, and wrote about "the dim tunnel over burbling water," and "the tall, narrow tollbooth with majestic spire," but "empty, unmanned." She wrapped up the description with: "At the end of the covered bridge, or the opening, depending on which way you enter, I looked down into the clear water and saw a school of tiny minnows. There were hundreds, maybe thousands of them, all wriggling and squirming as they fought against the current, each struggling to lash its way upstream. For some reason I felt compelled to take a coin out of my pocket and drop it into the center of the school, which provoked such a tizzy of confusion that the minnows scattered and lost their momentum and were all carried away in the opposite direction."

She laughed when she thought of what June, who considered herself "a modified Jungian," would make of that description.

Charlotte sealed the letter in an envelope, addressed it, and would have carried it outside to the mailbox, except that there were no stamps in the desk drawer. Instead of being annoyed by this discovery—as something unexpected might usually annoy her—on that morning, Charlotte welcomed the absence of stamps as an excuse to get out of the house for a while. Perhaps if she frittered away the day an hour at a time, kept her mind on trivial things, maybe tomorrow would bring a return of the old peacefulness.

Thirty minutes later, after she had showered and dressed and put on a little lipstick, she drove four miles to the post office on the opposite edge of town. After nearly half a year in Belinda, the quaintness of the post office still amused her, still reminded her of the post office in Ike Godsey's general store in the old television serial *The Waltons*. Belinda's post office was little more than a counter and cubicle inside a butcher shop. Shortly after moving to Pennsylvania, Charlotte had written to June, "You can stand at the post office window and buy a stamp, move three steps to your right and order a nice rump roast. One-stop shopping! How quaint is that?"

Now with a new letter in hand, Charlotte threw open the door to Shinder's Meats and stepped inside. The postmistress, Cindy, still petite but acquiring the fleshiness of middle age, thickening in all of the least attractive places, had been leaning forward on her post office counter and jabbering away at Rex Shinder, who was trimming stew beef at the butcher's block table behind the meat case. Both fell silent and looked to their right when the little bell above the door tinkled.

"Well, hello, stranger," Rex said. Charlotte, at their first meeting months earlier, had assessed his age in the midforties range, perhaps a few years younger than Cindy. He was as bald as a cue ball and built like a wine barrel. Charlotte could never look at him without being reminded of a wrestler from Pittsburgh named Bruno Sammartino, who had been active in the sixties and into the late seventies. As a little girl she used to sit on her father's lap to watch Bruno and "Jumpin'" Johnny DeFazio and "Haystacks" Calhoun and all of the others as they knocked and threw one another around the ring. "They're all a bunch of frauds," her father would tell her, one arm wrapped around her waist, a glass of Chivas and melting ice in his other hand. "But we love them, don't we, sweetheart?" When she thought of her father now, this was the way she liked to envision him, when he was strong and articulate, a venerated English professor and Lost Generation scholar with a secret fascination for choreographed violence.

A couple of times since coming to Belinda, she had slipped and called Rex "Bruno." Now she always took the time to smile at him for a moment and remind herself, *Not Bruno, Rex*. She had begun to suspect that her smile might have given him the wrong impression, because ever since Christmas, whenever he looked at her, she was sure she saw the twinkle of testosterone in his eyes. Not long after that visit, she wrote to June, "Rex tried to chat me up again today. Unfortunately the poor man had a gob of beef fat stuck to his cheek just below his left eye, flung off his mighty cleaver, no doubt. It sat there and quivered like a big throbbing mole every time he grinned at me. He has a beautiful smile but that quivering pink mole kind of made my throat thicken and my stomach burble. I don't think I'll ever be able to look at him again without searching his face for another glistening gob of fat."

On this day, he immediately stopped trimming chunks of stew beef to call out, "Well, hello, stranger." Cindy chimed in, "What a nice surprise! Where you been keeping yourself?"

This was followed by the usual volley of words from Cindy. "So how's everything out there at your place? Got enough wood to get you through? Your pipes didn't freeze up last week, did they? Temperature drops as low as it did last week, you got to keep a close eye on those pipes. Big drafty place like yours . . . You staying warm all right? Rex, you got any ideas on how to keep this lady warm and toasty through the winter?"

Meantime, Rex, grinning and blushing, went to work organizing the chunks of meat atop the cutting board, rearranging them on the block as if to piece them back together into a cow.

Eventually Cindy made change for Charlotte's dollar, peeled off a stamp, and stuck it to the envelope. She stood there reading the address, eyebrows slightly raised, mouth getting ready, Charlotte knew, to produce yet another query about what is New York City *really* like.

"By the way," Charlotte said, a preemptive strike, "is there such a thing as a hunting season on crows?"

"You need to get rid of some?" Rex asked. Suddenly his eyes were large with hope. "Wouldn't be no problem for me to come out there sometime and get rid of them for you."

"He would too," Cindy said. "Probably even bring half a filet with him so the two of you can celebrate afterward."

Rex blushed so violently that his face took on the color of raw beef.

Charlotte said, "I only ask because I've been seeing this little boy going into the woods across from my place. He looks to be nine, ten years old maybe? Big mop of black hair? And he's always carrying a shotgun or rifle of some kind that's nearly as big as he is."

"Twelve," Cindy said. "Twelve, Rex?"

"Seventh grade, yep. So yeah, I'd say twelve."

"Jesse Rankin," Cindy said. "Cute little boy, isn't he? Him and his mom live in that old single-wide about a half mile down the road from you."

Charlotte nodded. "Okay. I know where you mean."

Rex asked, "He's not causing you any problems, is he?"

"No, no problems. It's just that I've seen him going into those woods several times . . . and later on I hear gunshots, you know? And then the crows all go flying out of the trees."

"Shooting crows," Rex said with a chuckle. "I got more'n my share of them back when I was his age, I'll tell you that."

"So it's legal, then?"

"Oh, all the boys do it," Cindy said. "Crows, chippies, rats at the dump . . . If it moves, they'll shoot at it."

"So it's not illegal?"

Rex said, "I think there might be some kind of season on crows nowadays. But nobody pays any attention to it if there is. I mean, kids these days could do a lot worse than taking potshots at birds. And believe you me, they hit fifteen or sixteen years old, they find a lot worse things to do."

"If Jesse is bothering you somehow," Cindy told her, "I can say something to Livvie next time she comes in."

"Livvie is his mother?"

"She does the cleaning over at the generating plant. Night shift. Cleans all the offices over there. Plus she's got some places in town she cleans during the day."

"My gosh."

"Works her skinny butt off, that's for sure." Now Cindy flashed Charlotte another wink, then leaned over the counter and said to Rex, "She's not all that bad looking either, is she, big boy?"

"Who's not?" he said, as if he had not been following every word of the conversation.

"Livvie Rankin. Who do you think we're talking about?"

"What about her?"

"Just wondering why you don't go after her instead and quit wasting your time pining over Mrs. Dunleavy here."

Rex turned away then, banged another heavy chunk of beef onto the butcher's block and hacked away at it, his big ears as red as fresh blood.

"It's pronounced Dunn-levvy," Charlotte reminded Cindy. "And it's not Mrs. anymore, it's Ms."

"I'm a good fifteen years older than her," Rex said.

"Livvie wouldn't care. You take her a nice big package of your buffalo meat, she won't give a hoot how old you are."

To which Charlotte asked, "You sell buffalo meat here?"

"Inside joke," Cindy said.

Rex told her, "I don't chase after married women."

"Well, you ask me, in Livvie's case, somebody ought to. She sure is wasted on that one she's got."

"I can agree with that," Rex said.

Now Cindy turned back to Charlotte. "Some men just . . . Well, heck, you're divorced. You know what I mean."

"I'm not sure I do."

"He's the kind that almost never comes around. But when he does, you wish he hadn't."

"He doesn't live with them?"

"Thank God for small favors." She gave Charlotte a knowing look, conspiratorial, as if to suggest that they shared a secret or a common bond.

Charlotte said, "Well, I guess I should be going. I just stopped by to mail that letter."

"Two o'clock tomorrow afternoon and it'll be off to New York. Wish I was going with it."

Rex asked, "You don't need nothing else? I got some nice chops in. And the ham loaf was made just a couple hours ago."

"Why don't you show her your buffalo meat?"

"Good God, Cindy," he said, and buried half his body inside the display case where he busied himself with lining up the chicken breasts. And Charlotte thought, *Like corpses at Arlington.*

"Nice seeing you both again," she told them, and turned for the door.

Talk about a stranger in a strange land, Charlotte thought as she climbed back into her Jeep. She had emerged from the post office that day, the butcher shop, that surreal little hybrid she had thought of as a throwback to an ancient time, feeling unpleasantly odd and awkward to the point of claustrophobia. More than a year earlier, when she had been pouring over guidebooks and real estate brochures, the word invariably used to describe Belinda and similar small towns was *quaint*. Initially she had relied on the word herself whenever she described her new hometown to June or Margo at the gallery or to any of her former friends and acquaintances. "Straight out of that Harrison Ford movie, *Witness*," she had told them. "Wide, quiet streets, clapboard buildings, clean, inviting storefronts, Amish buggies parked alongside visiting Volvos and Saabs."

Suddenly, however, the word *quaint* no longer seemed to fit. Not for the town and not for the farm itself, that wide bowl of land with its fields and trees and then, in the distance, those high, soft hills that people in the East call *mountains.*

Until that January afternoon, the woods and the farm and the amusing quaintness of Belinda had been her sanctuary and inspiration. Until then she had never given a thought to ever leaving it.

But now, four months later, winter gone, April budding on the trees, now not an hour after the sheriff's visit, she remembered the dead crow and now the missing boy, and in her mind they seemed somehow one and the same, and those woods outlying her house, those desecrated woods, and as she sat there in her darkened studio and felt the air grow tight and too warm and heavy in her chest, she wondered if she could ever feel at home in that shattered place or any other ever again.

10

GATESMAN had finished the eggs and hash browns, had finished the glass of orange juice and even the small bowl of applesauce Bonnie had set before him, and now, with nothing on the table in front of him but for a glass of water and the newspaper Bonnie had left behind, he felt, finally, something opening up in him, some small release of the pressure that, for as long as he could remember now, had pushed at the insides of his skull. Ever since she had unloaded the tray of food in front of him, then walked away, trailing her fingertips across the nape of his neck and saying, "Eat up, big boy. It's good for you," Bonnie had busied herself behind the bar, filling the ice bin and washing glasses, then shredding potatoes and chopping onions in the kitchen for the half dozen or so men who would show up shortly after the bar officially opened.

Whether because of the scent and simple fulsomeness of the food, or the act of eating alone while Bonnie moved about with very little noise, or the feel of her fingertips that still lingered on the back of his neck, Gatesman felt a strange and pleasant lightness coming over him. It was true that ever since the last time he had been with Bonnie he had avoided her, always set himself apart from her at high school football games, community picnics, and other public events. They had been together three times after Patrice's and Chelsea's deaths, and when he ended it, when he told her that it just wasn't right to be like this with his wife's best friend, Bonnie had told him, "That's bullshit. What's bothering you is that you like being with me. And after two years you're still unwilling to let yourself enjoy anything."

And now, in the barroom ten years later, he finally realized that she had been right. She had felt no guilt because she knew that Patrice would have felt no anger. Bonnie's touch and her kindness had made him let go of something he had hoarded too long, and now the pressure inside his head had finally relented, and when he looked at the newspaper now, he saw only watery squiggles of black on white instead of words and tragedy and the daily grief in two-inch columns.

Then came the roar of a car engine and the slide of tires on gravel. A few loud bars of Queen's "Bohemian Rhapsody." Then sudden silence. One door slammed shut and then another. Female voices laughing. The front door swung open and a tall thinnish redhead strode in, followed closely by her blond, more amply curvy twin. They spotted Gatesman at the same moment, stopped laughing, came to a sudden halt. Then, as if by some telepathic signal, they both threw their hands into the air.

"I'm innocent!" the redhead told him.

"I'm not!" said the blonde.

Then they both laughed and dropped their hands, and holding on to each other, they hurried into the kitchen.

A couple of minutes later, after introductions, Gatesman faced them from across the bar. The blonde, Joanne, fourteen minutes older than her sister, told him that Denny Rankin had been there two nights earlier, the night before his son's disappearance. "Do you remember how long he stayed?" Gatesman asked.

"Till we threw everybody out," she said.

"About two-thirty," Judy added.

"He was shooting pool by himself," Joanne said. "Other than that, it was just one couple and two single guys. He was the last one out the door."

"Left by himself?" Gatesman asked.

"All by his lonesome," Joanne said.

"He didn't say where he was headed, where he planned to spend the night?"

"I locked the door behind him," Judy said. "He offered me a twenty to go out to his truck with him."

"And you didn't take him up on it?" Joanne asked.

"Hell no."

Joanne looked at Gatesman and said, "She usually charges fifty."

"Whore," Judy said. She gave her sister a shove, and they both laughed and bumped against each other.

Gatesman waited until they settled down. "So he was here, left alone at two-thirty, and there's nothing more you can tell me, right?"

"Well," said Judy, and looked at her sister. They were on the verge of laughter again when Bonnie said, "Girls. Be serious."

"That's all," they said in a single voice.

Moments later, Bonnie walked with Gatesman to the door. He looked back at the girls giggling behind the bar. "You are a very smart businesswoman," he told her.

She put a hand on his arm. "I'm also good at other things. Like being a friend."

"Yes, you are," he said, and patted her hand. He knew that she wanted more and certainly deserved more but that he was not the man to give it to her. "Thanks for breakfast. And everything else."

He saw the way her face went soft then, saw the distance that came into her eyes. "Drive carefully," she said.

11

It was just after three in the afternoon, a full eight hours after the sheriff's visit, that the telephone rang in Charlotte's kitchen. She had spent most of the morning in the chair in her studio, the blinds closed. Later she had stood at the front door for a while, looking out through the wire screen until her body began to feel so heavy and her legs so weak that she stepped backward to the stairs and sat down. Only with a great deal of effort had she managed to drag herself into the living room and onto the sofa, where she was lying wide awake when the telephone rang. She listened to the first six rings without moving. Only when she recognized Mike Verner's voice on the answering machine—"Well, I guess you're outside getting that garden of yours ready"—did she sit up and stand and cross quickly to the kitchen.

"Mike, hi, it's me, I'm here now."

"Didn't mean to bring you running into the house. You sound all out of breath."

"No, it's okay, I was . . . just doing some cleaning down in the basement. What's, uh . . . what's going on?"

"I just wanted to let you know that a bunch of us are going to be heading into those woods out there in the morning. Didn't want you to get a scare when you looked out and seen cars all up and down the road. Sheriff's getting a search organized. Bringing in a couple of state boys and sniffer dogs."

Charlotte blinked at the wall. Felt the sunny room go dark. "He didn't say anything about that this morning," she said. "He said he'd been through there last night."

"Sheriff out to see you already, was he?"

"About seven this morning."

"Nothing like a visit from the law to get your blood moving in the morning, is there?"

"He said he thinks Jesse is with his father somewhere."

"Yeah, well, he finally tracked down Denny sleeping in his truck at a rest stop up at Benvenue. No sign of the boy. Plus, apparently the sheriff followed up on Denny's story about where he's been and who he's been with all this time, and I guess it checked out. Not that the sheriff could be persuaded to share any of the juicier details with me."

"So now he thinks that Jesse's still in the woods?"

"Naw, I don't think so. I think he just doesn't know what else to do. Besides, there's maybe a sinkhole, a burrow of some kind, even a hollowed-out old tree. It's hard to say all the places a little boy might've gotten into."

Charlotte tried to swallow but could not. Instead she cleared her throat. Then asked, "Would it be okay if I came along? On the search, I mean."

"Absolutely. Around first light you'll see the vehicles start lining up along the lane. Just come on over and join us."

"I will," she said.

"I'm just hoping we don't get drenched. Weatherman says there's a front coming through tonight. We might be in for a spring boomer."

Charlotte nodded but her mind was elsewhere. "Mike," she said. "I told the sheriff about Dylan being out here on the tractor yesterday. I told him how Dylan got off and went into the woods for a while. I wasn't saying he did anything because I'm sure he didn't. He wouldn't. But I just . . . I mean the sheriff asked, and I told him."

"Well that's what you're supposed to do when the sheriff asks you something, isn't it?"

"I suppose so. I just hope I . . . I mean I know Dylan couldn't possibly be involved in any way."

"I told Mark the same thing. He'll want to hear it from Dylan himself, though."

"He hasn't talked to him yet?"

"Naw, his class is off on a field trip all day. Far as I know, they're not home yet. They went to one of those wraparound movies about penguins or something. Then there's a museum or two and I think dinner at some place with belly dancers. I tell you what, if I'd had that kind of education when I was his age, I'd still be in school."

"So you're not at all worried then? About Dylan being involved somehow?"

"Not in the least. I mean, the boy's got some issues, no doubt about it. But hell—you know anybody who doesn't have issues?"

"No," she said. "Not a soul."

"Dylan will be okay, don't you worry. Meantime, I guess I'll see you in the morning."

"Mike, wait. I, uh . . . I was wondering if you would mind if I store some bags of garden compost in one of the barn stalls."

"Why would I mind? But put them upstairs where it's dry. Those stalls are pretty much open to the weather."

"But that's your storage space upstairs," she told him.

"How much room are a few bags going to take up? Besides, why go to all the trouble of having to haul the bags all the way around the barn to the pasture side? Set them inside the front entrance. In fact, now that I think about it, that shed of yours is only, what, twenty feet from your garden?"

"Yes but . . . I think I saw a snake under the shed last summer."

"What kind of snake was it?"

"I don't know, it was . . . pretty big, I think."

"What color was it?"

"Black?"

"Probably just a king snake. They're good to have around. They'll keep the rodents away."

"Yes, well, that's fine, I guess. I mean, in that case, he's welcome to stay. But I still don't want to go near the shed if I don't have to, not if there's a family of snakes living under it. So I'd really like to put the compost in the barn if you won't mind."

"Then put it upstairs where the bags'll be easier to get at. You can't have all that many bags."

"I bought a dozen."

"That's nothing. You got them in the back of your Jeep, right? So just drive on up to the barn door and stack them inside."

"But I'm afraid they'll get in your way when you come for a load of hay next time."

"I'll tell you what," he said. "Just leave the bags in your Jeep. After the search tomorrow, I'll run them up to the barn and unload them for you. What else are you using?"

"What else?" she said.

"What all are you planning to put in this year? Same as last year? You had, what—pole beans, squash, cucumbers, green onions . . ."

"I did peppers and tomato plants too."

"You have any interest in doing cantaloupe? Because I've got plenty of extra seeds. Not to mention sweet corn. I plant both the Bodacious and the Kandy Korn."

"I don't know, I'll . . . I'll have to think about it."

"How'd your tomatoes do last year?"

"The cherry ones did fine. But the Better Boys didn't produce at all."

"You could probably use some 21-7-7."

"Excuse me?"

He chuckled. "It's a fertilizer mix. I'll bring some of it along for you."

"You don't need to do all this, Mike. In fact, I wish you wouldn't."

"Don't worry about it. We'll have you growing blue-ribbon tomatoes in no time. I'll see you in the morning, okay?"

"Mike, wait."

He waited.

Charlotte forced a little laugh. "I already stored the compost in one of the stalls."

"Now, what did you go and do that for? It's bound to get wet down there."

"It will get wet when I put it on the garden too, won't it?"

"Yes, but first you'll have to carry those wet bags out through the pasture. A forty-pound bag of wet compost will feel more like sixty pounds."

"Well . . . I can use the exercise."

"I'll come out and move them for you," he said.

"Mike, stop it, please."

Even to her own ears, her voice sounded tight, too shrill. She wondered how it must sound to Mike Verner.

"I didn't mean to make you mad," he said.

"I'm not mad. I just . . . I was just so proud of myself after I carried all those bags into the barn," she told him. "I felt like I had really accomplished something, you know? And now you want to come out and undo that for me and prove that I'm really just a foolish city lady after all."

"Now, did I say that?"

"Not in so many words."

A few moments passed. Then he said, "You know . . . come to think of it . . . putting those bags in a stall might be a better idea than mine."

"And why is that?"

"Well . . . it just is. Stop asking so many questions."

She laughed again. "You're a good man, Mike."

"I wish somebody would tell my wife that."

"I will if I ever meet her."

"On second thought . . . no sense stirring up trouble, is there?"

She said nothing to that, only smiled to herself, felt her weariness returning, felt the morning looming out there on the other side of the horizon.

"By the way," Mike finally said. "What did you think of our Sheriff Gatesman?"

"He seems like a nice enough man, I guess."

"The question is, nice enough for what?"

"Oh, Mike."

"He's single, you know."

"You don't say."

"Been a widower for going on, what, a dozen years now."

"He never mentioned it."

"He wouldn't. They'd only been married about a year and a half when it happened. She rolled her car over an embankment out on Route 74."

"I heard about it from Cindy at the post office a while back. What an awful thing to happen."

"I guess so. Patrice and little Chelsea, both."

"How old was the child?"

"Four months. And she was the light of his life, you know? Both of them were."

"Jesus, Mike."

"Here's what makes it even worse. It was just a week or so before Christmas, and they'd been to the mall in Carlisle so that Chelsea could get her picture taken with Santa Claus. Cindy tell you all this?"

"No, just that there had been a car accident."

"Well, Mark was supposed to go with them to the mall—a family day, you know? But then there was this altercation up at Little Buffalo State Park, reported to be a shoot-out of some kind, but it turned out to just be a bunch of drunken kids shooting off firecrackers. But by then, Mark had sent Patrice and Chelsea off on their own. When they didn't come home and she wasn't answering her cell phone, he went out looking for them."

"He's the one who found them? Oh God."

"So be nice to him, okay? Be very nice, if you know what I mean."

"I know exactly what you mean. But, Mike, honestly . . ."

"He's a nice, lonely man. That's all I'm saying here."

"God, Mike, please. Don't do this to me."

"I happen to know that he thinks you're sort of special."

"You know no such thing."

"Charlotte, listen to me. I am the source of all knowledge. The sooner you accept that fact, the sooner you can start convincing my wife."

She laughed a high, strange, whimpering kind of laugh. "I really wish you hadn't told me about his family."

"Part of my job as the town gossip," he told her. "And one other thing."

"No more, Mike."

"Just this. I've got sixty Angus pooping machines over here putting out a fresh supply of manure every single day. That's what compost is, you know. So don't go wasting your money on store-bought again, okay? They sterilize that stuff and kill off all of the helpful bacteria. My manure, on the other hand, is crawling with it."

"I'm not one to impose on my neighbors."

"Hey," he said, "if neighbors can't give one another a little shit now and then, what kind of neighbors are they?"

Again, Charlotte smiled. His kindness made her want to cry. "Okay."

"We help one another out around here. You need something, you pick up the phone."

"I will."

"You can count on me to fulfill all of your seed, heavy lifting, and cow poop needs. All of your other needs, Mark Gatesman is the man you'll want to call."

"God. You just don't quit, do you?"

"That's a good opening for something dirty. But I'll save it until we know each other a little better, okay?"

She nodded but did not answer. The call had exhausted her in so many ways. She felt an urge to let her body slide down the wall, to find its natural resting posture as a heap crumpled into the corner.

"In the morning," he told her.

"In the morning," she said weakly, and hung up the phone.

12

THUNDER rumbled in the early evening, high and distant in the darkness. Charlotte sat alone in the living room with the television on, but she was unable to concentrate on the Lifetime movie, something about a young girl trying to locate the half brother she had never known. Charlotte had fixed a plate with a few crackers and slices of fontina and a half dozen Greek olives, but the plate went untouched, though the bottle of white merlot did not. Because the movie's dialogue struck her as more distracting than engaging, she finally muted the sound and put on a Michael Bublé CD instead. The music, however, struck her as inconsistent with the rumbling night, so she searched through her CDs until she found the Berlin Philharmonic's recording of Mozart's *Requiem*. Then she went through the house and turned out all of the lights. By the time she settled onto the La-Z-Boy with her feet up and a light fleece blanket laid over her and the last of the merlot in her glass, the first movement was well under way, and a forceful rain was blowing hard and tapping like a thousand fingernails against the living room windows.

She dreamed that she was sitting in a lawn chair in her backyard in the early hours of morning. She was very old and her feet were bare and cold in the wet grass. There was just enough chill in the air to make her think it must be September already, or maybe October, and she was glad to have a mug of hot tea cupped in her hands, its subtle fragrance of oranges warm on her face and the cup warming her palms and fingers. She could still hear the rain, but it was falling against her house, gurgling down the drain pipes, but not touching her, some ten yards away. The night was very dark, the sky overcast. She could make out five stars in the Big Dipper plus the hazy reddish glow that was either Mars or a communications satellite. She was aware of being very old in her dream and very tired, yet she did not wish to go inside the house where she could be warm and dry and alone. She wanted to remain outside awhile longer, looking at the stars and asking them, *Who's up there?* and waiting to see if one of them winked at her in any fashion that could be interpreted as a response. She found that if she stared at the stars long enough, their fuzzy edges would elongate somewhat, stretch out a bit like hazy wings, and it seemed then that she might be staring at the negative image of a daytime sky, the sky black instead of sunlit, and the birds, instead of black, were full of light.

After a while she became aware of somebody walking toward her from the direction of the pond. She could not see him at first but only felt him coming. The figure of a man was perhaps twenty-five yards away when he finally began to take form in the darkness, but he came to a stop, still sufficiently distant, at least fifteen feet away, so that the features of his face were not distinguishable and he remained little more than a silhouette imposed upon a lighter darkness. Even so, she could feel his eyes on her, and she felt emanating from him a not unkind emotion, something neither particularly warm nor cold but interested and curious. She was not afraid of him, but neither was she comfortable with his presence. She felt that he was looking at her much as she had been regarding the stars. When he finally turned and walked away from her and disappeared completely in the darkness again—not just concealed by the darkness, but more like a man who, walking into a deep pool of water, gradually returns to water himself, actually becomes the water—she was overcome with a terrible sorrow, a sense of loss that rose up out of the darkness to surround and engulf her, a sorrow so intense and suffocating that she awoke herself with the breathless violence of her sobs.

13

All night long the wind whistled and pulled at the house. The windows rattled sometimes and the house seemed to be straining to hold on to its foundations, and Charlotte had the peculiar feeling that the darkness itself was doing the blowing, that it was trying to pull her up by the roots and hurl her away.

After waking from the dream of the man made of shadow, after sobbing for a long while until she convinced herself that it had only been a dream, she had dragged herself up the stairs and crawled into bed, but she could not sleep well for thinking about the morning. At times she felt feverish and at other times she shivered, and the few times she dozed off through the next five hours, she always awoke with a start.

The dawn came gray and dirty as she lay listening to the rain gurgle down through the gutter and drain pipe. She was not aware of when the gurgling stopped, but when she heard distant voices, she knew that the search party was beginning to gather.

She climbed out of bed and went to the window. The four vehicles parked along Metcalf Road near the edge of the woods were indistinguishable in the mist except as two sedans and two pickup trucks, and near the tailgate of the last truck, two orange embers glowed dully in the mist, moving as the men moved the cigarettes to their mouths and away again.

She stood there for several minutes, still feeling the sadness of her dream and the awful hollow heaviness it had invoked in her. There was also the very strange feeling that things were happening peripherally or behind or above her that she could not discern, that her head could not turn fast enough or her eyes could not be quick enough to catch the activity. It was a feeling she had experienced only once before, in the city with June, who had insisted that they visit the Guggenheim for the King Tut exhibit, so Charlotte, who had wanted only to suffer her head cold alone in bed in an unlit room, took four antihistamines and a Valium on an empty stomach and joined her friend.

Consequently, every artifact in the exhibit appeared menacing and evil to Charlotte and seemed to permeate sinister intentions. The same was true for all of the other visitors and especially for the security guards. The old lady docents who stood by smiling or prattling on helpfully were frauds of the highest order. Charlotte had felt that the moment she walked past any of these individuals they immediately dropped their facade and whispered conspiratorially about her.

That had been a very long morning for her, and this one, she knew, promised to be even more of an ordeal. As she dragged herself away from the window and into the bathroom, she was aware of a pressure accumulating against her, as if the air itself had force and weight and was pushing against her chest and down onto her shoulders.

In the bathroom she splashed warm water over her face and pulled hard at the corners of her eyes. The smallest, most routine movement felt alien. Nearly thirty minutes passed before she was able to prepare a half pot of strong coffee and pour it into the largest cup she could find, an old German beer stein she had saved from her college days, and then to lace up her Timberlands and pull on the tan Carhartt jacket with the quilt lining—items she had once thought of gleefully as part of her "country ensemble." She then jammed her floppy wide-brimmed gardening hat down low on her forehead and, shuffling like an ancient crone, hands cupped around the beer mug and holding it close to her face, made her way outside and toward the lengthening line of vehicles parked along the road.

A heavy dew still covered the ground, and the air was so cold that her ears and nose stung. The steady wind made her cheeks feel tight, and she wished then that she had taken the time to put on some makeup and conceal the damage done to her by the night.

She estimated that there were between thirty and forty people standing around in small groups, some still along the macadam road and some already in the stubbly field, all waiting for the sheriff to put them into motion. She was aware of their eyes on her as she approached. She tried to anticipate what they must be thinking. *She's the one who would have seen him last. She's the one who told the sheriff about Dylan. She's the one . . . She's the one . . .*

She looked down at the broken cornstalks, watched the water accumulate around her boots. She held the mug of coffee close to her face and felt the warmth and steam soothe her eyes. *If at any previous moment in your life,* she told herself, *if you had made a decision other than the one you made . . . you wouldn't be here now.*

Where would you be? she wondered, and forced herself to imagine the most pleasant alternative. You could be strolling through a souk in Morocco now. Studying the silks or the fragrant bins of spices. You could be sipping café au lait at a brasserie. You could be lying in the arms of your ceramics prof from Smith. *No,* she told herself, *he must be in his seventies by now.* Then, *I don't care, I wish I were there with him. I wish we were far away from here.*

She was still twenty yards from the last vehicle in the line when Mike Verner broke off from a small group and walked out to meet her. He handed her an orange plastic vest. "Mornin'," he said. Charlotte answered with a grumble that she hoped would amuse him.

But he, too, was in a somber mood and did not laugh or even smile. "Rough night?" he asked.

She knew how she must appear to him. Puffy face, red eyes and nose—the look of somebody who has been dragged screaming over rough ground. "Couldn't sleep," she told him. "Sought refuge in a bottle of wine."

"Me neither," he said, "except that I watched television. Same numbing effect except that you don't feel quite as bad in the morning."

"Now you tell me," she said.

Soon the sheriff called everyone together and a few minutes later had them spread out in a line with their backs to Charlotte's house. They stood an arm's length apart, local farmers and retirees, Gatesman and one of his deputies and two state troopers.

Gatesman said, "We'll send the dogs in ahead and let them do what they do best. The rest of us should just try to maintain the line more or less and keep our eyes open. What you're looking for is anything at all that's not a natural part of these woods. Any signs of a disturbance in the surroundings that doesn't look natural. I mean, hell, you all know what we're here for. Just keep your eyes and ears open, that's all you can do."

A state trooper leading a German shepherd on a leash started into the woods near one end of the line, and halfway down the line a man in coveralls and boots started in as well, pulled along by a small beagle straining at its lead. The others followed a few moments behind, trudging, Charlotte thought, like pallbearers. She imagined how they all must look from her farmhouse, gray figures in a mist, their orange vests winking behind the trees like the dying lights of huge, exhausted fireflies. Every once in a while she heard somebody murmuring to somebody else, but she could not distinguish the words. She tried to keep her attention on the ground, but the sibilance of whispers distracted her.

For several minutes the routine continued without change. Then suddenly the little beagle made a quick movement to its right and pulled its handler out of his easy step. A little gasp caught in Charlotte's chest when she saw where they were headed—straight toward the fallen tree where she had first come upon the boy, the place where he used to sit.

"Slow, deep breaths," June used to advise her. "Sloooowly in through the mouth. Then blow it out just as slowly. I know you feel like you're suffocating but you aren't. You can control this, don't let it control you. Slowly in . . . slowly out. That's all there is to it."

Charlotte had thought she'd left that sniveling, panicked version of herself behind. Thought she'd left her behind as a ghost in June's office. But now she watched the beagle sniffing all around the log, pulling its handler in a wide, erratic circle. The pain radiating through her chest and crushing the air from her lungs made her think that this time, truly, the heart was in real danger, overtaxed and insufficient.

But a minute later the beagle stopped sniffing at the wet ground. It looked up at his handler. The man said, "Let's go then," and pulled the dog back toward the center of the forest. Only then did Charlotte realize that she, too, had come to a stop, she and half the line on both sides of her, all waiting for the moment of discovery, the surprised call of either tragedy or relief. Now, with the dog moving again, the others resumed their pace as well.

Every now and then someone fell out of the ragged line to look closely at the ground, to scuff away the leaves from a shallow depression, or to stoop and squint into a fallen log. When this happened, all the searchers in the vicinity slowed and waited, all hoping for the shout of discovery. But their were no shouts, no voices raised. They moved on solemnly, eyes scouring the leaf-matted earth, every step a little heavier now.

Only by turning her head to the left or right could Charlotte get a full picture of the woods. The woods seemed to her far denser than they actually were, close on all sides and dark around the edges in a way they had never been. Ever since the searchers had entered the woods, her field of vision had become constricted, her breath shallow and leaden, so that she felt herself to be walking down a tunnel made of trees, a tunnel walled in by darkness and holding insufficient air. She thought of Pissarro's *Path Through the Woods* with its walls of trees and its blind turn in the narrow path, but then told herself, no, those trees were heavy and black in their leafiness, but there are no leaves in these woods, no path; the limbs here were bare and black unless she lifted her gaze into the canopy where the reddening buds made a domelike roof, a porous cover backlit by the rising sun so that the sky glowed like a fresh bruise.

She thought of the painting she could make of this scene, all grays and black, people and trees, bodies leaning slightly forward, all eyes on the ground, three-fourths of the canvas somber and colorless, only the topmost section brighter. But then she told herself, *Stop it. How dare you?* and she brought her eyes down to the ground again, brought her attention back to the damp brown earth.

After a while Charlotte could see the light through the far end of the tree line, a clouded yellow glow. She had never walked the entire way through the trees before, had never been interested in what lay beyond the trees—another field, the road, the houses, the town—but only in the woods themselves, the hushed silence and the cool ensconcing shade. But now, just as they were about to step out of the trees on the far side and into the adjoining field, something she had been holding on to with every breath now broke loose in her. She started shivering and sobbing and was helpless to hold it back. Mike Verner moved close and laid a hand on her shoulder, then rubbed his hand in a circle on her back, the plastic vest crinkling with the movement of his hand. Only when she had managed to get her sobbing under control did he lift his hand away from her. Then, without speaking, he stood there with the others as they watched the dogs sniffing at the broken cornstalks.

Between her own soft sobs, Charlotte could hear other women weeping too. Every once in a while a whimper, a sniff. Somebody blew his nose. One man, as the group stood facing the sun rising far across the road and the distant hills, the woods at their backs, softly recited the Lord's Prayer.

Charlotte watched him until he had finished. Then she looked for the dogs again, but they were being held on shortened leashes now as their handlers and the state troopers and Gatesman and his deputy stood together in a defeated huddle.

Livvie Rankin's trailer was visible fifty yards away on the

opposite side of the road. Charlotte turned sideways to the sun and put her right hand to the side of her head so that she could see the trailer more clearly. It seemed to her a wretched place to have to live.

She calculated the trailer's length at maybe twenty-five feet, its width half as much. *Hardly bigger than my living room,* she thought. The exterior was a faded yellow accented with one broad stripe of brown around its middle. The roof had been tarred so many times and so carelessly that great gobs of hardened tar hung all along the roof's edge. In the distance the tar glinted wetly, still damp with dew, so that it looked as if it were melting. The screen door hung open, torn away from the topmost hinge, which made it dangle lopsided above the two concrete steps. The yard was small and brown and unhealthy, the grass brown and sparse. A pale blue concrete birdbath sat just a few feet off the stoop, and though Charlotte could distinguish a small, dark shape inside the birdbath's basin, she could not identify it. She only knew that it was not moving, it was not a living thing.

"Okay, everybody," the sheriff called, and when he said nothing more, the searchers, until then still strung out in a loose rendition of line, began to coalesce toward him.

Finally he told them, "Listen, folks. I've been talking with the state boys and the dog handlers and everybody agrees that there's not much use in going back through those trees again. Between Livvie and me and all of you good people, we've covered every inch of it at least a couple of times. If Jesse was anywhere in those woods, we'd know it by now."

"So what now?" a man called out.

"Now you folks go on home or back to your work," the sheriff told them. "We appreciate all of your help. And just keep praying for him. We'll find him yet, I know we will."

Charlotte wondered if he really meant that or if it was just part of the script. She watched him then as he went up the line collecting the plastic vests, thanking everybody individually. She noticed that his fingertips inadvertently touched hers when she handed him her vest.

"Sorry to take you away from your work," he told her. She winced, reminded of her earlier thought, so hateful, so selfish, and she answered, "This is way more important than anything I do. Or will ever do."

He regarded her curiously for a moment. She felt uncomfortable under his gaze and looked away. Quietly the sheriff moved away from her. She turned slightly and saw Mike Verner grinning.

He said, "Did I see a spark of electricity just now?"

"If you did," she told him, "it's because your brain has short-circuited."

He laughed softly and touched her shoulder as she moved away from him, out toward Metcalf Road and easier walking. Mike fell into step beside her. "I've got that fertilizer I promised you in my truck."

She was grateful for a change of subject, a return to normalcy or at least the attempt. "Is it too early to be putting it on?" she asked.

"If you can work the soil, you can put it on."

"Would you mind dropping it out beside the garden?"

"Happy to," he said. "You want me to drive up to the barn and haul back some of your store-bought manure for you?"

"I guess I'll deal with just the fertilizer today. How much do I owe you for it?"

"Including the tax? Zero dollars and zero cents."

"Mike . . ."

"I get it wholesale," he said.

"So how much do you pay for it?"

"I get it in bulk. I had that bag already."

"And how much did you pay for it?"

"Charlotte," he said, then looked down at her and smiled, "stop being a pain in the ass, okay?"

"You're the pain in the ass," she told him.

He kept smiling as they walked. They stepped over a shallow drainage ditch and onto the macadam. A minute or so later he asked, "You going to be okay?"

She stared straight ahead down the road. "It's not me that matters right now."

"Jesse might turn up yet. You never know."

"Mike," she said, but nothing more. A familiar bubble of despair was ballooning in her chest now, cutting off the air.

"It doesn't look good, I agree. Still . . . You just never know about these things. I've always believed it's best to stay optimistic until there's no other choice."

No other choice but the awful truth, she told herself. She felt her eyes beginning to sting again, felt the congestion rising in her head and her lower field of vision start to shimmer. Without turning to face him, she put her hand out and squeezed his arm once before increasing her pace. "Thanks for everything, Mike," she said, and with two quick strides she pulled away from him. He smiled and nodded and made no attempt to detain her.

14

SHE spent the rest of the morning in what she thought of as a state of collapse. For more than three hours she lay nearly motionless on the La-Z-Boy in the living room. She had removed her boots and gardening hat in the mudroom and had unbuttoned her coat as she walked through the house but then fell into the chair without removing the coat. The room grew warm with sunlight. In contrast to her limbs, which felt too heavy to move, too weak and spiritless, her mind thrashed wildly with a mad tumble of thoughts. Again and again she tried to order those thoughts, to lay them out in a coherent chronology of the past two days, but they would not surrender to order; they shuffled and looped through her mind in random clips and fragments.

She slept for a while, then awakened with a start, thinking she had heard a gunshot. She sat up, gasping for air. The house was silent. Her hair was damp with perspiration. She felt the sweat between her breasts and under her arms. She heeled down the footrest and stood and wrestled the heavy coat off and let it fall to the floor, then stood there panting, blinking, rubbing the sweat off the back of her neck. She could hear and feel the blood hammering in her temples, could feel the thump of her heart. "Do something," she told herself. "Or you're going to go crazy."

She turned sharply and crossed toward the stairs, pulling her sweatshirt off along the way. Then her T-shirt. Then the bra. All fell behind her on the stairs. At the top of the stairs she wriggled out of her jeans. Shed her panties. Her socks. Then she stood beneath the cold spray of the shower until she was shivering, and until she could breathe again, until the tunnel relented and allowed in some light.

15

IN the early afternoon Charlotte stood at the post office counter, handed Cindy a ten-dollar bill, then pocketed the change and the book of twenty stamps. She was aware of Cindy chattering as usual, aware of Rex out from behind his display case this time, hanging bags of beef jerky on a rack, aware even of herself being aware of it, but there seemed a distance and an unreality to everything she saw and heard, as if she were watching herself in a play on a stage.

Charlotte: So apparently our search of the woods this morning didn't turn up anything important.

Cindy: Which in itself is important, don't you think? Nothing must mean something, seems to me. As many times as that boy has been in those woods, and for those sniffer dogs to come up empty? Sounds suspicious to me. Rex? Am I right or am I right?

Rex, working hard to keep his eyes averted, to not be caught in the act of admiring Charlotte in her loose khaki slacks, the pale blue blouse, the expensive loafers he knew he could never afford to buy for her but would do so anyway if ever she asked: This isn't CSI, you know.

Cindy: Evidence is evidence. There's always something left behind. There's always a scent trail.

Enter a skinny little lady with a stiff blond bouffant; she speaks the instant she steps over the threshold and continues talking as she cuts a glance at Charlotte then crosses quickly to the meat display case: You have any good T-bones, Rex? I need a couple of T-bones, you know how I like them, and a pound of ground chuck. How you doing there, Cindy? Looks like spring might be coming after all, doesn't it?

Rex: Coming right up.

Cindy: Mrs. Dunleavy and me was just talking about the search this morning. About how those dogs couldn't find a darn thing.

Bouffant Lady: Donnie said the rain will do that. All that rain and soft ground. They should have had those dogs out on day one.

Cindy: Donnie would know, I guess. *(To Charlotte)* Donnie teaches at the Vo-Tech. Body shop.

Bouffant Lady: That was him and Bailey this morning.

Charlotte: Bailey?

Cindy: That cute little beagle.

Rex: Best rabbit dog in the county.

Bouffant: It's like Donnie says, though. You can't expect even a prizewinning nose like Bailey's to perform miracles.

Rex: I hear that state police canine was all but worthless.

Bouffant: You can say that again. Just leave out the "all but."

While Bouffant Lady pays for her order, Charlotte pretends

to be interested in the post office's latest philately tacked to the wall, three mounted and limited photos of the Philadelphia Eagles, with accompanying stamps.

Cindy: Those can be a good investment. The kids love them. You don't have any kids, Mrs. Dunleavy?

Charlotte *(wincing slightly)*: No, I don't.

Cindy: I've got some other ones for girls too. Ballerinas, I think. *(And she starts digging around in her filing cabinet drawers.)*

Charlotte: Maybe around Christmas, okay? Don't bother for now.

Cindy: I'll remind you, come about Thanksgiving.

Charlotte smiles, then turns to the Bouffant Lady: So what does Donnie think, I mean about where—

Just then, the bell above the door tinkles and in walks an older gentleman, sixtyish, tall and thin with a full head of silver, slicked-back hair. He's wearing neatly pressed chinos, a pale green knit shirt, and a light jacket. He smiles at Charlotte when he first enters.

Gentleman: Afternoon, all.

Cindy: Jack. How's the flower business these days?

Gentleman: Bright and blooming. *(To Bouffant Lady)* But never as lovely as you, Maggie.

Bouffant Lady *(pats his arm on her way to the door)*: Sweet as sugar, same as always.

Gentleman proceeds to the meat counter and orders two skinless chicken breasts. Cindy looks at him, looks at Charlotte, gives her a wink, and jerks a nod toward the gentleman. Charlotte scowls and shakes her head no, though the truth is she noticed him at the search that morning. Even in her ruined state, she couldn't help but admire his poise, his aplomb, the dignified carriage she used to consider her own but lately found impossible to muster.

Now she has a pained look on her face as she considers how tasteless her role in this play is, how tasteless this play and all of its players are.

Gentleman *(to Charlotte)*: Damn shame about that boy. I was really hoping we would find something.

Charlotte: It breaks my heart.

He nods, then faces the display case again, stares at the meat. Now Cindy reaches over the counter, gives Charlotte's sleeve a tug, and jerks her head at the gentleman again, all with a hot adamant gleam in her eye.

Charlotte: So are there . . . any theories circulating? Any credible scenarios being proposed?

Gentleman: Credible? I really don't know. It's difficult to ascribe credibility in the total absence of anything concrete, don't you think?

Charlotte nods. He gives her a brief, warm smile, pays for his chicken breasts, then heads for the door.

Gentleman: Have a good day, all.

Cindy *(who can hardly wait until the door eases shut behind him)*: So? What do you think?

Charlotte: What do I think?

Cindy: He's a retired professor. Runs a flower shop now, specializes in orchids. Just your type, if you ask me.

Charlotte: I only came here for the stamps, thank you.

Cindy *(to Rex)*: You plan on making a move, big boy, you better quit your dillydallying! *(To Charlotte)* He's shy but he's as honest as the day is long. Course, it all depends on whether you prefer the brawny type or the brainy type.

Rex *(with a scowl aimed straight at Cindy)*: I think I'll go cut up a pig.

Cindy *(as soon as Rex disappears into the back room)*: On the other hand, why even have to choose? Keep one for the pillow talk, and one to do the heavy lifting. *(And here she gives Charlotte a knowing look.)*

Charlotte, feeling suddenly lost, disoriented, pats her pockets: Did you give me my stamps?

Cindy: In your right side pocket. And I'll tell you something else about him, too, if you want to know it.

Charlotte: Thanks, but I need to—

Cindy: Just don't ask me who told me this because I promised I'd never tell *(and here she cuts a glance toward the back room)*. But from what I hear, he's built like a bull in more ways than one.

Charlotte is unaware of what she says in response or if she says anything at all. She removes the stamps from her pocket and looks at them, some foreign curiosity, as she crosses to the door, as she enters into the sunlight, too bright, and retreats to her vehicle, the safety of metal, closed glass, and locked doors.

16

THE moment the green Jeep swung into the driveway, Dylan looked up from the porch steps, sat straighter, his eyes glistening with torment, mouth squinched tight with fear.

At first Charlotte failed to recognize him. The sunlight coming in through the windshield was too bright; it stung her eyes. Only then did she remember the sunglasses she kept in the compartment to her right, and she reached for them as the Jeep rolled forward over the gravel driveway. Then the recognition came to her, Dylan Hayes, and the world went tight and dark around its edges again, her chest tightened, and her hand fell away from the sunglasses, went back to the steering wheel, guided the Jeep up close to the garage and brought it to a halt.

She tried to sound normal as she approached the porch, but her voice was pinched, throat raw. "Isn't this a school day?"

"I can't stand it there anymore," he said. "The way everybody looks at me."

She paused in front of him, had no words, no idea of what to do or say.

"I'm not blaming you," he said, and at this her heart lurched, because his words confirmed what she had been trying to push away. "But I wasn't in those woods for no forty minutes. It was no more'n five."

She stood there breathing so fast and hard through her nose that she could hear the inhalations, could feel them matched by a racing heart.

"Sheriff didn't mention you by name, but I know it had to've been you, told him that. Who else would've seen me?"

"I didn't . . ." she started, but faltered, stumbled against the truth.

"All I did was to go in there to take a crap. That's all I did! I was back on the tractor again in five minutes at most."

"I never said you were in there for forty minutes, Dylan. I said I heard the tractor starting up again maybe forty minutes later."

"Well I don't know how that could be because I left it running the whole time. I never shut it down until it was back in Mike's barn."

"I'm sorry, I don't know what . . . whether I misspoke or the sheriff misheard, I don't know what to tell you. I was doing chores here in the house, I . . ." The way he looked at that moment, the way he looked up at her, she felt small, tiny, a smudge, a smear of spilled paint.

His eyes showed his panic, but he sat as still as a stone in his big, muddy boots, big, raw hands squeezed together between his skinny legs. Only his eyes gave him away, those dilated pupils huge and dark, as shiny as black water.

"I never accused you of anything," she told him, "I swear. I never suggested to anybody that you had done anything wrong."

"That might be so but the thing of it is . . . he thinks I'm lying about it. Just before you got here, he made me show him where I'd been. Where I was when I took a dump, you know? But I couldn't find it. I mean, I know where it was, I know exactly where I was because of this low branch I was holding on to when I squatted. Except now there's nothing out there. Nothing but leaves. I mean, how could that be?"

"Maybe an animal or something . . . Maybe the rain."

"I never even seen that kid!"

A part of her wanted to go to Dylan now, to take his hand, sit beside him, collapse against him.

"I could go to prison for this," he said.

"No, no, that will never happen, I'm sure it won't. They have to have evidence to even charge you. There has to be solid evidence of some kind, and there isn't. There *isn't* anything, right?"

He shook his head as if nothing she said mattered. "Most of the kids at school won't even look at me. The ones that do just stare like I'm some kind of pervert or something."

"It has to be terrible for you, I know, but . . . I mean, there's no evidence of any kind. There's no reason for you to be so worked up over this. Nothing is going to happen to you, I promise."

He regarded her with glistening eyes. "You know what Reenie asked me this morning? When I stopped to pick her up for school?"

She waited, said nothing, couldn't even shake her head in answer.

"She wanted to know if I liked doing it to little boys."

"God, Dylan. Jesus, I . . ."

"I always walk up to her door to meet her, you know? I mean, she's always lugging a bunch of stuff to school with her. Books, gym clothes, her clarinet . . . you know? So I'm standing there at the door when it opens, but she just steps out and gets right up in my face and you know what she says? 'Just tell me one thing,' she says. 'You like doing it to little boys?' "

He was crying in earnest now, the tears streaming down his cheeks. "And I fucking slapped her for it! I mean, I wasn't even thinking, I just hauled off and did it. I didn't mean to, I swear I never done nothing like it before, I just—"

Charlotte's own cheeks burned as if slapped, needed to be slapped, deserved his pain. She moved closer to him now, put a hand on his shoulder, though she was uncertain if it was to comfort him or steady herself from falling. Then she sat on the edge of the porch beside him, sat huddled as he was huddled, bent forward, brittle, hands clamped between his knees.

"It will be all right, I promise. Nothing is going to happen to you, you didn't do anything. I know you didn't."

He trembled and wept. "I can't even tell you what she said to me after I slapped her. I can't even repeat it."

"It will be okay," she told him. "I promise it will."

"I wasn't in those woods for no forty minutes. You've got to tell the sheriff you were wrong about that."

"I will, I'll tell him."

"You promise you will?"

"I'll call him. I'll tell him I wasn't even paying attention, I wasn't watching, it was just a guess, that's all. Just a bad guess is all it was."

"I swear to you that all I did was to take a quick dump and then climb right back onto the tractor."

"I believe you," she said. "I believe you with all my heart."

Even after he left, she could not move. After he stood and walked away, disappeared around the corner of her house. After he passed through her backyard, into the long fields at the rear of the house. After he had probably reached Mike Verner's farm, was probably talking to Mike, probably still proclaiming his innocence. Even then Charlotte remained on the edge of her porch, hands clamped between her knees, knees squeezing hard, eyes squeezed shut, not wanting to see this world again, this place, this idyllic life so suddenly gone so irremediably wrong.

17

In her studio, the dimmest room on the first floor, the room whose scents and memories comforted her, she opened her cell phone. It took the sheriff a while to answer the call; in fact, the recorded greeting had already started on his machine before he picked up. The sound of his actual voice, as soft and nonthreatening as it was, came like a swat to knock away the relief she had felt just seconds earlier when the recording started.

"Marcus, hi. This is Charlotte Dunleavy. I apologize for interrupting your afternoon."

"Is it still afternoon?" he said. "Feels like it should be at least midnight by now."

"I know," she said. "Such a long, unhappy day." She had recognized the weariness in his voice because it echoed her own, and she would have liked to have ended the conversation there, that shared moment, shared recognition in the gravity of the air they breathed, though miles apart. It was the closest thing to intimacy she had experienced in a long time, and now that she felt it, she felt, too, how sorely she had missed it.

But her promise to Dylan Hayes, her obligation to the boy, was impossible to avoid. She said, "I had a talk with Dylan a few minutes ago."

"Where are you?" Gatesman asked. His voice was more animated now, almost brusque. "At your place?"

"Yes. He came here."

"Tell me what he said, Charlotte."

"He didn't threaten me or anything, if that's what you're thinking. He was distraught, Marcus. The boy is terrified."

"And maybe rightfully so."

"Not if you're basing your suspicions on what I told you yesterday."

"Oh?" he said.

"You realize I was just guessing, don't you? About how long he stayed in the woods?"

"You were estimating, is what I thought. That's different than a guess, isn't it?"

"I know I told you forty minutes, but . . ."

"But now you think you were wrong?"

"Now I think I might have inadvertently misled you. That I might have implied something I didn't mean."

"Well," he said, "how about if you tell me what you did mean?"

"I saw him get off the tractor and go into the woods, yes. But afterward . . . It's not like I stood there at the window watching his every move. I started vacuuming . . . no, I was lying on my bed. Yes, I was thinking about my work, my painting . . . My mind was elsewhere for I don't know how long. The truth is, I forgot about Dylan entirely."

"Until you heard the tractor start up again."

"Until I became aware of the sound of the tractor again."

"Not *start up*?"

"I don't know. I honestly don't. What I mean is . . . you know how sometimes at night or whatever, you're sitting there alone in your house, and suddenly you become aware of some sound? Maybe it's the refrigerator running, maybe it's a bird outside, it could be anything. When I lived in the city—I mean, God, there were sirens going off all the time. Horns blaring down on the street, traffic noise, phones ringing in other apartments. You just learn to tune it out, you know? I mean, it doesn't stop, it never stops, but you tune it out. Then every once in a while it just sort of registers again. And suddenly you're hearing it."

"As if it just then started up again."

"Exactly!"

"So what you're saying is . . . maybe the tractor had been running a lot longer than you're aware of."

"I'm sorry, Marcus. I never meant to imply . . . or to implicate or . . ."

"I understand," he said.

In his silence then she heard his desk chair creak. She pictured him leaning back in his chair, staring up at the ceiling.

"And why was it Dylan came to see you?" he asked.

"He knew it had to have been me who told you he was in the woods for forty minutes. Who else could have seen him get off the tractor and take something from behind the seat?"

"Do you think now you know what that thing was?"

"It was a roll of toilet paper, Marcus."

"You didn't know that when I first asked, though."

"He told me, and then suddenly it was like, aha, yes, of course, of course that's what it was. I mean, I see it happening now, I see him climbing down off the tractor, reaching behind the seat . . . I can even see it in his hand. It's as clear as day to me now."

"That's how the memory works sometimes. He says it was a roll of toilet paper, and now that's what you see whenever you think back on it."

"Marcus, really, honestly, I mean, let's think about this. Could that boy have gone into the woods, found Jesse, done something to him, hidden the body where nobody can find a trace of it, and then climbed back on the tractor and spent another two hours or so spreading lime like nothing had ever happened?"

"If he was in there for forty minutes, maybe he could have."

"Marcus, please. You're a sensible man."

His chair creaked again. She imagined him swiveling around to face the window, gazing out onto the street.

She told him, "You know as well as I do that Dylan didn't hurt that child."

"I never said he did. But something happened to Jesse. It's my job to find out what."

"I understand. I just wanted to let you know that I . . . I really have no idea whether Dylan was in the woods for forty minutes or four minutes. I'm sorry if I implied that I did."

She could hear another phone ringing in his office, and she wondered what it must be like for him. One human tragedy after another. A good day would be a day when the phone didn't ring. Did Marcus ever have a good day?

"Can I put you on hold for just thirty seconds?" he asked.

"Of course," she said.

Is this how God feels? she wondered as she waited. Was there ever a day, an hour, when He wasn't bombarded with prayers and pleas? Carnage everywhere He looks. Flesh and spirit coming apart at the seams.

"Oh God," she said aloud, and thought about hanging up the phone, clicking it shut, clicking everything shut.

"You still there?" the sheriff asked.

"I'm here," she said.

"Sorry about that. But anyway. I just wanted to say that I appreciate you calling. And to make sure that, you know, he didn't put any pressure on you or anything like that."

"Dylan? My God, no, nothing. He never so much as implied it. He's frightened to death, Marcus. He's just a child really. Just a frightened little boy."

Gatesman was silent for a moment, then asked, his voice softer now, "Are you crying, Charlotte?"

"I just . . . I feel so bad for everybody. For everybody involved."

"It's hard, I know. This kind of thing . . ." He would have said more, wanted to, but then told himself, *Now isn't the time.*

Finally he said, "Okay then. Thanks again. You take care of yourself, okay?"

"You too," she said. And the closeness she felt for him at that moment, the impossible closeness, it took her breath away, hollowed her out and made her body ache with emptiness. She waited, hoping for more, *Do you want me to come over? Could you use some company tonight?* But there was only silence, two people silently waiting. And finally she folded up her phone.

18

THREE *years,* she told herself. *Four years this July. Four years so alone.*

If only Mother were here, she thought. *Mother always knew what to do. Somehow she always knew.*

She had known about Mark, Charlotte reminded herself. And she did her best to warn me. But I wouldn't listen. I was always so goddamn smart, I wouldn't listen to anybody.

On the day Charlotte's mother died, her family was all at the hospital with her—her husband, her daughter, her son-in-law.

Daddy was on one side of the bed, Charlotte remembered. *Holding Mother's hand as always. God, how he adored her. His first marriage, what little I know of it, hadn't been pleasant, though the few times he talked about it, he blamed himself for much of the unpleasantness. It takes two, he used to say. Two to make things work, two to break it beyond repair. I wonder if he was insinuating that he had cheated on his first wife? Abused her verbally or psychologically?*

Even physically? I can't envision that he ever did. On the other hand, maybe that's always been my problem. Me, an artist. An artist with a woefully limited vision.

Yes, Charlotte thought, bringing herself back to the day of her mother's death, *Daddy was sitting there holding one hand, I was holding the other one. She was in a lot of pain, I think, despite the morphine. But she was lucid as hell. At one point she squeezed my hand so hard that I lifted my head to look at her, and she was lying there with her eyes wet and shining but smiling the most beautiful smile.*

"It's so ironic," she had said. Charlotte leaned closer because her voice was weak. "What is?" she asked. And her mother answered, "That the organ that gave me my greatest joy is now going to take me away from her."

Charlotte remembered struggling to keep her tears to herself but to small avail. "You're not going anywhere," she had told her mother. "I won't let you."

Her mother had smiled a soft, indulgent smile, then closed her eyes awhile. Charlotte's father had leaned forward then and rested his forehead on the corner of her pillow.

Several minutes later, Charlotte's mother opened her eyes again. "Listen," she said, and Charlotte leaned close. "That man . . ."

Charlotte followed her mother's gaze to the doorway, where Mark stood each time they visited the hospital. Each time he would come into the room and kiss the older woman's cheek, then eventually retreat to the doorway to stand there with his back against the frame. And that was why, when Charlotte's mother said *that man*, Charlotte had immediately turned to look toward her husband, and found him, as usual, not even looking in their direction but smiling at something down the hall.

"What about him?" she had whispered.

Charlotte's mother regarded her daughter then, but no longer with a smile on her lips. She held her daughter's gaze for a long time but never finished the sentence, only squeezed Charlotte's hand until her own eyes closed again and her grip went slack.

Charlotte's mother lasted another four hours, and during that time her eyes never opened. She spoke only one more time, though in a whisper so small that only Charlotte's father heard. He then answered, "I won't, sweetheart. Never."

Charlotte later asked him what her mother had said, and he told her, "Don't let go."

Charlotte had never been entirely convinced that her mother had been speaking only to her husband, only asking him to never let go of her hand, which was what Charlotte's father always believed. Charlotte wondered if perhaps those final words were somehow the completion of the previous unfinished sentence, if *that man* and *don't let go* had in some manner constituted a single thought. After her father had relayed the final words to Charlotte, she had turned to the doorway, empty now, and had become suddenly annoyed that Mark had wandered away at some moment prior to her mother's passing, was probably in the lounge or the cafeteria or at the nurses' station flirting with a candy striper.

Had her mother been telling her to not let go of that man? Or, more likely, had she been warning her to not let go of something *because* of that man? To not give away something she should keep for herself?

During the year of Charlotte and Mark's courtship, then the eight years of marriage, Charlotte's mother had never warmed to her son-in-law. And Mother, Charlotte remembered, was an exceedingly warm person. *But sometimes I would catch her looking askance at him, her eyes narrow and her mouth in a hard line, just like that day in the hospital.*

Two years earlier, Christmas Eve at Charlotte's parents' house, had been another example of that look. Charlotte had opened her gift from Mark, saw the Tiffany box, opened it, and saw the two-karat diamond ring. While she gasped and gaped, Mark started chattering about what a fortunate man he was, what a wonderful wife Charlotte was, on and on until Charlotte blushed with embarrassment. It was then Charlotte had glanced at her mother and saw the way she was regarding her son-in-law. As if he had just let loose a ripping loud fart, Charlotte thought.

Later, when alone in the kitchen with her mother, Charlotte had said, "You don't really like Mark much, do you?"

"Of course I do," her mother answered. "He's your husband."

"I saw the way you were looking at him. And it wasn't the first time."

"And how was I looking at him?"

"Like he disgusts you."

Her mother had chuckled softly. "No, sweetie. That's not it at all."

"Then what is it?"

"Sometimes . . ." she said.

"Sometimes what?"

"Sometimes he just goes on too long, I guess. He gushes."

"And you find that . . . what? Suspicious?"

"Why? Do you?"

"Do you think I should?"

Several seconds passed before her mother responded. "I guess I was just listening to him go on and on about you, and wondering . . ."

"Just say it, Mother. Wondering what?"

"Wondering if he says those things to you in private."

"Of course he does. All the time."

"Good. Then that's just the way he is. He adores you and doesn't mind expressing it."

But, of course, Charlotte had lied to her mother. And that was why Charlotte had gasped and gaped so at his extravagance. Neither generosity of objects nor compliments had been natural to Mark. *Anyway, not where I was concerned,* Charlotte remembered.

And then, she told herself, then came the night at Tambellini's. Our usual Thursday night. Summer in the city. The thick stench of simmering concrete and carbon monoxide.

They were seated as usual at a small table near the back of the room, the area Mark always requested. They were waiting for the salads—his, the house, hers, the *caprese.*

And just like always, she remembered, his damn cell phone started vibrating atop the table. It was always something important, of course, some junior partner to advise, a client to calm down, one of the paralegals with a question that couldn't wait until morning. And, same as always, he picked up the phone, looked at the caller's number, then said, straight off the script, "It's too noisy in here. I'm going to step outside for a minute." Every single Thursday night. *And I was too stupid to question it,* Charlotte thought. *He's a busy man, I told myself. Wasn't he always telling me what a busy man he was? I never even thought to ask him or myself, "Why not take those calls in the men's room or even the coatroom?" Not until* that *Thursday night anyway.*

Because the Tiffany diamond incident had been her first nudge of awareness. Her mother's deathbed look at him had swung the door of suspicion wide open.

What made Mark's Thursday night disappearing act at Tambellini's especially suspicious for Charlotte was that Thursday night, right after the cannolis, was their night for sex.

The man would lay not a finger on me all week long, she

reminded herself, and felt the anger blossoming again, just as it always had in June's office, the anger and then the heat and sting of tears. Because by the time he handed the server his credit card on Thursday nights, he was playing footsie with his wife.

Or just sitting there grinning at me with that I-need-to-fuck-you gleam in his weasely little eyes. So this time—unlike all the other times—my bullshit detector was screaming like a banshee.

"This might take a couple minutes," he had told her, then stood and made his exit, the phone to his ear. But this time, instead of turning her attention to the other customers, instead of entertaining herself by checking out hairdos and jewelry and footwear, this time Charlotte watched him all the way out the door. She knew from past experience that he would stand there just on the sidewalk, in plain view through the front window, for fifteen seconds or so. Then, ever so nonchalantly, same as always, he would wander out of view.

But this time, instead of sitting there patiently as she had always done—*instead of sitting there sipping my wine like a good insipid wife,* she thought—this time Charlotte stood and laid down her linen napkin, walked to the door, and peeked outside. And there was her husband, striding briskly down the block, cell phone nowhere to be seen.

The rear door swung open on a black Lexus parked at the curb, and Mark climbed inside. *And that's when I knew,* she thought. *That's when I absolutely knew why my mother had looked at him and said "That man . . ." I finally understood, without the shadow of a doubt, why he insisted on going to Tambellini's every Thursday night. For the pasta fazul, my ass.*

If Charlotte had not followed her husband down the street that night, ten minutes later he would have come strolling back inside, pretending to be annoyed about having had to take the call. Then, halfway through the entrée he would have slipped off his Italian loafer, always the right one, and slid his foot between her legs. He would have winked at her with his mouth full of mascarpone.

And, of course, she remembered, *I'd let him fool around like that. I wanted it. I'd been wanting it all week long. A real kiss, a lingering touch,* any *authentic display of affection. So what did I care if it took a plate full of semolina to get him aroused?*

Until that night. When Charlotte yanked open the rear door on that shiny black Lexus, and her husband looked out at her staring in at him, he made no move to cover himself or to pull away from the woman with her face in his lap. He kept his hand on the back of her head. The dome light had come on when Charlotte yanked the door open, so she could see clearly the look in his eyes, and what she saw wasn't fear or surprise but excitement.

I think the sonofabitch actually pushed her head down harder, she told herself. *I think he came in her mouth the moment he realized he'd been caught.*

Afterward, when Charlotte and her husband met at the elevator outside their apartment, with him coming up and she and her suitcases waiting to go down, he looked at her and smiled sheepishly and said, "You have to understand how *bored* I get."

"Get out of the elevator," she told him. But he would not.

"I'll take the stairs," she said.

He said, "Baby, wait," and reached out and grabbed hold of one of the suitcases, pulled it and Charlotte into the elevator with him, and held her by the arm so that she could not exit. She repeatedly jabbed the *L* button until she felt the jerk of descent.

He released her arm then and dropped the suitcase to the floor and leaned into the corner. "I never go all the way with her," he said. "It's just prelude, that's all."

"You did tonight, though, didn't you?"

He tried for another sheepish grin, but this one came out as a smirk. "It's the only time I see her," he said. "I swear."

"Fuck you," Charlotte told him. Then the pain returned, another nauseating wave. She staggered back against the chrome wall. "So that's the only way you can get aroused enough to fuck me? Is that what it takes for you?"

He answered with a smirk and a shrug.

"How much does she cost?" she demanded.

"Don't," he said.

"I want to know. How much are you willing to pay to make you horny enough to want to fuck your wife? Tell me!"

"She charges five hundred dollars."

"Two thousand a month," Charlotte said. "You're paying her two thousand dollars a month. She gets twenty-four thousand dollars a year from you, and I get maybe twenty minutes of mediocre sex once a week."

"I knew you would get nasty about this," he said.

"Nasty? You lousy, rotten, stupid bastard. You ruin our marriage, and I'm the one getting nasty? What, you never heard of Viagra? Five dollars a fucking pill!"

"It's not physical, you know that. It's all mental. If you'd just relax and look at this rationally . . ."

The elevator bucked to a stop then; the door slid open. Charlotte jerked her suitcase off the floor and stepped out. "*You're* mental," she told him. "You're sick and disgusting." And she headed for the lobby doors.

"And you," he said, his voice increasing in volume now, "are, as always, unbelievably provincial. I thought you were an artist. You're supposed to be creative. Instead you're just plain boring."

She made the mistake then of looking back at him. She was

already halfway across the lobby, the doorman had pulled the door open for her, she had only to step over the threshold and be free.

But I just had to turn around and look back at him, she reminded herself. *Just like Lot's stupid wife. So not only did he get the satisfaction of seeing the tears streaming down my cheeks, but I had to witness that damn smirk of his one last time.*

She spent the next two years trying to scour that smirk out of her consciousness. And she thought she had done so. Moved to Pennsylvania, bought a farm, remodeled it to suit nobody but herself, started a brand-new life. Made her own schedule: slept, ate, worked, hiked, did whatever she wanted whenever she wanted to. She had at long last reached the point where she could close her eyes at night and not see Mark's god-awful handsome face with its haunting and obliterating smirk.

Then came the boy who shoots crows.

19

Midmorning the day after the search of the woods, Charlotte sat on the concrete edge of her rear porch. She had made a pot of coffee that morning using eight coffee singles, but even this cup, her third in a little more than an hour, did not ease the heaviness of her eyelids or lighten the heaviness of every movement. Her intention was to start the labor of working the soil in her garden, mixing in the fertilizer Mike Verner had left, and thereby distract herself one spadeful at a time from the horrors of the previous days. But she had made it no farther than the edge of her porch, had stood there awhile after her second cup of coffee and considered the distance to her garden shed, the effort required to step inside, pull down the garden rake from the rack of hand tools, go back to her garden, hack open the bag of fertilizer, spill the mix over the soil, and then drag the rake through the earth, push it forward, again and again and again several hundreds of times. The mere thought of walking to the shed exhausted her. Only two weeks earlier she had spent a quietly joyful evening poring over the new seed catalog, reading about all of the new varieties from which she might choose and envisioning the abundance of her garden come late summer, the scent of a sunny kitchen with an ever-present basket of green and yellow squash arranged in an edible bouquet: the plump tomatoes, cucumbers, red and green sweet peppers, and yellow banana peppers, the bright little jalapeños like little penises, the clumps of carrots, the scallions, and all of the herbs in little jars of water lined up across the windowsills. But this morning she had gazed upon the brown, rectangular plot and felt no joy. Her mouth no longer watered and she no longer thought of the dizzying thrill of biting into a fat tomato, warm from the vine. That morning she had appraised her garden plot and told herself, *I'll have another cup of coffee first.*

The crows had fallen silent and flown off hours earlier. In the silence, she felt only a stupefied slackness in a body no longer her own. When Mike Verner's voice echoed through her house—"Hey, Charlotte! Good morning!"—her recognition of his voice was not immediate, and the sound only made her clutch the coffee mug even tighter.

"I'm in your house," she heard, "and walking toward your kitchen. Don't bother to get dressed on my account, I'm naked too." She smiled then, but also felt how detached she was from that smile, how Mike's humor registered only on the surface, only lingered on the air for a moment, and then was quickly gone.

"I'm on the back porch," she called over her shoulder.

"I think I smell coffee," he said.

"Follow your nose. You'll find it."

"Aha!" he said a few moments later. Then, "Cups?" he asked.

"Where cups usually are."

She heard a couple of cabinet doors open and close, then nothing, and thirty seconds later he stepped out onto the porch. "Good morning, Miss Charlotte. How's everything out here at Green Acres this morning?"

"Pensive," she said. "How's everything with you?"

He sat beside her, took a sip of the coffee, made a face, but quickly changed it to a more neutral expression. He said, "*Pensive* is one of those words I forgot to learn in high school. I'm guessing, though, judging from the look on your face, that it means something like sad."

"Thoughtful," she said. "But yes, in a sad way, I suppose. It is a sad day, isn't it? Sort of like my coffee."

"It's not all that bad. Your coffee, I mean. Just not what I'm used to."

She said nothing for a moment. Then looked at him and said, "Did you bring more bad news this morning?"

"Jesus, is that what I am? The messenger of bad tidings?"

"You have too much work to just sit and enjoy a cup of coffee with me, I know that much. So what's up?"

"You're a little out of sorts this morning, aren't you? Yesterday took all the starch out of you."

She smiled. "My mother used to use that expression."

"It's a good one." Then, "Used to? She's no longer with you?"

"It's going on five years now. Ovarian cancer."

"I'm so sorry, Charlotte."

"She was one of the lucky ones. Went very quickly."

"If you have to go, and we all do, that's the way to do it." He sipped his coffee, considered her yard, his field beyond, the distant sky, the far unseen. "How about your father?" he asked.

"He's been in a nursing home the last couple of years. Started having these little ministrokes not long after Mother passed. Last time I visited him, he didn't even recognize me."

"Jesus," Mike said. "Life really sucks, doesn't it?"

"Right now it seems like that's all it does. How about your folks? Are they still with you?"

"Only by telephone. They have a condo down in Naples, Florida. They belong to a senior citizen's swingers club. Orgies every night."

She looked at him for a moment. "You're such a liar, Mike."

"I'm just speculating, of course."

"More like fantasizing, maybe?"

"Hey, a man's gotta have something to look forward to."

She set her coffee mug on the concrete, then put her hands atop her knees. "So back to the original question. What brings you here this morning?"

"So you're not in the mood to talk about orgies right now. Okay then, moving on. I just came by to make sure you knew about the thing for Jesse tonight."

For a few moments she had hoped for a slow revitalization at work as the result of Mike's company, an opening up of her sun-filled yard, but now, at the mention of Jesse's name, the world darkened and shrank in on her again. "What thing?" she asked.

"I figured you might not have heard. There's going to be a candlelight thing over at the elementary school tonight."

"A candlelight vigil?"

"That's the word I couldn't think of. You know how words sometimes do that? Just disappear from the memory banks for a while?"

She said nothing.

"I lost *vigil* sometime in the middle of the night. Couldn't lay a hand on it all morning until you just now gave it back to me."

"It happens," she said.

"Too much of late. But anyway. It's starting around eight, I guess. Why it's being held at the school, I have no idea. From what I hear, the boy hated school with a passion. Spent as little time there as he could get away with."

"In the gymnasium?"

"Probably outside is my guess. Supposed to be a clear night and all. You want Claudia and me to swing by about a quarter till and pick you up?"

"No, I . . . I guess if I go I'll drive over myself."

"Not that you're obligated or anything."

"I know."

"Just thought it might be a good way to, you know, get involved with the community. Nobody's going to hold it against you, though, if you decide not to come."

"No, I want to. I just . . ."

"Things like this," he said, "it's always seemed funny to me. If it weren't for things like this—weddings, funerals, you know what I mean—people might not even talk to one another anymore. Everybody's too busy being busy."

"I'll probably be there. Watch for me, okay? You might be the only person I know."

"You bet. The thing'll probably last only an hour or two at most. A lot of crying and praying, then back to our busy lives."

"There might be some music too," she said.

"Oh yeah?"

"I went to one for John Lennon."

"No kidding. Where was this?"

"It was actually on the first anniversary of his death. 1981. In that park in Manhattan they named after the song. Strawberry Fields."

" 'Strawberry Fields Forever.' That must have been something."

"I stayed in bed for two days afterward. Just didn't want to move."

"Well, yeah. I imagine this one will be rough on some people too. So if you don't feel like going . . ."

"I do, though. I mean . . . What are people saying about me, Mike? I mean because of my house being right here beside the woods . . ."

"Nothing. Nothing at all as far as I know. Hell, whatever they're saying about you, they're probably saying about me too. So who gives a rat's ass, am I right?"

She could tell that he was lying. "Dylan, though," she said. "He has some thoughts about me, I'm sure."

"Naw, he knows you cleared things up yesterday with the sheriff."

"He does?"

"Sure. His parents, you know . . . his dad especially, he's stayed in fairly close touch with the sheriff. Mark told him you called. Said as far as he's concerned, Dylan's story checks out."

"Thank God for that," she said.

"So about tonight. It's no problem to swing by and pick you up. Save you the trouble of driving there yourself."

"I appreciate the offer, thanks. But I'll meet you there, okay?"

"We'd come in Claudia's Sonata, by the way, not my truck. I was thinking maybe we let her drive, you and me can ride over in the backseat together. See if maybe we can get some practice in for when we all move to Florida."

She wanted to laugh but it came out as a single-syllable grunt.

"I'm not saying we have to actually do anything in the backseat. Not on the way over, anyway. On the way back, okay, if you can contain your natural attraction for me that long."

"That's why I think it's better if I drive myself."

"How about if I throw in a video camera?"

"Now you're getting out of hand."

"I'm on my sixth cup of coffee this morning, can you tell?"

"You're on something, all right."

"But, hey, since you've been to one of these things already and know how they work: Are we supposed to take our own candles or what?"

"Usually whoever organizes the vigil will provide them. Was it a church group?"

"One of the teachers, I think."

"Even though Jesse hated school?"

"So I hear. I don't have to wear a coat and tie, do I? Like for a funeral?"

Her heart, which had been quieting again to the lull of Mike's slow baritone, now jumped like a stomach-hooked trout. "Funeral?" she asked. "Is that what this is supposed to be tonight?"

"Naw, nobody's giving up on him. Not publicly anyway. There's one of those AMBER Alerts out on him. You've seen it on the local news probably."

"I hardly ever turn the television on. Maybe the History Channel, Discovery Channel, an old movie now and then."

"This thing tonight is just to show our support, you know? Claudia says it's mainly for the boy's mother."

A sudden flare of brightness, then a darkening, a tightening down to tunnel vision again. "How is she, Mike? How is she doing?"

"Claudia? Mean and spiteful as ever. By the way, when I introduce you to her tonight, try not to look surprised if she turns around and pops me a good one on the jaw."

"What?" Charlotte said, because the conversation seemed broken now, the edges did not match.

"I told her back when you and me first met that you're fat and ugly," he said. "Even more so than she is. And that takes a lot of doing. Any chance you could put on a hundred pounds or so before tonight? Maybe twist your face up a little and pull out most of your teeth?"

"Oh, Mike," she said.

"Just giving you fair warning, is all." He set his cup on the concrete, then stood. "We'll see you tonight. If you have a Kevlar vest, probably wouldn't hurt to put it on."

She watched him walking away then, around the corner of the house and toward the front. Only ten minutes later, as she sat there staring straight ahead, did she realize that she had never heard Mike's truck arriving in her driveway that morning, nor had any sound of departure reached her ears. This realization about herself, the ease with which she was able to drown out reality by sinking into a swamp of self-pity, her self-absorption, her narcissism, it struck her with the force of a blow, and she understood suddenly how wholly she had deserved those smirks of contempt, the look from Mark, the look from Jesse, and that it was by her own selfishness that she had come to this point in time, this world of darkness and grief, this fear without end.

20

GATESMAN spent the morning returning phone calls, reading and signing a small pile of the endless paperwork that came and went from his desk. With each chime of the old clock in the courthouse corridor, he felt another portion of heaviness accumulating in his gut. What he did not know was whether the heaviness was real or psychological, only that something wasn't right inside him. He felt bloated, his belt too tight, even though he had skipped breakfast again that morning. But he kept his discomfort to himself. He knew that if he so much as hinted of the tender spot in his lower abdomen, Tina would take it upon herself to make an appointment for him with Doc Stevens. She might go so far as to schedule a colonoscopy. And Gatesman could envision no good coming from any such procedure or investigation.

When the clock in the hallway started chiming again, and then continued to chime long after he thought it should have stopped, he opened his cell phone and saw that the time was twelve o'clock. He turned in his chair and looked out the window. *The morning is gone,* he told himself. *Where did it go?*

The day was bright and clear. Vehicles moved up and down the street outside his window. Pedestrians hurried past. *Everybody is going somewhere,* he thought. *There's always somewhere else they have to be.*

For a reason he could not discern, his thoughts turned to Livvie Rankin then. The last two times he had visited her, she had seemed inordinately still. She, among all the people he knew, had stopped trying to be somewhere else. What she wanted was to be some*time* else.

And then he asked himself, *Isn't that what you want too?*

And he acknowledged, *Yes. That is exactly what I want.*

He wished he could walk away from his office and the courthouse and the town of Belinda and go up into the mountains with his wife where the air was not so heavy, where the lake was cold and sparkling clear and they could sit on the porch of a rented cabin and hold hands and not speak and feel almost weightless in their happiness. The sunlight would dance across the surface of the lake like a scattering of silver leaves. A red canoe would be overturned on shore beside somebody's dock, and maybe a little girl would be standing on the dock and plinking stones into the water.

But he knew that he was wishing for what he could never have, especially not now. Not after what had happened two days ago. Another child gone under his watch. He did not know if he could bear the weight of that error. Nor the knowledge that there was nothing he could have done to prevent it, not this time or the next time, not unless he did the impossible and herded all the children together into one place and stood guard over them 24-7.

Worst was the weight of what might yet occur. He had the

sense that even more ugliness was building out there in his jurisdiction, maybe more to do with Jesse, maybe not. In any case there would be more of it, always more of it. There might yet come another day with the sunlight and the red canoe and the little girl, some other little girl, but as for the weightlessness of happiness, as for Patrice and Chelsea, none of that could come again. The last time had been the last time.

Up until a few days ago, he had from time to time been blessed with what he now perceived as a kind of ignorance, blindness, that cautious optimism that fuels all of human perseverance, that maybe he was finally done with most of the darkness, was maybe able now, with mindfulness and careful tread, to venture out beyond the shadows. But now Jesse was gone and Gatesman could find no trace of him, did not even know where else to look for him, and now Livvie's hard life had closed and hardened all around her, and there was nothing Gatesman could do for either of them.

"You can't help anybody," he told himself.

The day was clear and bright and the lake in the mountains would be so pretty now, and in a couple of days the trout season would open. *But you should probably skip the first day of trout season this year,* he told himself. *You should probably skip the entire season.*

21

All through the morning and well into the afternoon, the sounds and the scents of the search stayed with her. If she stretched out on the La-Z-Boy and closed her eyes, Charlotte could hear again the whispers of all those footsteps moving through damp leaves. The scent of those leaves, of slow decomposition in dim, damp light, seemed to be stuck low in her throat and could not be dislodged no matter how often she tried to clear it. When she moved throughout the house, she avoided mirrors and all reflective surfaces. If she glimpsed herself even peripherally, she was quick to look away. She could find no place in the house to rest, though she could not remember ever being so weary.

Several times that day she stood in front of her easel to consider the image half-completed on the canvas. Amish boy, Amish girl. The grizzled, grinning biker. *How long ago did I do that?* she wondered. It had only been four days, yet the lines seemed to have been drawn by somebody else, the sketch some relic of the long ago.

The painting was no longer hers, but she understood what the painter had been trying for, she could see the possibilities. The perspective of the biker wasn't quite right—she noticed that when she stood just to the right of the easel; the rear wheel should be pulled just slightly closer to the viewer so that the biker appeared to be driving deeper into the scene instead of merely across it. *I could fix that if I wanted to,* she thought, but she made no move to do so.

What kept her from reaching for the charcoal pencil was an unsettling sensation of being watched. She was aware of herself as both inside and outside the room, one self standing near the easel, thinking painterly thoughts, the other watching from a short distance away and thinking, *You fraud.*

As evening approached, her restlessness and weariness grew. Only with the television turned on could she keep herself from moving from window to window, peering out from behind the curtain or blind. The programs she found most soothing were the slow-paced, quiet ones on the Discovery and National Geographic and History Channels. For twenty minutes or so, she fell asleep to the ponderous, graceful movements of elephants bathing in dust, but when she woke she was momentarily anxious and surfed through the channel guide for several minutes before coming back to the elephants.

Finally the blue readout on the DVD told her that it was 6:30 P.M., and she said to herself, "You can get ready now, Charlotte."

But even after she was showered and dressed, she kept finding little things to tend to. She took the garbage from the kitchen receptacle to the larger container on the back porch. Then she told herself, *You might as well do the rest of them too,* so she also gathered up the little wire basket in her bathroom and the tall wicker basket beside her desk and emptied those into the trash as well. Then she happened to look up at the kitchen light as her hand went to the switch to shut it off, and she noticed that the plastic shade over the light had several black specks inside it, some dark blurs that she knew to be dead flies. So she climbed onto a kitchen chair and removed the shade, emptied the flies into the trash, and washed and dried the shade before putting it back in place. She did the same with the shades in both bathrooms and the two overhead lights in the upstairs hallway. Then the light in the downstairs foyer. Then she thought, *Maybe I should just stay home and give this house a good cleaning.* She took the vacuum out of the hallway closet, but then suddenly she was out of breath and her heart was racing and every beat felt like a bruise inside her chest. "Oh God," she said aloud, and leaned against the closet door, forehead to the wood, until the panic gradually subsided.

"You have to go," she told herself then. "You have to."

A few minutes later she went into the living room and looked at the DVD. The readout said 8:05 P.M.

By the time she had the Jeep out of the garage, the first few lines of an old Moby Grape song were playing on a continuous loop through her mind. *Eight oh-five . . . I guess you're leaving soon. I can't go on without you, it's useless to try.* She was able to drown the lyrics out finally only by grabbing a CD from the four she kept in the console, shoving it into the player, and turning the volume up loud. She wanted only sound, no words, no memories or associations, just noise she could feel on her skin and in her teeth, noise to drum all thoughts from her brain, so all the way to the elementary school she swam through the punishing current of the Trans-Siberian Orchestra's *Beethoven's Last Night*—swam, she told herself, like an old, barren salmon struggling upstream to die.

22

THE parking lot at the elementary school was jammed full, and the only parking space Charlotte could find was out along the highway. She parked with the Jeep's right wheels inches from a drainage ditch. She could see hundreds of cars and trucks but not a single person in sight.

She climbed out of the Jeep and closed the door softly and stood there on the gravel shoulder. There on the highway, she was enveloped in darkness. The sky was black, no moon and no stars visible. The air was cool but clean-smelling, with just a hint of wood smoke from somebody's chimney. The nearest light was forty yards away, across the schoolyard at the corner of the parking lot, a sodium-vapor light mounted at the top of a thirty-foot pole.

Nobody even knows you're here, she told herself. It would have been a more comforting thought had she believed the anonymity could last.

Then she heard the singing. The words were indistinguishable, little more than a muddy drone of voices, but a wavering melody made its way to her through the darkness, broken bits of which she thought she could identify as John Denver's "Sunshine." She thought it a strange choice to be singing in darkness for a surly little boy whose favorite place had been the darkened woods. *But maybe it's his mother's favorite song,* she thought. *Or his father's. They probably don't have much money for music. Or maybe it's not even that song at all.*

She thought the night felt more like October than April. A crisp night of gathering excitement. Football season. Homecoming. The high-voltage drama of adolescence.

But no, this night was an ending, not a beginning. Charlotte wondered if any candlelight vigils anywhere had ever ended with happiness. Were missing children ever returned safely to their families? Did all those songs and prayers ever pierce the heart of heaven?

Now that her eyes had adjusted to the darkness, she was able to pick out a couple of dim stars. Then she saw that they did not twinkle, they hung like tiny sequins on black velvet. Satellites, probably, she told herself. Tin cans beaming signals. Tonight's episode of some stupid reality show. The four-hundredth rerun of *Blazing Saddles*.

She stood there on the side of the road and searched from one corner of the sky to the next. Then suddenly she remembered her dream the night before the search in the woods, the shadow man who had approached her, and suddenly she was afraid standing there alone. Across the road were a few houses separated by wide, vacant yards, and behind the houses, a row of trees leading toward a ridge. She shivered with the thought of somebody rushing toward her out of that darkness. She reached into the pocket of her stadium jacket and closed her hand around the key chain and crossed quickly toward the school building and the light behind it.

The elementary school sat at the bottom of a gentle slope, and behind, on a low plateau, were two football fields. The nearest, maybe fifty yards behind the building, was the high school team's practice field. Then came a sharp rise of twenty or so feet, and on another plateau of sculpted land were the game field and the high school. Sodium-vapor lights at the rear of the elementary building made all this visible to Charlotte, though the two football fields themselves were unlit but for the watery, flickering glows of several hundred candles in the center of the nearest field. It seemed to her that the entire town must have been gathered there, everybody from all the little trailer court hamlets, the isolated farmers and their families, the entire scattered school district. She had not known there were so many people in the entire county.

Her stomach lurched with every step. By the time she reached the rear of the crowd she was shivering uncontrollably, despite the heavy jacket she wore and the gray wool scarf wrapped twice around her neck. She kept both hands in her pockets, came to within two feet of the nearest people, and would have paused there, hung back, invisible at the rear, except that a man turned at her approach and smiled. He greeted Charlotte with a nod and took a step to the side. "Come on through here," he told her. "You won't see nothing but people's heads from back here."

She wanted to tell him that that was all she wanted to see. But he kept smiling and waiting, so she continued forward, moved into the space he'd made for her. Immediately others turned to look at her, and they, too, moved aside. She continued to inch her way forward, though she could not help wondering, uncomfortably, why all of those strangers continued to make room for her to advance. At first she thought it an act of simple rural courtesy, but halfway through the crowd she became aware of people leaning close to one another, whispering, edging away to let her pass. She understood then that these strangers who had never laid eyes on her all recognized her immediately because she was not one of them. She did not dress like them or look like them, and she could only be the woman who lived in the house not a hundred yards from where the boy had disappeared. She could only be the woman who had told the sheriff about Dylan Hayes. She could only be that painter lady from the city, that outsider in their midst.

The blood was pounding so explosively in Charlotte's head that despite the continued singing of hundreds of voices, the music did not register to her as anything but a loud drone. Then it was as if her ears suddenly became unstopped and she heard the words, "When evening falls so hard, I will comfort you. I'll take your part . . ."

She came to a stop then and stared straight ahead into the broad back of a tall man, and she let the music come to her and tried to breathe more easily and allow her heart to calm. Soon her field of vision began to expand as if the tunnel she had been in was fading away, and she saw that she was well inside the crowd now, only ten feet or so from the front. Nearly every person but her was holding a paper cup with a little candle flickering inside. Some of them, men and women both, also held a can or bottle of beer, a soda can, or a cup of convenience store coffee in their free hand. Some of them whispered to one another. A few had set the paper cup and candle between their feet. A teenage boy and girl not far away were kissing.

The woman standing next to Charlotte was a small, round

woman wearing a denim jacket over a gray hoodie. She turned to Charlotte and said, "There's candles up front."

"Thank you," Charlotte said. "But I'm okay."

"Eldon," the woman said to the man in front of her, and jabbed him on the shoulder so that he turned to look. "Move aside and let this lady through."

"Really, I'm fine, thank you," Charlotte said, but the woman took her by the arm and pulled her forward, all but thrust her through the opening Eldon had made, at which point the person in front of Eldon moved aside as well, and the next person and the next, and Charlotte, smiling awkwardly, felt she had no choice but to be pulled forward by this tide of courtesy, no choice but to be drawn into the open circle at the heart of the crowd.

The open space was perhaps twenty feet wide. At its center, on the ground at the base of a bamboo patio torch, was a mound of flowers, pictures, letters, and cards all stacked around a large corkboard that leaned against the bamboo torch. Two people stood shoulder-to-shoulder behind this display. The woman, Charlotte knew, could only be Jesse's mother, a thin thirty-something woman, pretty but looking so worn, so exhausted by grief. She stood huddled into herself and stared at the ground near the mound of flowers. The fire from the torch threw flickers of light across her face.

The man beside Livvie Rankin was one Charlotte recognized as a man she had seen on a few occasions while driving through town. Each time she saw him, he had been standing on the sidewalk, apparently locked in earnest conversation with somebody else, their conversation so earnest, on his part at least, that it always appeared to be on the verge of an argument. Each time Charlotte had driven past this scene, she had felt compelled to glance back once or twice to reassure herself that the men were not fighting.

So you're Denny Rankin, she thought. He wasn't much taller than his wife, maybe five-nine to her five-seven, but he held himself as stiff as a sword and stared hard past the flame, his gaze going into the darkness just above the top of the crowd, the bill of his ball cap pulled low, his arms crossed tightly across his chest. What held Charlotte's attention was the turn of his mouth, the full lips in a tight, one-sided, very critical smile. *That's Jesse's mouth,* she thought.

Then a hand touched Charlotte's shoulder. She jerked away at the touch and turned quickly.

"Hey, it's only me," Mike Verner said. He had to lean close so as not to shout above the singing. "Sorry if I surprised you."

Beside him stood a petite, smiling woman with a pretty, slightly freckled face. She leaned past her husband to reach for Charlotte's hand. "I'm Claudia," she said.

Charlotte thought the woman's hand felt rough and dry, but it was also warm, and in an instant her other hand also closed around Charlotte's. "It's so nice to meet you finally," Claudia said. She stood no taller than five feet two and had a delicate kind of beauty, a pale Irish complexion and shining auburn hair.

Charlotte leaned close to her and said, "Your husband is a big, fat liar."

"Oh yes, he certainly is. What did he lie about this time?"

"He said that you're fat and ugly."

"Well, I could stand to lose a few pounds."

"Where? You don't have an ounce of fat on you."

"Actually, I was referring to this hundred and ninety pounds standing here beside me."

Mike grinned as if the women's sudden alliance against him was a personal victory. "I'm glad we found you," he said. "So many people showed up, they had to move this thing off the front yard. I hope half this many people show up when I disappear."

Claudia shushed him, flashed her green eyes at him. He drew an imaginary zipper across his lips.

To Claudia, Charlotte said, "I wish I had brought some flowers or something."

"Some people are throwing a dollar or two in that little cardboard box. To help Livvie out."

"I didn't even think to bring my purse."

Claudia looked up at her husband. He reached for his wallet, then held it open in front of Charlotte. "An interest-free loan," he said. "But no free toasters."

Charlotte told him, "You're an inveterate liar but a very nice man." She thumbed through the inch-thick wad of bills, then extracted a twenty. "You mind?"

"Well, I kinda had that one earmarked for a lap dance at the Sugar Shack."

Claudia gave his hand a little slap. "He ever sets foot in the Sugar Shack, he won't have need for money or anything else, and he knows it."

"I'll pay you back tomorrow," Charlotte said, then immediately stepped into the open space and crossed toward the torch, six stiff steps over beaten-down grass. Her intention was to drop the twenty into the shoebox, which was already half-filled with other bills, handwritten notes, and what, as she drew closer, looked to be a St. Christopher medal. Charlotte's knees threatened to buckle as she drew closer to the display, but she managed to close the distance finally and to let the bill flutter out of her hand. She could smell the burning oil in the torch and could hear the singing going on all around her, "How Great Thou Art" now, the lyrics mingling also with the scent of cigarette smoke, the chilled scent of the air, all of it wrapped together in a softly buffeting wave that took Charlotte's breath away and made her feel simultaneously tiny and too conspicuous.

She became aware of standing motionless too long and told herself to move. She lifted her gaze out of the cardboard box, looked at the mound of flowers surrounding it, mostly wildflower bouquets from the nearest Walmart, but also some florist shop roses, bunches of tulips and lilies, gladioli and sprigs of yellow forsythia, hand-printed and colored sheets of paper and cards, everything banked against a corkboard that leaned against the bamboo stake.

Pinned to the center of the corkboard was a five-by-seven of Jesse, his most recent school picture. Pinned around this photo, framing it, were four pencil drawings. They were primitive drawings, childlike, but when Charlotte looked at the first one, then immediately at the other three, she heard her own sudden intake of breath, then the exhalation, and her chest felt suddenly empty, hollow with disbelief.

Under other circumstances—at the school's open house, for example; at a community picnic; at a local art contest she had been asked to judge—Charlotte might have looked at those sketches and thought, *For a twelve-year-old, they're very good.* But these were Jesse's drawings and Jesse was gone. These drawings had been made by the hand of a boy who had disappeared within view of Charlotte's house. Under those circumstances, Charlotte was stunned.

Pinned directly above Jesse's photo—and he wasn't smiling in the photo, but almost, with just a corner of his mouth in a tentative lift, while his chin was low and he regarded the camera with hooded eyes, suspicious eyes, the very same eyes with which he had once regarded Charlotte—was a sketch of a collie in profile. With a few careful strokes, Jesse had captured not only the fur hanging down from the animal's chest, but the lifelike lilt of its tail, and even something of the animal's dignity and intelligence. The talent was raw but obvious to Charlotte's trained eye. The other three sketches were equally good and honest: the trailer where he and his mother lived; a hawk on a branch; and the one that broke her heart in half, the woods in deep shadow. This last one was the most impressive, because with cross-hatching and white space, he had instinctively lit up the cheap poster paper with the play of light and shadow—so real that she could sense in those lines the faint shimmer of what the woods must have meant to him, its comforting silence and hushed, breathing soul.

Later Charlotte would remember those sketches and remember, too, the cold, desiccating wind that swept through her. She would remember that the night went suddenly black and rushed in to crush her from all sides. She would remember that the world collapsed like the closing iris of a camera until all she could see, as if at the end of a long tunnel, so painfully clear though seemingly miles away, was Jesse's photo, his face, those sad, wary eyes and the hard line of an almost-smile.

"Thank you," she heard, a weak, feminine voice, as unexpected and quickly gone as the sputter of a candle. But Charlotte knew in an instant who the voice belonged to, and though she did not want to look up, did not want to have to face Jesse's mother and her irremediable grief, she was unable to resist as her gaze rose and her head lifted, and there she saw Livvie Rankin with her small, sad smile, and Jesse's mother told her, "He'll be back," in a voice so soft and hoarse that it could only be a mother's voice, "I know he will."

The darkness roared in at Charlotte then from all sides; it

roared inside her head, a black storm without sound of its own but demolishing all other sound. Later, alone in her bed, Charlotte would try to remember those moments but could find not the smallest trace of what had happened next, of how or when she had returned to the edge of the crowd to stand again with Mike and Claudia, of the songs they might have sung before the evening ended. She must have walked with Mike and Claudia back to her Jeep, or at least as far as the parking lot. She must have driven home, or how else would she have ended up in her own bed? A week earlier she might have considered it incredible, unbelievable, that a person could conduct herself in a normal manner for an hour or more yet have not a moment's retention of that hour. Isolated pieces of memory were visible, individual instants, but they had no correlation to the whole, no contiguity, and drifted across the blackness of that hour like old clips of celluloid, a few frames each: Sheriff Gatesman standing off on his own, his little smile and nod; Denny Rankin with his hard mouth frowning as he looked at her; a deer in the road, a small doe, frozen by her headlights, then turning to flee, skittering and falling onto a hip, then clambering to its feet again and finally bounding into the weeds.

Charlotte could find nothing more of the last hour of that evening, no matter how long she searched the dark ceiling. She lay on her bed, atop the blankets and comforter, still wearing her stadium jacket and knit cap, still wearing her shoes.

23

For a while in the morning, Charlotte stood before her easel, considering the lines, warming her hands with a mug of hot tea, trying, too, to warm herself with the reminder that this was just another day, a day like any other. Her eyelids felt heavy because she had slept very little, and her body weary. *But it's just another day,* she told herself. *There's no reason why you shouldn't paint.* The light through the windows was soft, the gray light of an April dawn. *But at least you opened the curtains,* she told herself. *At least you made a start.*

She saw again that the lines on the canvas were not quite right. They did not convey what she wished to convey. What she wanted was for the viewer to take in the entire canvas, the Amish boy and girl, the old biker, the buggy coming down the road, but then for the whole to coalesce around a single image, a single image that in this case was situated off to the side, the Amish buggy, so that the viewer would be drawn closer, would step up to the very side of the buggy and peer into its dark interior, see there the young husband, just a boy himself, with the reins in his hands, a few fine, long whiskers on his chin, the girl-wife beside him, and the toddler on her lap, pulling forward to see the old biker, the baby's eyes wide with wonder. What Charlotte wanted was for the viewer to be pulled *into* the painting, and very nearly into the buggy itself.

She sipped her tea and wondered, *Who did you learn that from?*

From Boudin, of course, she thought. The way he makes you walk that little scrap of beach in *Rivage de Portrieux*. Makes you crowd onto the jetty with all the other people. Makes you stroll the dock in Rotterdam. And then there was Degas too, Monet, Cézanne sometimes. And Cozens.

And Chase's studio, she thought. How every time I look at it I ache to duck under the curtain and through the doorway to his easel in the farthest corner of his studio! Or to walk that wide dirt road to Clara Southern's Warrandyte Hotel. And Lilla Cabot Perry's woods and barn—how could anyone not go sneaking into that dark rectangle of door, or try for a peek through the window of that little house in the woods? *What sly dogs they were,* she told herself. *What seducers!*

She went as far as to cross to her table and set down the mug of tea. But when she reached for the charcoal pencil, when she held it between her finger and thumb, Jesse's four sketches appeared in her mind's eye just as she had first seen them the previous night, his photo centered between them. And she dropped the pencil and turned away and walked out of her studio and pulled shut the door.

24

WHEN she awoke on the La-Z-Boy, the living room was full of light. She glanced at the cable box. 8:37 A.M. A truck was rumbling down the highway, a fading drone. And there was something else, too, a memory. Claudia had said, "A couple hundred dollars dropped into a collection box is one thing. But what Livvie needs right now is to know that her neighbors care. That we're all praying with her." She planned to bake a few loaves of banana bread and take them to Livvie in the morning, this morning. "She's probably not even feeding herself," Claudia had said.

And Mike had told her, "You go ahead and whip up a seven-course dinner if it makes you feel better. I'll cart it over for you."

Charlotte heeled down the footrest and went into the kitchen.

25

"CHRIST Almighty," Gatesman said out loud. He was alone in his vehicle in the hospital parking lot, had only seconds earlier heaved himself inside and slammed shut the door. He never swore in front of his deputies or anybody else, but on occasion he allowed himself the luxury of a few explosive curse words delivered in solitude, never in his own home, never where the spirits of Patrice and Chelsea might be lingering, nor in the courthouse, where Tina or some citizen in the anteroom might hear. But in his car with the windows up was just fine. "Goddamn it all to fucking hell," he said.

He hated hospitals. He hated the smell of them, the sound of them, the very atmosphere that filled them. He had had a dream last year of himself dying in a hospital room, tubes and wires hooked up to his body, machines beeping, a terrible weight crushing all the air from his lungs. In his dream he lay there gasping, paralyzed by the invisible weight while nurses calmly strolled past his door, ignoring the beeps of alarm.

Coming to the hospital, or even driving past it, always reminded him of that dream. But what angered him now had nothing to do with his own death. "Now you have to go hunt that little fucker down again," he told himself.

Gatesman had long ago ceased to be surprised by the cruelty and stupidity of his own species. But what continued to amaze him was the tolerance otherwise intelligent people displayed for allowing certain obviously defective specimens to wander around at will.

26

It was nearly three in the afternoon when Charlotte parked her Jeep in the little gravel driveway that ran almost to the trailer's door. She was glad to see only one vehicle already parked there, a tired-looking Datsun hatchback at least a dozen years old. Somebody had painted the whole contraption sage green, even the naked rims. Both rear fenders were banged in, and there was a long crack in the windshield. Denny Rankin, she knew, drove a small, red pickup truck. *So that's Livvie's car,* she thought.

I should buy her a car, she told herself. *Have it delivered with a note:* From a friend. But how to keep it from her husband? That would be a problem.

She shut off the Jeep, lifted the Ovenware dish with its hot pad off the seat, and held it atop her lap. The trailer looked unoccupied, even abandoned. All the curtains were drawn. No gleam of light behind them. No whisper of music or drone of television in the air. Charlotte sat there in the Jeep with the dish of braciola in her lap, felt her stomach turn over at the scent of baked sauce, and hoped that Livvie was not at home.

Two minutes later, Charlotte changed her mind, decided to go home, toss the braciola in the trash. She started the Jeep again and lifted a hand to the gearshift. Just then the front door came open by a few inches, and Jesse's mother peeked out at her. Charlotte lifted her hand off the gearshift, held it up behind the windshield in a motionless wave. Livvie cocked her head a little, opened the door only wide enough that she could step through and put one leg over the threshold, one stockinged foot on the first concrete step.

Charlotte pushed open the car door, leaned out. "I'm sorry, I didn't mean to disturb you."

Livvie opened the door a little wider, brought her other foot down onto the gray concrete. Her face was pale, no makeup, hair hanging straight. She was wearing blue jeans, a pale orange sweatshirt, and gray cotton socks. Something about the sight of her unshod feet caused a pinch in Charlotte's chest.

Livvie said, "Is this about Dylan?"

Charlotte did not understand the question. She slid her legs around, held on to the baking dish, and stood just outside the Jeep. "I brought a dish of braciola. So you don't have to, you know . . . I'm sure you don't feel much like cooking."

Livvie said nothing, and for a few moments the women stood looking at each other, both confused, both attempting to process the words they had heard and to find some sense in them.

Livvie was the first to respond. She came down off the three concrete steps and started toward the Jeep. Only when she was halfway there did Charlotte react. "Wait," she said, "let me come to you. You don't have any shoes on."

Livvie stopped and looked down at her feet. Then offered

Charlotte a little smile. To Charlotte's eyes, she had never seen a sight so pathetic, so swollen with heartache. She crossed to Livvie as quickly as possible, but felt, even as she moved toward her, hands flat under the hot pad on which the baking dish rested, that the manner in which she carried the heavy amber dish must have looked, as it felt, artificially ceremonial.

"People have been bringing me food all day," Livvie said. "There's no way I can eat it all. I wouldn't want it to go to waste."

"It's braciola," Charlotte said, and again felt a disconnect, as if they were trying to communicate through a strong wind that blew every other word away.

"Will it freeze?" Livvie said.

Charlotte stood there in front of her, holding the dish, looking down at the foil cover. Then understanding clicked into place. "You want to freeze it? Sure, that's fine. I'd seal it up in a freezer bag first though. Otherwise you'll get freezer burn."

Livvie nodded but did not reach out for the dish. She kept her arms wrapped around herself. There was a plaintiveness in her eyes, some plea Charlotte could not decipher.

Charlotte asked, "Did you say something about Dylan?"

"I hope they catch him. I really do."

"Dylan ran away?"

"Denny. My husband."

The conversation felt strangely dreamlike to Charlotte; dizzying.

She asked, "Dylan and your husband ran away?"

"Denny did. After what he did to Dylan."

Again the pinch in Charlotte's chest, but sharper this time, prolonged and deep. "What did he do?"

"He nearly beat him to death."

"Your husband beat up Dylan?"

Livvie nodded. "The sheriff came by around five this morning looking for him. But he never came home last night. He went out drinking after the thing at the football field."

The palms of Charlotte's hands stung from the heat of the braciola, but the pain gave her something to focus on, something to help choke down the churning sickness.

She understood that Denny had beaten up Dylan, that Denny was gone now, yet the pieces of information seemed broken. Nothing fit together. "I'm your neighbor from down the road," Charlotte said. "The old Simmons place."

"Somebody told me last night. Thank you for the money."

"Oh, that. I . . ." She had forgotten about the money borrowed from Mike Verner. "I'm Charlotte. Charlotte Dunleavy."

Livvie said, "Maybe you could take it to Dylan's family instead."

"Take . . . the money?"

"The dish. The . . . what did you call it?"

"Braciola. It's a meat dish."

"I wouldn't want it to go to waste," Livvie said.

"Is he going to be all right? Dylan? Your husband beat him badly? With his fists, with . . . ?"

"He's in the hospital, is all I know. All broken up. Denny's not a big man but he's a mean drunk. Sober too, I guess."

Charlotte felt a semblance of understanding then, a fitting together. The two women stood facing each other, neither speaking for half a minute. Livvie offered a thin, sad smile. Charlotte offered one of her own.

Finally Charlotte turned back to the open door of her Jeep, set the Ovenware dish on the middle of the seat, and climbed in. She turned the key in the ignition but realized only when she heard the grinding noise that the Jeep was already running. She thought then that she should say good-bye before driving away, turned to look out the door, and was startled to see Livvie standing there beside her.

"What was it you called it?" Livvie said. "The dish you made?"

"Braciola?"

"I don't think I know what that is."

"Oh, it's a flank steak. Beaten thin and then rolled and stuffed. And baked in a marinara sauce."

"It sounds good," Livvie said.

"Are you sure you won't take it?"

"People have brought so much," she said. "People I've never even talked to before."

Like me, Charlotte thought. "I haven't made it in a long time. My ex-husband used to love it."

"I'm sorry about not being able to take it. I wouldn't know where to put it. The refrigerator's full already."

"It's my fault, I should have realized. I just wanted . . ."

Livvie reached inside then and laid a hand on Charlotte's arm. "I know," she said. "It's all right."

In an instant Charlotte's head seemed filled with tears, throat constricted, sinuses congested. She looked away, stared through the windshield.

Livvie said, "Maybe you could make it again sometime for Jesse and me. He's a big meat-eater. It's about all I can get him to eat."

Charlotte turned to look at her, felt Livvie's hand still on her arm. She said, her voice far stiffer than she intended, "You're going to ruin your socks standing out here without any shoes on."

Livvie drew her hand away. "I hope I didn't offend you or anything."

"God, no, no it's just . . . no, not in the least."

"It was kind of you to bring it over. I really appreciate it."

"Listen, I understand, I really do. It's my fault, really. I should have called first."

"You don't have to call," Livvie said. "We're neighbors."

"We are," Charlotte said.

"It's nice to meet you finally."

"I wish we had spoken before. Before any of this."

Livvie smiled again. "Anyway, you know Jesse."

The statement jolted Charlotte and made her flinch.

"He said you asked him about school. Why he wasn't at school one day."

"I did," Charlotte said. She felt herself choking, unable to swallow.

"Sometimes he plays hooky, I know. I probably shouldn't let him, but . . . it's not an easy place for him. He's small for his age. He gets teased a lot."

Charlotte looked away again, stared at the watery windshield.

"Well," Livvie said, and took a step backward. "Anyway. Thank you for not reporting us or anything. I'm not going to let him play hooky like that anymore. We might move, I don't know. I mean, if Denny comes back . . . I don't know," she said.

Charlotte wanted to drive away. She wanted to pull the door shut and slam the gearshift into place and just drive. Just drive and keep driving.

But Livvie had not moved. Charlotte turned to look at her. Tear pools shimmered in Livvie's eyes. She was hugging herself again, squeezing tightly.

Charlotte said, "He likes to draw."

Livvie nodded and smiled. "He's good at it too."

"I saw the drawings last night. He's very good."

"I have a hundred more I could show you."

"I'd really like to see them."

"We'll come over sometime and say hello. We always pick berries over across the road from you."

"Do you?"

"Blueberries. They ripen around July, usually. We'll bring you some next time."

Charlotte could make no reply, could think of nothing to say that sounded sincere.

"There's a patch of them in the field over the road from you," Livvie said. "But it's around behind some trees. You probably can't even see it from your place. We'll show it to you some time."

"Thank you," Charlotte said.

Livvie nodded and smiled.

Charlotte nodded and smiled.

Then, abruptly, Livvie turned and made her way over the gravel, up the cold concrete steps, into her ruined home. Charlotte pulled the door shut and backed out of her driveway, backed onto the road and drove home. Her chest ached. She saw the road as if it were underwater, as if she were driving through thick water. She heard somebody moaning with every exhalation.

27

THE Jeep slowed to a stop at the mouth of Charlotte's driveway. She held her foot on the brake, leaned forward over the steering wheel, and wept. For the next several minutes she was unable to move.

When she sat upright again, she stared down the driveway at her farmhouse and yard. *My home,* she told herself, though she no longer felt any warmth there, had no desire to go back inside.

I made you, she thought, and remembered the joy she had taken in the remodeling, the joy of moving in, the joy of signing the mortgage papers. She had made a home for herself out of the passion of her work. The passion of painting. *But where is the joy now?* she wondered.

She remembered what June had told her once, that the word *passion*, from the Greek, also means *grief*. "These days we think of passion as a source of joy," June had said, "a driving ambition, a compelling lust for somebody or something. But those wise old

Greeks. They realized that yes, of course, passion is all that, but it's also grief, because how can a person long for something—for love or sex, fame or beauty, money or success—without fearing its inevitable loss? And what is that kind of fear but the future tense of grief? And what is grief but a recognition of what we can never have again?"

"All we can do," June had said, "is what the Buddhists advise. Try to find the joy in sorrow."

Charlotte gazed at her farmhouse, the yard, the outlying fields and buildings, the barn. *All I can see,* she told herself, *is the sorrow in joy.*

28

GATESMAN cruised the bar parking lots from the west side of town to the east. After the last one he asked himself, *Where else?* Then he decided to check the truck stops along the interstate. He knew that he should have had his deputies doing this, and he had alerted them to be on the lookout for the pickup truck, but he also knew that he was in no frame of mind to be sitting at his desk now, had no patience for the trivial complaints and selfish requests that flowed across his blotter. Besides, he felt responsible. *Whether I am or not is another matter,* he told himself. *Anyway, it's how I feel.*

As he drove he considered the confluence of incidents over the past few days. He wanted to believe that each of the separate incidents had been accidental. Most crimes, he knew, most violent incidents, were the result of an act of passion, an accidental surge of adrenaline, a sudden impulse, a perfect storm of chance. Only a very low percentage of crimes were premeditated. For that reason he continued to believe that Jesse's disappearance was the result of some accident, that Charlotte Dunleavy had unintentionally implicated Dylan Hayes, that Denny Rankin had been induced by the combination of excessive alcohol and paternal fear to confront Dylan, and that Rankin's ensuing rage had flared up unexpectedly, with no malice aforethought. *It's like a twelve-car pileup on a foggy night,* he told himself. *Just one big chain-reaction accident.*

It's what all of life is, isn't it? he asked himself. *Life starts out with an accident, the accident of birth. Even the planned ones are accidents when you think about the thousands of things that could go wrong. And in most cases life ends with an accident. If an accident is any event that goes against plan or expectation, an outcome that goes against the odds whether it is desirable or not, then my guess is that the course of most lives is determined not by one's will but by one's adaptation to the storm of life's accidents.*

In the courthouse, the 9-1-1 dispatchers' office was located just across the hall from his, and now and then Gatesman would pause in the doorway to eavesdrop on the calls coming in. On occasion, all three dispatchers, two women and one man, would be handling calls at the same time. This generally happened on Friday and Saturday nights in the summer, usually on full-moon nights. *But those are just the accidents that get called in,* Gatesman told himself. *Those are just the pleas for help.*

There's all the other ones too, he thought. *There's the blow to the head, there's the ruptured appendix. There's the cancerous cell, the cerebrovascular accident. The teenage pregnancy, the miscarriage, the icy road, the argument . . . the office seduction, the rejection, the telephone call in the middle of the night. There's the blind-side hit, the sucker punch, the bean ball, the helmet-to-helmet blow. There's the flame that leaps from candle to curtain. The cigarette that falls out of the ashtray.*

There's the earthquake, the hurricane, the landslide. The beautiful doe in the middle of the road. There's the flash of the skirt on the sidewalk. The insult, the compliment, the wink, the smirk. The something or other that pulls at your heart, that turns your head, that makes you look the other way.

Jesus, Gatesman thought as he scanned the houses and bars and the bends in the road, *the infinitude of chance!*

What sadist crafted this existence?

29

THE nearest hospital was twenty minutes away in Carlisle. At the information desk in the hospital lobby, Charlotte inquired of Dylan's room number, then took the stairs to the fourth floor because she did not want to encounter anybody in the elevator. As anxious as she was to reassure herself of Dylan's well-being, she was in no hurry to face him. She hoped that the door to his room stood open so that she could glance inside, see him sleeping peacefully or, better yet, laughing at some stupid show on the television, and then she could slip back to her Jeep and drive back to the solitude of her house. Every step she climbed seemed steeper than the previous one. Near the top she experienced a moment of dizziness, thought she might topple over backward like an old birch, and so she clung tightly to the handrail until she felt able to drag herself up the last few steps.

She had been walking too briskly down the corridor and came upon Dylan's room too quickly, stood squarely in the open doorway before she told herself, *Here. This room.* 423. Dylan's mother and father were in the room with him, Mama in a green vinyl chair pulled close to the bed, holding Dylan's big, childish hand in hers while she stared at the far wall. Dad was in a chair on the other side of the bed, staring up at the television mounted near the ceiling on a little platform; the screen was black and empty. Charlotte understood with just a glance what both parents were seeing at the end of those hundred-yard stares. They were seeing the end of their fragile dreams. *You live a good, decent life,* they must have been thinking, *you work hard and go to church and do the best you can with what little you've been given, and this is what you get for it. You get your only son lying battered and swollen in a hospital bed. You get a blizzard of accusations and gossip that will cling to you now like stink, a stink that might fade in time but can never be completely scrubbed away.*

To Charlotte, Dylan's parents looked as button-eyed, as sagging and limp as rag dolls.

Dylan looked even worse. His mouth was swollen and bruised, the lower lip split open, one eye blue-black and swollen shut. One ear was stuffed with cotton and looked twice its normal size, and his naked chest had been made somehow even thinner by the yards of elastic bandage wrapped around his ribs. His nose was the color of a beet and humped at the bridge, with two strips of white tape over the hump. The thumb of his right hand was in a splint, the pinky and ring fingers taped together. His stare was as vacant as his parents' and went straight up to the ceiling.

Whether it was another moaning exhalation from Charlotte or just the adamancy of her thought that she should move, step away, Dylan rolled his head slightly and saw her there in the doorway. "Hey," he mumbled, his voice raspy with phlegm.

Immediately Dylan's parents looked her way. She felt suddenly pinioned by their eyes.

"My God, Dylan," Charlotte said, "are you all right? I mean how could this . . . why would anybody do this to you?" Even as she heard her voice and its detestable shrillness, she felt her neck and face flushing scarlet, felt the sudden heat of her skin.

Dylan's father pushed himself to his feet. "Let's go get us some coffee, Mother. Son, you ready for that milkshake yet?"

Dylan's mother did not answer or acknowledge her husband. Her eyes were fierce and locked on Charlotte's, remained on Charlotte even as the woman released her son's hand, then stood abruptly and crossed toward the door. She was not a small woman, as tall as Charlotte but fuller-bodied, filled out by the daily grind of rural life. Charlotte stood aside to let her pass, but Dylan's mother turned toward her and stood close, their faces only inches apart.

"You're the woman who told the sheriff my son hurt that boy." Her soft monotone did nothing to soften the blow of her words.

"No, I didn't say that, I didn't. In fact I called him afterward and told him I was absolutely certain Dylan did *not* hurt Jesse."

"Did a lot of good, didn't it?" she said.

Her eyes were gray-blue, dirty ice, and Charlotte felt herself shrinking beneath the gaze. Felt her bones turning brittle. Felt exhaustion shutting down her brain so that she could think of nothing else to say, wanted only to close her eyes and drift into a black unconsciousness.

"Come on, Mother," Dylan's father said, and took his wife by the arm. He would not look at Charlotte as they squeezed past. She stared at the floor until their footsteps faded around a corner.

"You can come in if you want," Dylan said. His words were raspy and deep and he cleared his throat after speaking. Charlotte wondered but did not have the courage to ask if he had been punched in the throat, or if the paramedics had to force something down his esophagus.

With tentative steps she approached the bed. She stood looking down at the chair where his mother had sat, the indentation in the cushion. Then she looked at Dylan. His hand still lay exactly where his mother had placed it, fingers splayed across his chest. Charlotte wanted to seize that hand but she did not. She wanted to touch the boy, lean down close to him, but she did not.

"I'm so sorry, Dylan," Charlotte said. "I don't know what to say, what to do about this. Is there anything, something I can do for you?"

"I can't stay here anymore," he said.

"But you need to stay until they release you. You need to let them tend to you."

"I mean in this town. I can't stay in this town now."

"But what . . . ? I mean . . . there's school and . . . you have your work . . ."

"Do you know anybody might give me a job somewhere? The farther away, the better."

"Dylan, you can't," she said. "You have your senior year to think about. Just a couple of months left now, right? And what about your parents? Surely they don't want you thinking like this."

"They want me to go. Thing is, they don't have any money."

"Your parents want you to leave?"

"That asshole's going to come back and kill me, I know he will."

"You mean Jesse's dad?"

He nodded. "If not him, somebody else."

"Where did this happen?" she asked, and immediately thought, *As if that makes any difference.* "How did it get started?"

"It was at the football field. Must've been around midnight sometime."

"After the candlelight vigil?"

Another nod. He cleared his throat again, grimaced when he did so. "There was just twenty, thirty people still hanging around. Standing around drinking. I was just laying on the front seat of my truck in the parking lot. I hadn't even gone up to the field or anything. Just wanted to be there, is all."

"Were you by yourself?"

"Who else would I be with?" He licked his bottom lip where it had cracked open and was bleeding again. "I heard these steps coming toward me and I sat up to look. And he just reaches in through the window and grabs me around the neck and starts hammering on me."

"Oh God, honey, I'm sorry. I'm so sorry that happened."

"At some point he yanked open the door and dragged me out onto the blacktop. Nobody even tried to stop him. They was all just standing around, laughing, you know? It wasn't like I was fighting back or anything. He'd already busted me along the head a couple of good ones."

Charlotte lowered herself into the green vinyl chair. She reached for his hand to pull it close, but her grip was too desperate and he winced, his entire body jerked, and she released him, pulled back, clamped her hands between her knees. She heard the little whimpers coming out again, detested them but felt incapable of silence.

"He just kept stomping and kicking at me," Dylan said. "He's a grown man for chrissakes. And I never even did a goddamn thing to that boy!"

He was crying and Charlotte was crying, and with every breath she felt emptier, more hollowed out, so that soon she was sitting on the edge of the chair cushion and leaning toward him, then she lowered herself further until her forehead rested on the edge of the mattress. She could not control the sobbing now or the way her body shook. She could hear Dylan sniffing and clearing his throat, and then he startled her by laying a hand atop her back, in the space between her shoulder blades, and though his hand was warm and heavy, she took no comfort from it; that is, the intended comfort of his touch entered her emptiness and became its opposite, so that it felt, she would later remember, like a cold wind howling down an abandoned well.

It wasn't long before his hand lifted away. The place where he had touched her felt burned, and the phrase *frozen fire* came to her mind. She forced herself to sit upright. She pulled two tissues from the box on the stand beside his bed, wiped her eyes and nose and tried to pull herself together. "You need to stay with your family," she told him. "The police will find the man who did this. And then he'll go to jail for it."

"He might, but what about the rest of the town?" the boy asked. "Everybody believes the same thing he does."

"That isn't true, Dylan. People *know* you. They know you would never do such a thing."

He looked at her and blinked once, then again, and winced a little with each blink. Then he said, "There's nobody else I can ask to help me."

All Charlotte wanted was to close her eyes. She ached for forgetfulness and sleep. "How long before they release you?"

"They said maybe tomorrow. Next day at the latest."

"All right," she told him.

"Dad said I should drive to Lancaster or Harrisburg and try to sell the truck for a coupla thousand. Then I should get on a bus and go someplace else."

She nodded. "How about Muscle Shoals? Isn't that where you always wanted to go?"

"I got three broken fingers," he said.

She had barely enough breath to speak. "Can you come see me before you go?"

"I'll be leaving in the middle of the night. So nobody sees which way I'm headed."

"Nobody will follow you," she told him, but his fear was too great and she had no authority to conquer it.

Minutes later Charlotte rode the elevator down to the lobby. When she stepped outside the hospital, she was taken by surprise by the warmth of the sunlight. She had expected winter on its darkest night.

30

A day and a half after her visit to the hospital, at exactly 2:37 in the morning—and Charlotte knew this because she was lying awake in her bed, having felt, ever since dusk, the barometric pressure of the world gradually increasing—a loud rap rattled her back door. And it simultaneously rattled her, even though she had been anticipating it. It jarred her into a sitting position, then all the way off the bed as she climbed to her feet.

She went to the window and looked out. There in her driveway, pulled close to the garage, visible in the dim light of a gibbous moon, was a pickup truck. The previous night she had brought a flashlight to her bedroom, so now she retrieved it from atop the dresser and aimed the light at the truck.

Blue, she reassured herself, then shut the light off and set it atop the dresser again.

Next she slipped a chenille robe over her flannels, stepped into her slippers, felt for the bulge in the robe's pocket to reassure herself it was still there. Then she cinched the robe around her waist and headed downstairs.

In the mudroom she flicked the yellow bug light on for just a few seconds, long enough to make absolutely certain that it was Dylan Hayes out there huddled close to the back door. Then she brought him inside, through the mudroom and into the kitchen, which was lit only dimly now by the bulb in the KOBE range hood over the stove.

He looked hardly better than he had in the hospital. Some of the swelling in his nose and ear had gone down, but the bruises were yellowing. He moved and looked at her with a furtiveness she considered new to him, foreign, this brash, gregarious kid who until now had never seemed to give a rat's ass for the opinions of others, had never shown any fear except for the fear of being too conventional. He stood just inside the kitchen threshold, backed up against the wall as if to minimize his presence, even though to recognize him from more than ten feet away would require the eyes of a cat; the thirty-watt bulb showed the stove top clearly but little else.

And Charlotte thought, *He actually looks guilty. He looks like a criminal.*

She was aware, too, of the shiver of pleasure that ran through her with that observation, as well as the sudden, though somewhat more detached, disgust she felt for herself at that moment. Dylan stood there leaning against the wall, huddled into himself, eyes averted. He reminded Charlotte of the scene in *To Kill a Mockingbird* where Robert Duvall as Boo Radley hides behind the kitchen door.

She asked him, "Are you sure you want to do this?"

"I don't see as I have much choice."

"If you leave, it's only going to make you look guilty."

"Everybody already thinks I am."

"But it's what you *know* that's important."

"That's easy to say. Would you like it if everybody looked at you like you was some kind of a pervert?"

"But there's not a bit of evidence against you. You can't even be charged with anything."

"It don't matter, don't you understand? Around here, people will always look at me like I done it."

She realized then that both she and Dylan were shivering, even though the thermostat was always set at seventy-two and the furnace blower was rumbling in the basement. She looked at Dylan a few moments longer, then slipped both hands into the robe pockets. She cupped her right hand around the fat bulge in the pocket.

"I was planning to leave sooner or later anyway," he told her. "I hate this fucking place."

"What about Reenie?"

He blew a puff of air through his lips, closed his eyes for a moment, and shook his head.

"Do you know where you're going? After you sell the truck, I mean."

"I got an idea. But I'd rather not say."

They stood in silence. Dylan regarded the floor while she studied his face. A part of her wanted to talk him out of running away, thought about offering him a job of some kind, painting the house, mowing the yard, free room and board—anything to keep him from a desperate, unnecessary flight. Another part wanted to hurry him on his way.

Finally she withdrew the envelope from her pocket, then nudged it against his hand until he took it. "Jesus," he said. "It feels like a lot."

"It's going to take you a while to get settled. You need money to live on."

"I've got three hundred of my own," he said.

"The money you'd been saving for an engagement ring."

He answered with a grunt of self-rebuke. "She was one of the first to turn against me. Can you believe it?"

Charlotte felt an overwhelming need to touch him, so she laid a hand on his arm. "You'll find the right girl, Dylan. Somebody kind. Just so long as you treat her the same way. Don't let this sour you."

He nodded, but soon he was sniffing and blinking back the tears, trying his best to stifle them.

"Will you write to me?" she asked. "I want to hear how you make out. Okay?"

"All right," he said.

"It will mean a lot to me."

She heard her voice, heard the words coming out of her mouth and knew that she meant them, but also knew, also recognized a simultaneous thought: *I want him gone.* Moments later, after an awkward good-bye—he had moved closer as if to embrace her but then backed away half a step, so that she leaned into him and kissed his cheek—she relocked the door behind him, turned the stove light out, and made her way back to her bed.

It's for the best, she kept telling herself in the darkness. *You know it's for the best.*

After a while she got up and went into the bathroom and took two Ambiens with a swallow of water. Perhaps an hour later, she fell into a dreamless sleep from which she did not awake until 12:53 in the afternoon. That she awoke feeling rested, if not wholly refreshed, came as a very welcome surprise.

31

SHE stood on the front porch with a mug of tea in her hands—it was the Harney & Sons' Irish Breakfast, a strong black tea that she had sweetened with organic honey purchased last fall at a little roadside stand ten miles down the highway—and looked out across her yard and thought, *Maybe this year I'll get a riding mower and take care of the lawn myself.* The previous summer she had hired a two-man crew from town—boys barely out of their teens, but they had done a good job keeping everything neat. They had even hauled away the grass clippings every week and, in the fall, had vacuumed up the leaves and hauled them away, too. *But this year I want to do it myself,* she thought.

It was only then that she realized why the day seemed so bright. There was no tunnel vision that morning, no dark periphery to her field of vision. Not twelve hours earlier Dylan Hayes had stood in her kitchen, but he was gone now, and with him had gone the heavy air and the sense that life was closing in on her. The world seemed a wider place that morning, though not without its sadness—the sadness would always be there, the sadness and regret—but on that fine afternoon she felt ready, finally, to accept the world on its own terms again.

What is, is, her friend June often said. *Happiness can only be achieved when we accept what cannot be changed.*

"What is, is," Charlotte said aloud. She sipped her tea and allowed herself a smile.

I can be a better person, she told herself. *I can live every day trying to make amends for how I've been. All the terrible things I've done and never meant to do. I can accept what can't be changed, but there are lots of things I* can *change. Lots of things I will.*

It seemed a very long time since she had felt such energy. *How long?* she wondered, and, counting back, she was amazed to realize that only ten days had passed since she had last worked on a painting. *Ten days! It feels like months at least!* she thought.

Minutes later, as she rinsed out her mug at the kitchen sink, she told herself, "You should go see Daddy today."

She had not visited her father in the nursing home since Christmas. That winter he had deteriorated quickly after three or four mini-strokes. She thought of them as tiny explosions in his brain, miniature suns going supernova, flaring up brilliantly for a nanosecond before going forever black. The Christmas visit had been very hard on her. The staff at the home had dressed all of the residents in red and green elf hats with jingle bells on them, and the result, to Charlotte's eyes, was the antithesis of festive. Her father had barely moved in his chair, never once lifted his eyes to look at her. She had slipped a small Godiva chocolate, his favorite sweet, into his mouth, but the melting chocolate had oozed out over his lower lip and she had had to keep wiping it away with tissues until the wafer dissolved. The sight of her once-vigorous, doting father reduced to a feeble stranger had left her in a melancholy mood for weeks, and afterward, each time she thought about visiting him again, the image of that haggard old man with chocolate drool on his chin kept her away.

But now, mid-April, with her kitchen warm and bright again, she told herself, "I'll go see Daddy."

While she showered, put on makeup, and dressed, she planned her day, going over it again and again, calculating the minutes and hours. First she would go to the bank and withdraw three thousand dollars to replace the money she had removed from her safe the previous night. The bank would be closed by the time she returned from the nursing home, and she was not comfortable with the idea of having no emergency money in her safe. So she would drive to Belinda, make the withdrawal, return home, and put the money in her safe, then swing north and follow the Susquehanna River all the way to Williamsport, then north on U.S. Route 15 to Wellsboro, her hometown until she was eighteen years old. If she felt like it after visiting her father, she might even treat herself to a garlicky lamb steak at the Steak House. *But if you're going to do that,* she told herself, *you'd better phone ahead for a reservation. You know how busy they get.*

What she looked forward to most was the slow drive up Main Street and back down again after nightfall. New streetlamps fashioned to resemble old gaslights had been placed on a grassy median down the center of the wide main drag, and at night they lit the town to look like a movie set, something out of an old Frank Capra film. She might even stop at Pudgie's afterward for an ice cream cone, one scoop peppermint and one scoop cherry vanilla, then sit for a while in the Green where she could look at the lighted fountain splashing around the whimsical sculpture of Wynken, Blynken, and Nod. What she missed was not so much the hometown itself but what she now thought of as the lightness of her past, those years when all the weight lay on the future and it was a desirable weight, to be gathered one gold coin at a time, and not at all like the weight she dragged behind her these days, unspendable, a cache of knowledge and experience no sane person ever sought.

But for today, she told herself, *I will forget about all that. Things are lighter today. Things look better.*

She was even looking forward to the drive north, the scent of forest, the clarity of higher latitude and altitude. Afterward she would drive home in the soothing darkness, and tomorrow she would wake up early and go back to work on the painting.

"*Umbauzone,*" she told herself. "That's what I'll call it." The title for her painting had come to her out of nowhere. An ending, a beginning, a reconstruction, continuous transformation—life as a Möbius strip, an endless loop with unexpected twists.

Smiling at the aptness of the title—*In German, even! What the Amish speak among themselves!*—she headed for the garage. Along the way she glanced at the mulch and flower beds, told herself what plants she would put in each bed this year, imagined the splashes of color placed here and there and there. As soon as all danger of frost had passed—*maybe this weekend if the long-range forecast looks good*—she would drive to the nursery.

She unlocked the garage door and swung it up, and almost immediately she heard the noise, a loud buzzing sound. Because of the high windows on three sides of the garage, she could see everything clearly, but the noise startled her and for several seconds she did not move from the entrance but stood there listening intently, afraid to progress. At first she thought *rattlesnake,* but the noise was incessant, it did not stop. Then she peered into the rafters, tried to spot a wasp's nest. But the rafters were clear except for the spiderwebs.

Then she became aware of the clicking sound mixed in with the buzzing, and that sound she recognized. Flies knocking against glass. There were certainly flies at each of the garage windows, but not nearly enough to account for the unrelenting buzz. Only after two tentative steps along the side of the Jeep and an increase in the volume of the buzzing did she notice the shadow moving across the inside of the driver's-side window.

She stepped up to the door and leaned closer. A mass of darkness seethed across the inside of the glass, almost bubbling. Another mass of flies was crawling over the windshield. There were flies, she saw, on every pane of glass inside the vehicle, but especially in the front. The Jeep was literally abuzz with them. They made a muffled, but no less ominous drone, and for a few moments the sight and sound of those thousands of fat black flies disoriented her, made her dizzy with incomprehension.

Then she remembered. The braciola. She had left it on the car seat. She had driven from Livvie's trailer to the hospital to visit Dylan, and then, returning home, had been so distraught that she had rushed straight into the house without giving a thought to the braciola. For most of four days, then, she had never left the house except to walk to the mailbox, and all that time the Jeep had been a little greenhouse, incubating flies by the thousands. And they had all been gorging themselves on spoiled meat, laying their eggs in it, fucking and feeding and doubling their numbers every few hours or so. Charlotte gagged at the very thought of it.

She wanted to run away from the Jeep, away from the garage—

wanted to run away from everything. All of her previous hopefulness evaporated in an instant. It seemed to Charlotte that the flies were mocking her, buzzing, *This is your fucking life, Charlottttttte. Get used to itttttttt.*

She stood motionless for a long two minutes, even reached into her jacket pocket, wrapped a hand around her cell phone, thought about calling Mike Verner. Then she told herself, *No. No, damn it. You made this problem. You made all these problems. Now you have to deal with them.*

In the end she could think of no solution but to hold her breath while she raced around the Jeep, flinging open all the doors. In an instant, the muted buzzing became a chainsaw. She ran out of the garage, swatting at her head long after the flies had left her, and retreated to the porch. Flies flew out of the garage, they flew back in. Even from the porch she could hear them clicking against the garage windows, bouncing against the windshield. They weren't going to leave, she realized, as long as their rancid feast remained there on the front seat of the Jeep.

Her stomach churned. She fought down the nausea, swallowed and swallowed. Finally she went into the house, dropped her purse on the hallway table, went upstairs and dug through a dresser drawer until she found a red bandana, tied it around her nose and mouth. In the kitchen she armed herself with a pair of oven mitts and a can of flying-insect spray.

At the mouth of the garage, she started spraying, filling the air with poison, swinging her arm from side to side. By the time she reached the driver's door, the can was empty. By now her eyes were stinging and she was afraid of going blind from the spray, so she tossed the can aside and ran back outside the garage, whipped off the bandanna, and wiped the dampness from her face. She could still hear the buzzing cloud, but she was out of ammunition. And the yard had grown dark around the edges again, the world was constricting.

She retied the bandanna over her nose and mouth, rushed back into the garage, seized the baking dish, and raced away as fast as she could, across the yard to the high weeds on the near edge of the field, all the while holding her breath and shaking her head violently to dislodge the flies crawling over her face. She would not look down at the baking dish because she knew that at least a corner of the foil would be lifted up and that inside would be a writhing bed of maggots and larvae. Flies buzzed up out of the dish and headed straight for her face, hummed in her ears, crawled through her hair, pelted her forehead.

Finally she was near enough to the weeds that she gave the dish a two-handed toss, hurled it as far as she could. She did not even wait to see it land and break and spill but turned and ran back to the house, still swatting at her head. One of the oven mitts fell off but she did not stop to retrieve it. She raced inside and slammed the door shut behind her.

She stood in the downstairs powder room, gagging over the toilet. When she had her breath back, she went upstairs, hurriedly pulled off her clothes, and stepped into the shower. Afterward she brushed her teeth and gargled and then sat in the kitchen wrapped in her robe. She could still taste the mouthwash, but she could also taste, or imagined she could, something maggoty and greasy. She made a cup of lemon tea, swished it around in her mouth before each swallow, and then made a second cup. Still, her tongue felt coated. Still, her stomach churned.

Initially she had no intention of retrieving the baking dish. She reassured herself that animals would come in the night to devour the contents—raccoons, stray cats, a dog, something to lick the glass clean. If the dish remained untouched till morning, maybe the turkey vultures would find it, drawn by the scent of putrefaction. Maybe the crows would come.

And let's say the sheriff happens to be looking in the woods again, she thought. *Or maybe he drives by and sees a half dozen buzzards sitting on the edge of my lawn. What then?*

Fuck, she told herself. *Fuck fuck fuck fuck fuck.*

This time she dressed in her gardening clothes, jeans stained with a hardened spatter of old paint, one of her father's discarded sweatshirts, white socks, and her Timberlands. Outside she opened the garden shed and dragged out the hundred-foot length of hose that had somehow become uncoiled over the winter. She hooked up the hose, turned on the spigot, dragged the hose toward the edge of the field.

It fell several yards short. By setting the nozzle on a tight stream, she was able to send it gushing at the baking dish, which to her surprise had remained intact, and to her dismay was lying facedown. For a moment she stared numbly as the water sprayed off the bottom of the dish. Then, disgusted by her own stupidity and carelessness, she threw down the hose and strode to the dish and flipped it over. For good measure she gave it a couple of bangs against the ground to empty it. All the while the flies attacked her. "Fuck you!" she told them. "Fuck everything!"

She sprayed and sprayed and sprayed. She sprayed until not a fly or maggot moved either inside the dish or on the ground. Then she sprayed until all but the baked crust of sauce had been rinsed from the Ovenware. Then she picked up the dish, dragged the hose back toward the house, left it lying there uncoiled. She shut off the fucking spigot. Carried the fucking dish inside, stuck it into a fucking garbage bag, rammed it into the fucking trash container on the back porch, went upstairs and took off her fucking clothes, and took another fucking shower and fucking climbed back into bed.

No escape, she kept telling herself. *No escape ever from this fucking mess you have made.*

32

Two days later she finally forced herself to visit the nursing home. The long drive had tired her, but the sight of the lovely grounds, the low, white buildings set against a backdrop of trees and the Tioga State Forest, was strangely soothing. She stood on the concrete veranda—all the chairs empty now, the air still too cool for the elderly residents—and filled her lungs with slow, deep breaths. *It does smell different here,* she thought, and wondered why she had not moved back to Wellsboro after the divorce, wondered why she had chosen an unknown town instead. She could only vaguely remember the impetus for her decision, something about independence, something about self-reliance.

Wrong again, she told herself, then swung open the door and went inside.

Lunch odors still permeated the corridors. *Meatloaf,* she guessed, and her stomach turned at the thought of it. All the food was soft here, cooked to a mush. In the locked ward where her father was kept, few residents could feed themselves, though many were still ambulatory and free to wander about in their pajamas and slippers. She found her father in the solarium, a wide sunny room with windows all along the south and west walls. A half dozen residents stood along those walls, peering out. A dozen or so others sat at small tables with boxes of dominoes or blocks emptied out in front of them. A single attendant in a cubicle in the rear corner of the room kept watch, though at the moment he seemed more engaged by his computer monitor and looked up only briefly when Charlotte came into the room.

Her father was seated out of the sunlight, alone at his table. His head was bowed, but he was not asleep, eyes open, staring, apparently, at his hands folded in his lap. A cardboard picture book lay open in front of him. Charlotte slid an empty chair close to him, sat and took his hands in hers. The pain in her chest, midway between her throat and sternum, burned like a thin blade.

"Why aren't you enjoying the sunshine, Daddy?" she said. She watched his face closely, but there was no reaction, not even an extra blink from his eyes.

She thought about gently lifting his chin so that their eyes could meet, but then she noticed the gob of something white stuck to his shirt front—mashed potatoes—and she leaned away from him, suddenly angry. She snapped open her purse, took out a couple of tissues and cleaned the food off his shirt. She balled up the tissues and stood, looked for a trash can, saw none, and marched to the attendant's cubicle. "Do you have a trash can back here?" she asked, and the young man, not yet thirty, scruffy-bearded and momentarily startled by her question, said, "Sure, under here," and nodded toward the small chrome receptacle beneath his desk. Charlotte tossed the wad of tissues in and turned away.

She took only two steps before turning back to the attendant. She said, "Doesn't anybody clean these people off after they've eaten?"

Again, the startled look. "Of course," he said.

"Well you're not doing a very good job of it, are you?"

He leaned a few inches back in his chair.

"And whose idea was it to comb his hair straight down over his forehead like that?" she demanded.

He opened both hands in a gesture of helpless. "I couldn't say for sure," he told her. "Sorry." She nodded and thought about turning away, told herself, *You should go now, let it go.* But she could feel something building inside her now, some anger out of all proportion to the situation, and she could not step away from it.

"Do you have any idea what that man has *done* in his life?" she asked. She could hear her voice rising, could feel the heat coming into her face, but could do nothing to stop it.

"That man has more education than your entire fucking staff put together!" she said. "His students have won Pulitzers and National Book Awards and fucking MacArthur Fellowships! And you can't even put a clean shirt on him and comb his fucking hair the way he's combed it for the last seventy fucking years?"

The attendant sat with both hands on the edge of his metal desk now, his chair pushed back against the wall. He looked up at her and spoke very softly, "I'm sorry, I'll let everybody know. We take good care of our residents, I promise you we do."

The anger broke in her suddenly and she felt the tears coming. "Not fucking good enough," she said evenly, then turned away and went back to her father.

She leaned into him and cried with her eyes pressed against the sharp rail of his shoulder. She wanted his scent but could smell only the nursing home. She wanted his warmth but the sunshine was across the room. She clutched both of his hands and lay against him and tried to remember the way he used to hold her. She would sit on his lap while they watched television together and he would wrap his left arm around her belly and sometimes hold her right hand in his and she would feel the rise and fall of his breathing against her back, the safe, warm steadiness of his presence.

Your hair smells like strawberries, babygirl, he might say. *Have you been rolling around in strawberries?*

She would giggle and tell him, *You're being silly. It's just my shampoo.*

She heard him ask, *Do you make your hair smell like that for your boyfriend?*

I don't have a boyfriend, Daddy. You know that.

Fess up, Lottie, he used to say. *Fess up now. Who's your beau?*

And she told him, *His name is Jesse, Daddy.*

And is he as handsome as me?

It breaks my heart to look at him, she said.

Jesse is a girl's name, isn't it?

No, Daddy, not always. Not this time, it's not.

And just where does this handsome boy live?

Just everywhere, Daddy. Everywhere I look.

Do you love him more than me, babygirl?

"Oh, Daddy," she told him, and she sobbed against his shoulder.

33

GATESMAN sat in his vehicle parked outside the mobile home. He had shut off his engine a minute earlier and could hear the heat crackling beneath the hood.

Mobile home, he thought, and the phrase sounded strange inside his head. *The last time you were mobile was when some truck hauled you away from the factory.*

Then he told himself, *Maybe you should just call her.* He didn't think she would be asleep already; it was only a few minutes after three. Maybe she did not sleep even after cleaning Mrs. Shaner's place. Maybe she was inside there, sitting at the window, waiting for the school bus to come by and drop Jesse off.

He swung open the door finally, climbed out, and went to the front door.

"Come on in," Livvie said after his three soft knocks, and he knew even before he stepped over the threshold that, yes, she had seen him outside in his vehicle, and now she would be sitting there waiting for him to come in and give her the news, *There's a witness claims she saw him getting into a dark blue van*, or maybe *There's this fella over in Elliottsburg, a registered pedophile. We're pretty sure he's involved in this.* Or maybe it would be, *We found his body, Livvie, I'm sorry.* What else could she be expecting by now, after all these days? The best news she could expect would be no news at all, no change in status quo, no witness, no pedophile, no body.

He looked at her there on the orange vinyl sofa, not even a cup of coffee in her hands, nothing but that hollow, waiting look. He closed the door, crossed to the sofa, and sat beside her. "How are you holding up?" he asked.

She said, "Do you have something to tell me?"

He looked at his hands. "I told the state boys that they need to be handling this. I just don't have the resources to do it right. Honestly . . . I don't have the know-how."

"So . . ." she said, "what does that mean?"

"Nothing, really, except that they'll probably be sending somebody around to ask you all the same questions I already did. They were with us when we went through the woods, so it's not likely they'll go all over that again. It's just that from here on in, you'll be dealing with them instead of with me."

"So nothing's really changed," she said.

"I guess that's right."

She didn't nod or otherwise respond.

He had never seen a person so still. "Have you heard from Denny, by any chance?"

"What would I hear?" she asked.

"Has he contacted you about anything?"

Five seconds passed before she shook her head no.

"And you don't have any idea where he might be?"

She looked at him, said nothing, then looked away again. "No."

"Well," he said, "I don't know if you'll consider this good news or bad news, but there's no charges against him for what he did to the Hayes boy."

"Why not?" she said.

"Dylan took off somewhere. He was supposed to come by the courthouse and sign a statement when he got out of the hospital. Instead he just packed up and left town. His folks claim to have no idea where he went to."

"Then it was Dylan," she said.

"Now, we don't know that, do we?"

"Why else would he leave and not tell anybody where he was going?"

"I don't know. Maybe he was scared of getting beaten again."

"But if he'd stayed and signed that statement . . ."

"Then, yes. We'd have had to pick Denny up for it."

"So then Dylan wouldn't have had any reason to be scared."

"Look," the sheriff told her, "the truth is that nobody knows anything. It's hard enough to understand why we do things ourselves, let alone figuring out other people's actions."

She continued to look at him without speaking, but the expression on her face was impossible to read. *She's probably not even seeing me,* he told himself. *She's looking somewhere else that's not even here.*

"I just wanted to let you know," he told her. "Denny's sure to hear it from one of his buddies sooner or later. I don't know if you want him back here or not, but . . . this is where he's likely to come."

After a while, she leaned away from him, leaned back into the corner of the sofa and closed her eyes. "All right," she said. "Thank you, Sheriff."

He did not interpret her dismissal as an insult. *It's nothing personal,* he told himself as he drove away. *Right now, I barely even exist as far as she's concerned.*

34

The crows were so noisy the next morning that they woke her. The evening before, after returning from the nursing home—there had been no ice cream cone afterward, no contemplation of the lit fountain and whimsical statue—she had opted for a glass of wine instead of fixing herself anything for dinner. For dessert she took two more Ambiens with another glass of wine, then lay back in the recliner with the television on. Just after four in the morning she awoke to a program on the History Channel, a dramatized biography of Clyde Barrow. She was able to lose herself in the footage for a while, watched the outlaw run from one crime to the next. *Men are so lucky,* she found herself thinking, *the way they can take whatever they want and feel no remorse. All that swagger and swinging testicles.* She thought the History Channel's version of Clyde Barrow's death much more realistic and therefore anticlimactic than Arthur Penn's operatic treatment of the event, and it was then that she began to lose interest in the program. The last thing she remembered before the crows woke her was the postmortem newsreel footage of Bonnie and Clyde. But even before she woke, the crows' squawking reached her in the living room and infiltrated her dream. She went from Clyde and Bonnie on the coroner's slabs to a Hitchcock nightmare of the crows laying siege to her house. Black, cawing clouds banging at every window, ramming impossibly long beaks through the door and the walls. Charlotte ran from room to room in her dream, looking for a safe place to hide but finding none. So many crows landed on her roof that the house began to creak. Eventually the roof upstairs collapsed and she raced back downstairs and cowered in her studio against the curtained window.

She could remember standing off to the side of the bay window and clutching the curtain while she peeked outside, dead certain that the crows were going to come swooping down the stairway at any second, smash through the studio's French doors, and tear her to shreds. In her dream she had her cell phone in her hand and was frantically punching numbers but could get no dial tone. Strangely, when she peeked out the window, the glass was clear, completely unmarked by feathers and blood, as if none of the thousands of crows had ever hurled themselves against the glass. She could see all the way across the field and to the row of trees now, and only then did she realize that the horrible midnight of her dream was now in daylight, the soft yellow light of a clear day a half hour after dawn. The nightmare soundtrack had ended. The only crows she could see or hear were the dozen or so real ones soaring and diving high above the trees. They were attacking three turkey vultures that had encroached on the crows' territory. The crows kept diving up and down at the buzzards like little kamikaze planes, but those big black airbuses just kept circling and circling in a leisurely gyre.

It took her a while to realize that she was awake and had walked to the window in her sleep. She stood there watching the birds for another ten minutes, feeling her heartbeat gradually slow and become close to normal again. When the crows finally chased the buzzards out of sight, all of the birds disappearing behind the trees, she went to the kitchen and prepared a cup of tea.

She did not want to settle in front of the television again and knew she could not paint, but she also knew that she had to keep her mind distracted, had to find something on which to focus her thoughts. She had found it interesting how the smaller birds, maybe a fourth the size of the turkey vultures, had acted so aggressively to protect their territory. She went to the computer and first researched crows. She read that some Native Americans think of the crow as the keeper of the Great Spirit, that others see it as a trickster and a shape-shifter, a creature free of the constraints of time, able to see into and occupy the past, present, and future simultaneously. Some believe that the crow created the world. The Alaskan Chuylens say that the crow can shape-shift into a handsome young man who can trick women into doing his will. In Celtic symbolism, seeing a crow is an omen that something special or unexpected will soon occur. Early American folklore held that a crow was a messenger bringing secret knowledge. Others view the crow as a messenger of death.

Charlotte then spent another two hours on the family *Cathartidae*, the "cleanser." She learned that the vulture is mute—unlike the crow, which can mimic human speech. Vultures can only grunt and hiss, usually to warn another vulture away from some meal of rotting flesh, but they allegedly grunt their loudest when fucking. *Just like a vulturous ex-husband I used to know,* Charlotte told herself. She thought it unusual and more than a little sad that such a graceful bird in the sky should lack a larynx, have no song to sing and no voice to sing one.

On one website she found a long essay by Lee Zacharias, a piece whose focus shifted back and forth between the vultures and Zacharias's father. There were two lines in the essay that Charlotte liked so much she copied them onto a sheet of lined paper: "The bird's muteness sits upon its shoulders. It knows what death tastes like, but cannot speak of the flavor."

In another passage, she read about vultures in the mountains of Tibet and was intrigued to learn that Buddhists there will hack a deceased loved one into portable pieces and leave them out on the rocks for the vultures. The birds will descend and swiftly carry the pieces away to be devoured. The practice is called *jhator*, a sky burial. Charlotte thought it equally gruesome and poetic.

After that long morning at the computer, Charlotte was unable to look at the crows or vultures or even to hear the crows cawing in the distance without thinking of them as presiding over a funeral, a sky burial, and remembering her father sitting like a corpse with his chin on his chest, and wishing she had the courage of doing him the honor of a *jhator*, wishing she had the courage and the wings and the crows' gift of song to spirit them both away.

35

WHEN Gatesman first purchased his cell phone several years past, the salesman had shown him how to download various ringtones, and together at the kiosk in the mall, they had listened to one after another until "Raindrops Keep Falling on My Head" played like a tinny little carillon in the salesman's hand and Gatesman told him, "That one." Gatesman soon learned that it was fine to be reminded of Patrice and Chelsea when in the mall, but not when Tina was relaying some urgent message to him in the field, or when one of his deputies called to ask how to handle a tenuous situation. It was not good, then, to be taken back in time to a place you wanted to stay forever, back to those feelings you were sure you would never feel again. It was not good to let the ringtone keep playing so that you could stay wrapped for a while in that sad blanket of memory. So, after less than a week, he had changed the ringtone to sound like an old-fashioned telephone. Unfortunately, even now, several years later, each time that quick trill of notes sounded, inside his head he heard Patrice singing, "Raindrops keep falling on my head, but that doesn't mean my eyes will soon be turning red . . ." And usually, each time he reached for the phone to snap it open and shut off the memory, he told himself, with some mix, depending on the situation, of amusement and annoyance, *Pavlov's dog.*

On this night he heard the phone ringing in the distance, and in his sleep he saw himself in the bentwood rocker with Chelsea asleep on his chest, while there across the room in a long rectangle of sunlight, Patrice in a yellow sundress danced inside the box of light, her legs and arms and feet bare, and the image was so painfully clear that he could see the soft, blond hairs on her forearms and he could feel the warm little breaths and heartbeats against his chest. Patrice kept singing and dancing, but the ring kept getting louder, and he could feel it pulling him away from her, he could feel them slipping away.

And then he was awake in a dark room and he could hear the cell phone ringing and vibrating on the night table. And this time, he said something other than *Pavlov's dog* to himself as he rolled over and reached for the phone.

Charlotte Dunleavy's voice echoed his own breathlessness, a strained and frightened whisper. "There's somebody trying to break in!" she told him. "I can hear him down on the back porch!"

He sat up quickly, looked at the clock on the other nightstand: 2:27. "Are your doors locked?" he asked.

"Yes, but I can hear him walking across the porch!"

"Sit tight," he told her. "I'll have a deputy there in a few minutes."

"You're closer, Marcus. Can't you come instead?"

"Maybe a minute closer. But the deputy's already dressed, I'm not." But by now he was standing by the chair in the corner, already reaching for the trousers he had hung over the back of the chair. He almost asked, "Are you sure it's not an animal of some kind?" But he knew what the answer would be. Frightened people *always* know that it isn't an animal, even though it usually turns out to be just that. So instead he asked, hoping, "Do you think it might be Dylan?"

"God," she said, "I don't know. I suppose it could be. But it's so dark outside, I can't see anything."

"You haven't heard from Dylan since before he disappeared?"

"No . . . no, not a word, why would I? Marcus, *please!* There's somebody down there!"

He shoved his right foot and then his left into his shoes. "Listen, I'm on my way to the car right now. But here's the thing. If it is Dylan, I don't want to frighten him away. So I'm going to be very quiet when I get there, okay? Are you in your bedroom?"

"Yes," she told him.

"Bedroom door locked?"

"Yes!"

"Okay. Watch for me out your window. I'll park at the end of your driveway. I'll blink my dome light on and off once so you'll know it's me."

"Okay," she said.

"Then you blink your light for me to let me know you're okay."

"I have a flashlight here," she told him.

"Even better. Once I know you're okay, I'm going to be sneaking around your house for a few minutes. If you hear any noises, I'll probably be the one making them."

"Okay," she said. "Are you on your way yet?"

"I'm headed for the car, Charlotte. A few more minutes."

"Thank you," she said.

"But listen. If I don't see you blink back at me when I get there, I'm going to come bustin' in."

"You'd better," she said.

36

FIFTEEN minutes before Charlotte made her call to the sheriff, a loud clank had brought her out of a light sleep. Again that night, she had fallen asleep on the recliner in the living room, had taken to the recliner a few hours earlier with the intention of watching an old movie with Charlton Heston and Orson Welles fighting and causing corruption in Mexico, but she had kept turning the volume lower and lower until the sound was completely muted, and then the light from the television bothered her, she had shut the television off. The clank awoke her suddenly a couple of hours later, and she sat upright and wondered who had turned the television off. Then a scraping sound across her porch boards told her that the raccoons were back, so she had climbed out of the chair and walked softly but quickly to the mudroom without turning on any lights.

A few days before Charlotte had moved out of New York, she had met with her former therapist and current good friend, June, for a final lunch at the little sidewalk café on West 48th they liked. As usual they split a half bottle of pinot grigio while waiting for their grilled chicken salads. It was then that Charlotte had said, "I have something to show you," and pulled her purse into her lap.

"You know how you've been insisting that I get some kind of protection?" Charlotte had said.

"And you finally did?" June asked.

"Not that I believe Pennsylvania is the wild frontier you seem to think it is."

To June, whose idea of roughing it was a Victorian bed-and-breakfast on Cape Cod, rural Pennsylvania was the Old West, a place filled with lawless men, rattlesnakes, and wolves. Now June said, "Look, you're a beautiful woman and you'll be living alone. You need to be cautious." She leaned closer around the side of the table. "What did you get?"

Charlotte opened her handbag and, without lifting it off her lap, leaned it toward her friend. "It's called a nine," she said.

June's eyebrows went up at the sight of the black pistol tucked into the purse with Charlotte's mascara and hairbrush. "Very nice," she said. She made a move to reach for it, but Charlotte pretended not to notice and clamped the bag shut again, then hung it over the side of her chair, close to her body.

"Weapon of choice for all us gangstas," Charlotte said.

What June did not know was that Charlotte only appeared to have taken her friend's advice. She knew that if she did not accede to June's wishes, at this final lunch and incessantly afterward, June would harangue her about the single woman's need for protection. So, for forty dollars plus change, Charlotte had armed herself with what appeared to be a nine-millimeter handgun. But Charlotte's model had a little cylinder of compressed gas concealed in the butt, and the magazine was filled with tiny copper pellets.

Ironically, after just a week on the farm, Charlotte was glad she had made the purchase. The first time she heard the rattling noises on her back porch, the previous summer, she had lain cowed and shivering in bed, with one finger poised on her cell phone's Call button, the 9-1-1 already punched in. She had told herself that if she heard glass break or wood splinter, she would jam down the button, then scream so loud to the dispatcher that, Charlotte hoped, the burglar or rapist or serial killer would be sent running. But all she heard was the garbage can lid hitting the porch floor.

She reasoned that a burglar or rapist or serial killer would probably not pause to rummage through her garbage. Her ex-husband might, however, for whatever demented reason he might have. So she had climbed out of bed, dug around in the closet until she found the pellet gun, then crept downstairs and into the mudroom. When she switched on the porch light, a pair of ring-tailed raccoons went scampering off into the darkness. Charlotte spent the next fifteen minutes scooping garbage up off her porch.

The next night, the raccoons were back. They skipped the following six nights, probably because, she told herself, they were busy picking pellets out of their butts. After being peppered a second time, the raccoons returned only once a month or so during warm weather. It seemed to take them approximately thirty days to forget that there was a big rock on the garbage can lid and a trigger-happy Dirty Harriet lurking behind the mudroom door.

After that first incident, Charlotte had kept the pellet gun on the narrow shelf of a coatrack near the back door. But now when she reached for it, on that dark night in April, the pistol was not there. She ran her hand back and forth along the shelf but felt nothing. The panic bubbled up in her as she wondered if somebody was already inside the house, and if somebody now held the air pistol and maybe had crept up behind her from the kitchen. It only added to her panic to remember suddenly why the air pistol was no longer on the shelf. In an instant the mudroom seemed sucked dry of all oxygen. Raccoons were no longer a possibility. Something or someone had come after her, the shadow from her dreams perhaps, the coalescence of all her fears.

She moved back through the mudroom and kitchen as quickly as she could but felt as if she were struggling to surface from an impossible, airless depth. She pulled herself up the stairs and into her bedroom. She seized the phone and took several deep breaths as she tried to get some air into her lungs. Then, using the light from her cell phone, she opened a drawer on the night table, took out the card Marcus Gatesman had given her, and, with a heavy, unnecessary pressure on the buttons, she entered his home number.

37

THE night was starless when Gatesman's car entered Charlotte's driveway and came to a soundless stop. He shut off the engine and extinguished the headlights. A half-moon hung pale and low in the sky. Through his half-open window Gatesman could smell the damp air; it carried a vague scent of wood smoke from somebody's chimney, a scent he had always liked. He waited a moment, turned his interior light on for just a second, then off again. A light in an upstairs window flashed once, then was gone. *There she is,* he told himself.

Gatesman climbed out of the vehicle and softly closed the door.

He stayed off the gravel driveway, kept to the soft grass. The only weapon he carried was a long, black flashlight, but he did not turn it on. Right now he wanted the darkness unbroken. The moon was weak tonight but sufficient to shade the world with different levels of darkness. The yard and the buildings were black; he was charcoal but carried or wore small bits that would catch the weak light and throw it back. His eyes, his belt buckle, the flashlight lens. He walked lightly around the west side of the house and kept his eyes narrowed, flashlight lens pointed at the ground, the hem of his sweatshirt pulled over and tucked under the belt buckle. He listened for the slightest of sounds, any moving glint of light or shadow.

Nothing. The back porch was empty. So, too, the yard. In his mind's eye he reconfigured the darkness—clothesline poles fifteen yards out, one metal cross just to his left, the other thirty feet to his right, two taut lines of plastic-coated wire traversing the sky at forehead level. A metal burn barrel farther left and another ten yards beyond the clothesline. Charlotte's garden plot at a sixty-degree angle to his right, between him and the farthest clothesline pole. No movement. No sounds.

Then a soft thud, a single distant knock on wood. He stood motionless. It had come from deep in the darkness, at least forty yards away. The barn. He walked briskly now, ducking under the clotheslines, long strides landing only on the balls of his feet. He kept replaying the thud in his head, homing in on it by instinct alone. It hadn't come from inside the barn, it had not been muted enough for that. Nor from the front or it would have been clearer. He made his way quickly to the rear of the barn, could hear the sibilance of his own footsteps but doubted that anyone else could. And when he saw a slender spear of yellow light dart past the lower corner of the barn, he froze for a moment, stood where he was, held his breath, and listened. The light had hit the yard like a splash, then had leapt back behind the barn.

Now he moved close to the wall, crept to the corner, and peeked around it.

Under the overhang that opened off the empty stalls, opened

onto the weedy pasture enclosed by a fence, a man stood facing the barn. He moved his flashlight beam up and down along the wall beneath the overhang. The light was weak, probably a Dollar Store model, nothing like Gatesman's own twelve-inch Vortex, 10-watt halogen bulb, 220 lumens. Bright enough to sear a man's eyeballs if necessary, sturdy enough to knock him unconscious. But none of that would happen tonight, because Gatesman had seen the man's face, saw it briefly illuminated by the weak yellow light.

"Hold it right there, Denny," Gatesman said.

Denny Rankin spun toward him, the light moving with him but barely strong enough to travel the five yards to where the sheriff stood. Now Gatesman turned on his own torch, threw the entire area and fifty yards beyond into white light.

"You trying to fucking blind me?" Rankin said, a hand raised to his face now.

Gatesman aimed the light at the hard-packed ground as he approached. "What do you think you're doing here?" he asked.

"Looking for the way in. What are you doing here?"

Gatesman came to within six inches of him, a tactical move made to emphasize the difference in their sizes. Rankin stood maybe five-nine in his heavy boots, still three inches shorter than the sheriff and at least eighty pounds lighter, a man all sinew and bone, gristle and spit. Gatesman said, "Lucky for you, you didn't find it yet. You're flirting with a trespassing charge."

"There's not a single sign around here and you know it."

"That doesn't give you the right to go creeping around on private property. So I'm going to ask you again, Denny. What are you doing here?"

Rankin blew a breath between his teeth. "You and I both know she had something to do with my boy being gone."

"There is absolutely no evidence of that."

"Fuck evidence. I know what I know."

"And what do you know?"

"I just know, is all."

"Then you don't know diddly."

"I know that those woods are right over there, and she's right down there in that house. And I know my boy. I'd bet dollars to doughnuts he's been in this barn plenty of times. Maybe she caught him in here once, got pissed off, and whacked him with something. You ever think of that?"

"I've been through this barn already. Inside and outside. Mike Verner's got some hay stored in there; otherwise the place is empty."

"Yeah? Well, maybe I'm the one needs to do the looking this time."

"I'm gonna tell you what you need to do, Denny. I understand that you're angry and frustrated. You *know* that I know how you feel. Losing a child is a hell of a thing. But I can also smell your breath, and I doubt very much you want to take a Breathalyzer tonight, do you?"

"You see me driving something? I fucking *walked* here."

"You're trespassing, you're drunk, and you're causing a disturbance at three in the morning. You want to go find out how the magistrate feels about that? After what you did to the Hayes boy?"

Rankin stared up at him. "You got any witnesses to that?"

"Dylan's going to turn up sooner or later, don't you worry. In the meantime, you give me the slightest reason to haul you in, it's a sure bet I'm gonna do it."

Every line and angle in Rankin's face was hard. "You need to go over this place again."

"Don't you tell me what I need to do."

Rankin stared at him a few moments longer. Then he turned away, a sudden pivot that made the sheriff tighten his grip on the flashlight. "You need to open your fucking eyes," Rankin said as he strode away, long, hot strides carrying him out into the pasture, shoulders hunched forward, weak light swinging back and forth over the weeds.

Gatesman thought about calling out to him, warning him to stay away from this place, but in the end, all he did was to throw the wide beam of his flashlight at Rankin's back to spear him in a shaft of white as he marched toward the trees.

Back at the house, Gatesman knocked on the front door. "It's me, Charlotte," he called. "Can you open up for a minute?"

He heard her feet padding down the stairs, heard the dead bolt snap open. Then she was standing there behind the screen with only the upstairs hallway light illuminating the foyer. The heat that had risen to his face during his encounter with Rankin suddenly cooled at the sight of her, or rather turned into a different kind of warmth, soothing and healing. She was wearing a long robe, blue flannel with primroses, and her feet were bare. Her eyes were frightened and she looked small, and her scent came to him through the screen door: a clean, soapy smell, a hint of strawberries.

He smiled. "Not a thing out here," he told her. "Not a sign, not a sound. Nothing."

She said, "I heard somebody rattling the doorknob. And I heard footsteps on the back porch. And just now I thought I heard voices."

"Well," he said, "let's just think about this a minute. 'Cause I'm not saying you didn't hear what you say you heard. But a raccoon can turn a doorknob, did you know that?"

"Are you serious?" she said.

"Plus . . . if somebody was trying to break in, would he *rattle* the doorknob? Or would he try to be quiet about it?"

"What about the footsteps?" she said. "Those weren't made by a raccoon. And what about the voices? Do the raccoons around here know how to *talk*?"

She was holding the neck of her robe closed with one hand, held her left arm across her belly. More than anything, he wanted to pull open the screen door, step close, and wrap his arms around her. What he didn't know was whether he wanted to do it for her sake or his own. The light from upstairs was soft and warm, and it illuminated the stairway behind her. He would carry her up those stairs like a child. He would feel her warmth and softness as she held herself against him.

He told her, "I'm not saying you're wrong, Charlotte. All I'm saying is, sounds are amplified in the night. Everything is. Even the way we feel about stuff. You'd think the darkness would have a dampening effect, wouldn't you? But instead it makes things bigger."

After a moment or two, she smiled. "I'm sorry I brought you out here in the middle of the night."

"You call me anytime. That's why I gave you that number."

"You want some coffee? I can make you a cup."

To him it seemed a long time before his answer came, before he could decide which answer to make. "You go on back to sleep. That's where I'm headed too. You might leave the porch lights on if you feel like it, though. That oughta keep the coons away. And what about that sodium-vapor light out at the barn? That still work?"

"It does, but it lights the place up like a football stadium."

"That's sorta the idea, isn't it?"

"I don't know if I'd be able to sleep in a football stadium."

He wanted to ask her then if she had trouble sleeping too. Wanted to ask if the darkness made her feel more or less alone. Instead he told himself that she was only being polite when she brought up the coffee. He told himself, *Look at the way she's holding the top of her robe together. And she's never once reached for the screen door to open it.*

Minutes later, driving home, Gatesman asked himself why he had chosen not to tell her about Denny Rankin skulking around. *Because it will only frighten her,* he answered. *It will only have her lying awake every night listening for him to come back.*

Okay, he thought. *But why couldn't you just say, "Listen . . . I think it would really be nice to hold you, Charlotte. I just want to feel what that's like again. A woman's skin beneath my hand. The way her mouth feels on mine."*

Why couldn't you say, "Look. People need to feel close to somebody."

Why couldn't you just say, "I get so lonely sometimes, I feel like I can't even breathe. Does that ever happen to you?"

38

THE days passed. She kept no tally. Instead she watched the History Channel, the Discovery Channel, old movies from the thirties, forties, fifties, and sixties, made-up stories evoking times recognizable even though they occurred before she was born. She read about crows and buzzards, read about objects—the history of the syringe (which led, not surprisingly, she thought, to the first morphine addict, the syringe inventor's wife), the morning glory vine (a beautiful killer that could kill in two ways, by slow strangulation if you were another plant, and with spectacular hallucinations if you ingested a few hundred seeds). She read about McPhee's oranges, Susan Orlean's orchids. She read Billy Collins's poetry, smiled at the thought of his gooseneck reading lamp trudging up close for a peek into the poet's grace, and then she asked herself which of her own possessions would miss her most. The teakettle? Her brushes? Her gardening hat?

She sat on the porch swing and thought about the walks she

had taken last summer and fall, the narrow lanes and logging trails she had explored, the wonderful excitement of getting herself lost—a different kind of lost, a kind that leads to discovery.

She slept erratically, afraid of her dreams. She wandered from room to room through darkness and daylight, peered out this window or that. Gazed into the distance. Watched cloud shadows crawl over her yard and garden shed, the weedy pasture, the silent, hulking barn.

On a couple of occasions she went for a drive, though she did not enjoy her Jeep anymore, no longer felt the pride of possession she had originally felt. In the city she had been at the mercy of her husband or some other driver, had to wait for taxis, buses, the subway, or friends to fulfill her transportation needs. Then, for a while here in the country, each time she reached for her Jeep keys, she had received a little jolt of adrenaline, a shiver of satisfaction. But now the Jeep felt tight and cumbersome, and no matter how many times she sprayed the interior or hung a new air freshener from the rearview mirror, she could always detect a low, rumbling odor beneath the artificial scents, as dark as distant thunder on a clear, bright day.

On those drives through town she was sure she could detect a new somberness in the air. The word *pall* kept running through her mind. One spring morning she noticed lilacs and crocuses poking their white and purple punctuations up out of the earth in several yards, the delicate little blue cornflowers sprouting along the highway; but on that same day she encountered not a single smile on the people she passed, and when she drove by the schoolyard, there were three teachers keeping solemn watch over the playground; and even the children seemed somber—no running or shrieking or high swinging visible, only children sitting in huddled clusters close to their teachers.

When she spotted Mike Verner coming out of the hardware store that morning, bouncing a small bag of wood screws in his hand as he headed for his pickup truck, she pulled into the nearest parking spot, climbed out, and hurried down the street to intercept him.

"Mike!" she called just as he pulled open his door. He stepped up onto the sidewalk to meet her. Though he smiled as she approached, Charlotte thought his eyes had gone gray and tired. "How you doing, beautiful neighbor?" he said in greeting, and she wondered if the sadness she saw and heard everywhere was real, if sadness could in fact permeate an entire town, a whole county, or if possibly she carried the contagion with her.

"I was wondering about Dylan," she said. "Have you heard anything? Any news where he might be?"

Mike held his smile in place but moved his gaze slightly so that he was looking past her, far down the gray sidewalk. Finally he looked back at her. "Not a word," he said. "I wish we would."

"Because I was thinking," Charlotte told him, "that I could send him some money, maybe. I mean, I know his parents don't have a lot to spare . . ."

He continued to look at her, continued to smile. She wondered how much he knew. Then he said, "It's tough, I know, but maybe the thing to do is to let a fella make his own way in this world. You depend too much on other people, you can go a little soft."

"It's just that I feel so bad for the boy."

He nodded and lost his smile. He looked across the street, then came back to her again. "People go around shooting their mouths off like it's a known fact Dylan hurt Jesse somehow. I tell them, 'If you know so damn much, where's the evidence?' It makes me so damn mad sometimes."

"How are Dylan's parents doing?'

He shrugged. "About what you'd expect. At least the state boys aren't saying Dylan's involved."

"The state police?" she said.

"They're handling it now, didn't you know that? Though *handling* might be too generous a word. They're pretty much convinced that Jesse's a runaway."

"Really?" she said.

He nodded, then looked at the packet of screws in his hand. "And maybe he is, who knows? I mean who the hell knows, Charlotte? Who the hell knows?"

"And Livvie, she's . . . she's gotta be . . ."

"Yeah," he said, "I imagine so."

39

On a bright day midweek, in the middle of the morning after another night of soft but steady rain, Charlotte sat on her porch swing with a slender book of e. e. cummings's poetry resting on her lap. She had read from the book well into the night and had returned to it shortly after waking. Whether it was the effect of her brief conversation with Mike Verner the day before, or the poetry, or the long night of rain, or the bottle of pink merlot that had accompanied the rain, Charlotte had slept for five straight hours, from around four A.M. to twenty minutes past nine, but instead of feeling rested, she felt undone by the combination of influences; she felt lugubrious, as unfocused as a bear stirring out of hibernation too soon. From the shaded porch, the colors all around her seemed especially vibrant, the grass green and lush after the rain, the new buds scarlet and full, and though the air was light and clean and she kept telling herself, *How beautiful, how beautiful*, still she could not shake her listlessness, the lassitude, the amorphous longing and sadness that seemed to fit no name.

It was into this atmosphere that the sheriff's car appeared out on Metcalf Road. It slowed as it approached Charlotte's driveway, then swung down the gravel lane and came toward her. Her heart did a little somersault, so she sat very still, she took slow and measured breaths.

Gatesman climbed out of his car, looked up at her, and smiled. As he ambled toward the porch steps he said, "Darned if it doesn't appear that spring might be coming after all."

"Officially," she said, "I believe it already has."

"People around here don't put much stock in what's official," he said.

It took her a few moments to realize that he was making a joke, poking fun at himself. "Ahh," she said, and laughed softly, and leaned back against the porch swing.

He put a foot up on the first step, laid a hand atop the rail. "How's the painting coming along?" he asked.

She looked at the book open in her hand. Laid her finger atop cummings's title, "in Just-." "It's coming along just fine," she said.

He nodded, then shifted his gaze slightly to the left, to the darkness behind the screen door. Then he brought his gaze back to her, smiled again, and looked beyond her to the right, over her shoulder and out the back of the porch. She watched his eyes and tried to imagine what he was seeing—the field, the shaded woods.

He said, "I like that one of yours you call *Horses in the Snow*."

She was momentarily surprised. "*Four Horses in the Snow*? Where in the world did you see that?"

He looked at her again and grinned like a mischievous boy. "I looked you up on the Internet."

"You Googled me?"

"I started out looking up that writer you said I resemble."

The pressure that had been building in her chest, that heavy ache, pushed up into her throat and escaped as an uncomfortable laugh. "Is that what you came here to talk about? My work?"

"Well," he said, and looked off toward the trees again, "I was just thinking that I need to go over to Harrisburg one of these days. Thinking I might go this Saturday. And I just figured that if you hadn't made it down there yet for sushi or whatever, maybe you'd like to ride along."

She began to tremble then. She was aware of the pressure in her sinuses, her throat constricting. She blinked, shivered, wondered, *Where is this feeling coming from?* Later, alone, she would identify a confusion of emotions, a tenderness for Gatesman, melancholy and wistful and grateful, plus an equally warm longing, even excitement, as she looked at his hands, his solidity and size, and his enviable stillness. But what made her tremble, what made her wrap her arms around her chest and shiver was the cold, fast river of fear gushing through all else.

He felt awkward in her silence and said, "It's all right if you're not interested. It was just an idea."

She leaned forward over the book, her eyes on the book now—*mud-luscious*, she read, *whistles far and wee*—and she thought about saying, "I want to, I do." And when she turned her head just enough to regard him, she almost did say it because it was so easy to imagine the pleasing scrape of his cheek against her own, to smell the clean, soapy smell of a man like Marcus Gatesman, a man who would never buy a ninety-dollar bottle of cologne, never pay more than fifteen dollars for a haircut, never even contemplate getting hair plugs or cosmetic surgery. She thought of all that in an instant, how wonderful it would feel to have him balanced above her, slowly pushing closer, the rush of heat radiating out from him and all through her to chase away, eradicate, obliterate the chill.

But it was all impossible and she knew it without a doubt. Bent over the book, holding on to herself, her head cocked to the side so that her eyes held his, she burst into tears.

He had no idea what to do. He started toward her, a tentative step. "Charlotte, I'm sorry, I . . . I didn't mean to say anything to upset you. I just . . . all I was doing was . . ."

She laid a hand over her eyes and kept sobbing. Her body shook and the swing shook and the chains creaked like rusty bones. When she heard him coming toward her again, two quick steps against the porch boards, she raised her other hand in the air, extended the palm toward him, and his footsteps ceased. "I'm okay," she said. "Just please . . . please . . ."

"Do you want me to go?" he asked.

No! she wanted to say, but instead she nodded once, then more adamantly again.

"Are you sure?" he said.

Each sob felt excruciating, a burst of agony in the center of her chest. She could no longer speak, could not look up at him. She felt capable of one action only and flung herself up off the swing, threw open the screen door, and all but dove into the house. She was halfway up the stairs before the screen door banged shut.

From her bed, face pressed to the pillow, she heard his car engine start. Heard the slow crunch of tires as he drove away.

Later that day she wrote a note of apology, sealed it in an envelope, and carried it to her mailbox. Halfway back to the house, the sobs bubbled up again. *Foolish foolish foolish woman*, they said, and she retrieved the note and crushed it in her hand and staggered back through the jagged sunlight to the concealing dimness of her house.

40

GATESMAN asked himself, *Why should you care?*

The sunlight glared off the windshield and stung his eyes.

He told himself, *You should have asked, "Is it me you don't like, Charlotte? Or is there something else wrong?"*

He told himself, *You shouldn't have left.*

He told himself, *Just do your work.*

41

SOMETIMES the house was full of light and sometimes fully dark. The usual demarcations of day and night had lost all relevance to Charlotte, and most times she could not recall how many days had passed since she had last known what day it was. Charlotte seldom left her house unless it was to sit on the front porch or the rear patio, and once a day to gather the mail from her mailbox at the end of her driveway. She had no curiosity about the mail and, after a glance, usually dropped it unopened on her desk or the kitchen counter and collected it each day only so that Lyle, the postman, would not grow suspicious or concerned to see it accumulating in her mailbox.

Sometimes the sound of crows cawing at daybreak or dusk caught her off guard, seized her as if the sharp cries were as real and cold as knives. Other times she would sit waiting for the birds to cry out, and when they finally did she would be taken by an overwhelming grief. She had read that crows were known to hold funerals for their fallen comrades, that they would gather around the flightless body and caw loudly, keening and mourning, only to fall into a sudden and empty silence akin to silent prayer. Then, in an instant, in perfect unison, they would fly off, a cloud of dark sorrow returning to the trees or sky.

Sometimes she would have to read or watch a movie or turn music up very loud. Sometimes she would drink an entire bottle of wine with Sinatra's or Bublé's or Harry Connick, Jr.'s voice blasting through the rooms. She ordered Ambien and Valium from an online pharmacy in Canada, and Ambien and Prozac and Vicodin from another. Sometimes when she took Vicodin and Valium together she would sit in her studio with the curtains drawn and she would imagine that she had shoved the past and the future down the steps into her basement. She heard little from the future, so she believed that it had been killed in the fall, but she could hear the past on the other side of the basement door, breathing heavily, summoning strength for another attempt at shattering the dead bolt.

Always there was a pain in her chest the weight of a cannonball. Always there were shadows in the corners.

42

THE morning she saw the figure stealing away from her barn—a gray-hooded figure visible only as a pale silhouette as it strode briskly, shoulders hunched, through the fog—she did not know at that moment whether it was morning or night and had to look at the clock on the stove, which read only 6:37, and then at the blue digital numbers on the microwave, which told her the same, and then she had to check the sky for the glow of either sunrise or sunset and saw that the world was at its brightest behind the barn, to the east. The sunrise looked like a fire burning in the woods behind the trees, and the fog was the fire's smoke, and the person hurrying through the smoke and toward Metcalf Road was maybe the person who had started the fire.

On the table in front of Charlotte were a ten-milligram Valium, an empty bottle of pinot noir, and a mug half full of tea. Charlotte put her hand around the mug, felt its warmth, and watched the figure moving quickly past her house. Then Charlotte went to her studio and peeked out the window and watched the figure hurrying away alongside the driveway. The figure did not step into the driveway but stayed to the damp grass until it reached Metcalf Road. It then crossed the two lanes of asphalt, jumped a shallow drainage ditch, and disappeared into the low brush on the opposite side of the road.

Charlotte remained at the window awhile longer, piecing together what she had seen. The glow of red behind the barn was, she knew, from the sunrise and not from a fire. The fog was fog, not smoke. The hooded individual had not been a large person and had moved with a certain degree of agility, an athletic, though stealthy, grace. That person, she knew, had come from her barn.

She thought of Denny Rankin. She thought of Dylan Hayes. She wondered if the fog could play tricks on the eyes, could make a person appear bigger or smaller than he really was.

When she crossed back through the kitchen to the mudroom, she glanced at the knife block on the counter and briefly considered grabbing one of the Wüsthof knives, the big chef's knife probably, something visibly frightening, but in the end she decided to go empty-handed and defenseless. It no longer mattered to her if she was attacked. She had come to think of violent confrontation as inevitable.

She did not move quickly as she laced up her boots and shrugged into the heavy jacket, and she took note of this fact, the almost-fatalistic fashion in which she dressed. *Just like when we searched the woods,* she told herself. She remembered every detail of that event, yet it seemed to have happened months or even years ago.

Outside she fell into a measured stride, neither fast nor slow but of the same unhurried pace with which not long ago she had strolled the back roads and lanes, the Nikon hanging from a strap around her neck, a small sketch pad in her pocket, a hickory walking stick in her right hand just in case she encountered an angry dog. This time her pockets and her hands were empty. She could feel the dampness of the light fog collecting on her hands and face. By the time she reached Metcalf Road, her skin was shiny wet.

The opposite side of Metcalf Road, across from her yard, was lined with thick bushes, aspens, and crabapple trees, none more than eight feet high but all crowded together, a wall of slender, entwining branches. In front of this ran a drainage ditch overgrown with weeds, and between the ditch and the bushes, a strip of tall scrub grass.

Only by scrutinizing the scrub grass could Charlotte discern where the hooded figure had moved through the brush.

As she stood there considering the path, Charlotte realized that something had quieted inside her. The anticipation of imminent violence was gone. A violent person would have cut a wider swath through the grass. An angry person would not flee. Whomever Charlotte was pursuing, he was not an angry, violent man intent on doing her harm. Charlotte doubted, in fact, that it was even a man.

She crossed the ditch and followed the slender path into the aspens. The branches were heavy with buds, though no leaves had yet appeared. She walked hunched forward, one arm raised in front of her face as she ducked branches and pushed others aside.

The wide clearing of tall scrub grass came as a surprise. Charlotte had often gazed across her front yard to the blue hills in the distance, the Tuscarora Mountains, but she had never guessed that this stretch of open land lay behind the heavy brush along the side of the road. She had imagined that the brush continued on and on until it met the stand of hardwoods approximately three hundred yards back, and that the hardwood forest continued all the way back to the mountains. Instead, here was a kind of prairie of knee-high grass. It ran as far as she could see to her right and left.

The slender path through this grass ran straight ahead another eighty or so yards, into a small copse of birch clustered in a circle. The sun was high enough now and the fog sufficiently thin that a pale, red glow lay over the grass like a tempera wash of crimson. Charlotte looked at the colors and the light and at the jewels of moisture glistening like pale rubies, and the pain in her chest began to pulse. *Why does beauty hurt so much?* she wondered. She dragged her hand through the grass as she walked and felt the coolness and the way the moisture sprayed up and away from her hand and the soft forgiving sway of the grass between her fingers.

She had only stepped past the first slender birch, had noted as she did so that it was a white birch, the bark like peeling paper—*The kind of birch Frost loved,* she told herself. *The kind we used to shinny up and ride to the ground*—when she became aware of the sobbing deeper into the trees, the small whimpering sounds that made her think of a child, so that she thought, *Jesse*, and almost said it aloud but didn't. She moved closer, more cautiously now, now for the first time deliberately softening her footsteps.

The hooded figure sat facing away from her, sat against the last birch before the clearing opened up again into tall grass and, ten yards farther, a long, low patch of blueberry bushes. The sun did not reach into the trees where Charlotte stood, but the figure was sitting on the edge of the sunlight, fully illuminated, too tall and slender for Jesse but still petite, a woman, her knees raised to her chest and her arms wrapped around her knees, her forehead resting on her arms as she quietly sobbed. She was wearing jeans and tennis shoes and a denim jacket atop a gray hooded sweatshirt with the hood pulled well forward, concealing even the sides of her face from view. Her canvas tennis shoes were soaked through from the wet grass, as were her jeans to the knees. Except for the clothing, all Charlotte could see was one ungloved hand, the right hand wrapped around the left elbow. The fingers were slender and long, the nails short—strong, feminine hands, red and chafed from the cold.

"Livvie?" Charlotte said.

The figure became very still, held her breath, and did not move.

"Livvie, it's me, Charlotte." She moved closer now, had her hand out to touch the woman's shoulder just as Livvie unfolded herself, lifted her head off her arms and dropped her arms from around her knees and turned to look up, but when Charlotte saw the face inside the hood, she was stopped momentarily by the sudden snag of her breath in her throat, but she recovered in an instant, and, saying "Oh God, Livvie," dropped to her knees and wrapped the other woman in her arms and held her close while together they wept in the soft, red sunlight on the dew-wet grass.

43

CHARLOTTE tried not to think about how energized she felt as she led Livvie back to the farmhouse. She did not like to admit that she had not felt so alert or purposeful for what seemed many, many days. Livvie seemed so small and helpless in comparison to the other Livvie, the adamantly hopeful one at the candlelight vigil; the thoughtful, unselfish one who would not accept Charlotte's braciola.

In the mudroom Charlotte quickly dropped to her knees to untie Livvie's sodden shoes. Despite Livvie's protests, Charlotte pried off the shoes and wet socks, then she dragged Livvie into the kitchen and had her sit at the little table while she dried the woman's feet and rubbed some warmth back into them with a clean dish towel. Then, ignoring her own wet shoes and the tracks they made across the tile, she filled a large mug with water, dropped a tea bag into the water, and set the mug in the microwave. While the water heated, Charlotte hurried upstairs, found her thickest pair of cashmere socks, returned to the kitchen, and pulled the socks over Livvie's feet.

Charlotte asked no questions until she had cleaned the blood off Livvie's face. She had questions to ask, a hundred questions, but even as her mind was racing with those questions, another part of her mind was piecing together a plan. For more than a week now she had felt heavy with despair, grew heavier with it day by day until she no longer knew or cared what day it was; then suddenly, during the past hour, something had changed, the fever of despair had finally and suddenly broken.

She could help this woman, she knew she could. She could change Livvie's life. And in so doing maybe save her own soul.

Is that selfish? she wondered as she dabbed at the dried blood on Livvie's swollen lip. *But isn't all altruism ultimately selfish? If there is such a thing as God's mercy, isn't even that a selfish gesture in the end?*

"So how did this happen?" Charlotte asked from the sink. She soaked the washcloth in warm water, wrung it out until the water ran clear, then dampened it, folded it into a small square, and placed it in the microwave for ten seconds.

"Is my nose broken?" Livvie asked.

Charlotte ran a fingertip down the bridge of Livvie's nose, then a finger and thumb along the side. "I don't think so. There's almost no swelling that I can see."

"It feels like it's broken."

"It's the cheekbone that you're probably feeling. That's where the real bruise is. I think we should get this x-rayed." She laid the warm cloth atop the bruise and held it in place.

"My lip's bad, too, isn't it?"

"About the size of a golf ball. You hold this cloth in place while I get another one for your lip."

"Aren't you supposed to put ice on a swelling?"

"Are you?" Charlotte said.

"Ice to bring the swelling down. Then heat. I think that's how it's supposed to be."

"I can look it up on the Internet," Charlotte said, but her mind was racing now with other plans.

"Can I just get some ice cubes, maybe? Wrapped up in a washcloth?"

"I have crushed ice," Charlotte told her. "That's even better."

Now that Charlotte knew what she would do while Livvie was there in the house and resting, she was feeling calmer and clearheaded. In her mind she could see the next hour or so playing out perfectly, with a quality of the inevitable that made her believe it was surely the right thing to do. She wrapped a handful of crushed ice in a cloth and handed it to Livvie. "Can you hold them both in place while I get you a couple ibuprofens?"

"Could I just maybe lie down on your couch a few minutes?"

"I think we need to go to the emergency room," Charlotte said, though she knew that Livvie would resist, and that she, Charlotte, would give in to the resistance. "What if your cheekbone is fractured?"

"Can we just wait and see when the swelling goes down? I don't have any insurance."

"You don't get insurance coverage from the generating plant?"

"They pay me as an independent contractor. All I do is clean."

"They're cheating you," Charlotte said.

"Plus, I missed work last night."

"Is that when this happened?"

"Most of it. Round two came about two A.M. or so." Livvie tried to smile with the side of her face that was not swollen, but the result was more of a grimace.

"You're amazing," Charlotte told her.

"Can you tell me that while you show me where the couch is?"

"You just wait right there for a minute."

From the medicine cabinet, Charlotte took two Tylenol PMs and a Vicodin.

When she returned to the kitchen, she placed the tablets in Livvie's hands. Livvie said, "These two are the ibuprofens, I guess. What's this big one?"

"For the pain."

"The ice is helping a lot already."

Charlotte handed her the mug of tea. "Take them all, Livvie. Don't try to tough this out. I already know how strong you are."

"I've never been a big fan of pills," Livvie said, but she reached for the tea mug all the same.

"Good," Charlotte told her after the pills had been swallowed. "Now let's get you upstairs to bed."

"Honestly, a few minutes on your couch is all I need. And then I'll get out of your hair. I'm sorry about disturbing your day like this."

"If you're really sorry, you'll quit arguing with me."

"Yes, Doctor," Livvie said. She allowed Charlotte to help her stand. They moved gingerly toward the stairs.

On the way up the stairs, with Charlotte's right hand atop Livvie's as it rode the banister rail, and Charlotte's left hand in the small of Livvie's back as she climbed one step at a time, Charlotte said, "So did you spend the entire night out in the barn?"

"After round two," Livvie said. "I didn't have much interest in doing round three."

"I bet it was cold, wasn't it?"

"I made a little hole in the hay. That helped to cut the chill."

Charlotte sat Livvie on the edge of the bed, then swung her

legs up and pulled the heavy comforter up to her neck. "Why didn't you just get in your car and drive away and leave the bastard to fend for himself?"

"That's why we had the fight and I couldn't go to work. He made me give him my car keys. His fuel pump or something went out in the truck."

Her voice remained matter-of-fact, and in her eyes and the turn of her mouth, Charlotte saw embarrassment and apology. "Do you *ever* complain?" Charlotte asked.

"I would if I thought it would do any good," Livvie told her with a smile.

Charlotte said, "You should be warm soon. This comforter is filled with goose down."

"Is this your bed?"

"The best one in the house."

"It smells like you."

"I'm sorry, I can get you a different pillow . . ."

"No, it's a good smell. That expensive perfume you wear."

Charlotte said, "I haven't worn any perfume for days."

"I smelled it that night at the elementary school. I wished you'd stood there longer. The smell of those torches was making me sick."

Charlotte only smiled and fussed with the comforter, made sure it was tucked in all around her. It wasn't long before Livvie's eyelids closed.

"What's it called?" she said.

Charlotte was unsure she had heard the question correctly. She thought about it for a moment, then answered, "Pink Diamond."

"Mmm," Livvie said, almost asleep now. "Like the dew on the grass at sunrise."

44

Now that Livvie was asleep, Charlotte allowed the anger to boil up and fuel her movements. She kept in her mind the look on Livvie's face in the blueberry patch, the small, bloody face all but covered in a gray hood, mouth swollen and crooked, the glaze of terror still in her eyes. Charlotte knew that she would need all the anger and strength she could muster to do what she felt she had to do, what every moment of the morning so far was leading her toward. She hurried down the stairs as quietly as she could and as her hand slid down the rail, she felt that she was sliding deliberately down a tunnel that would finally lead her to a clearing full of light and back to a semblance of the peacefulness that, three hours earlier, she believed she would never feel again.

The only article of clothing she had removed when she and Livvie returned from the blueberry patch was her jacket, but Charlotte felt no need for the jacket now. A deep flush of heat radiated through her muscles and bones. She grabbed the Jeep keys off the hook on the mudroom coatrack, stepped onto the back porch, very quietly eased shut the door, then turned and sprinted to the garage.

She did not pause to knock at the trailer, but shoved open the cheap wooden door so violently that it banged back against the wall. The sound awoke Denny Rankin, who had been sitting slouched back in a corner of the vinyl sofa, his legs splayed out wide. He jerked forward when the door banged open, and for a moment, only sat there squinting at Charlotte. On an empty sofa cushion was an empty box of tissues. Beside it were the tissues, now wadded up and bloody.

Charlotte stood just inside the door, waiting, letting the rage accumulate.

"What the fuck do you want?" Rankin said.

"Get up and get your clothes and get out of here," she told him. "And don't you ever come near her again."

He cocked his head a little and studied her. Then he slowly climbed to his feet. Took his time walking four steps to the door. He stood as close to her as he could without touching. Charlotte liked that her boots made him, in his dirty white socks, shorter than her.

She smelled his breath even before he spoke. "Get the fuck out of my house," he said.

His breath was not sour or beery as she had thought it would be but smelled of rot instead, and the stench reminded her of the dead opossum she had put in her car in early April, and it was this scent that caused her to flinch and momentarily weaken. But then she told herself, *You can't change any of that, you can only help Livvie.* So she drew in a deep breath full of rot and remembrance, and she looked at him and said, "I'm not moving. You are."

He did not take his eyes off hers, but she saw his eyes harden and she tensed at the same moment his hand seized her arm just above the wrist. An instant later she turned to the side, jerking her arm away so that he, holding tightly, was pulled into the open doorway. He released her almost immediately but it was too late, especially because she was able to get a free hand on his back now and to shove him forward. He flew face forward onto the hard ground.

When he came flying back into the trailer, his face was muddy and his eyes black with rage. It took him a moment to find her in the kitchen, to see her standing with her back to the sink, one hand lightly holding the other just below her waist. He stumbled in his fury to get to her, but still she did not move. She thought she knew what was coming and only hoped that she could survive it without losing consciousness. With luck he would hit her only once. Then she could retreat to her Jeep and call the sheriff and have Rankin arrested. The rest would fall into place when he was gone.

He came at her again, but again he stopped short. She was squeezing her fingers hard now, the left hand clenched around the right. He was so angry that he could not stop trembling. She could hear the air in his nostrils, quick, shallow inhalations, the exhalations blowing out hard. When she realized that he was not going to strike her, she held her hands even tighter, but smiled.

"You think I'm funny?" he said.

"I think you're hilarious. In a very pathetic, cowardly kind of way."

His breaths came quicker now, accelerating. She could feel how badly he wanted to hit her, how strenuously he was holding back. She thought of her father then and one of his favorite words, his name for their short bug-eyed neighbor who complained each time Charlotte's father's grass clippings flew into the neighbor's yard.

She looked at Denny Rankin and smiled. "Piss-ant," she said.

He grabbed her by the front of her shirt with both hands, seized her so viciously that she felt buttons popping and his fingernails scraping beneath her bra. He grabbed her and spun away and threw her out of the kitchen so that she went sprawling onto her hands and knees in the tiny living room. He strode up behind her and screamed, "Get the fuck out of my house!"

She stood very slowly, took a slow, deep breath before she turned to look at him. His fists were clenched but she did not care, he was finished now, she had made sure of that. She turned and went out the door and walked quickly to her Jeep. She could feel him following behind her, could hear in the dark distance his angry voice, but it was nothing more than wordless mutters to her now, sounds of no consequence. She climbed into the Jeep and locked the door and took out her cell phone.

Rankin was at her door now and had his face close to the glass. His mouth kept moving and she could see the spittle from his words, but it was all she could do to concentrate on getting the phone open, on hitting the call button and finding Gatesman's number on the list of recent calls, then scrolling to that number and pressing the call button again.

As the number rang, she looked up at the window. She watched Rankin's mouth moving and heard the sounds and this time the two came together and she understood.

"What did you do with my boy?" he shouted.

She heard Gatesman's voice in her ear but she could not respond. She could only stare at Denny Rankin glaring back at her.

Then Rankin slammed his fist against the glass. She jerked away expecting a shower of glass. But the window did not break. Rankin screamed something else at her, and then finally he strode away and back inside the trailer. She heard the beep of a broken call, a disconnection in her ear.

45

GATESMAN arrived approximately twenty minutes after her next call to him. With her second call, she had successfully reported the assault.

"Where are you right now?" he had asked.

"Sitting in my Jeep in the driveway."

"Whose driveway? Yours?"

"Livvie's driveway," she had said.

"Is Denny still in the trailer?"

"Unless he left out a back door, I guess he is."

"Then I want you to get out of there. Go back to your place and lock your doors."

But she was not finished yet. She had deliberately parked behind Livvie's battered Datsun so that Rankin would be unable to drive away. "I don't know if I can," she told the sheriff. "I can't even find my keys. I think I might have dropped them inside."

"Inside the trailer?" he asked.

"I think so, yes." She took the keys out of the ignition and slid them beneath a thigh.

"Jesus," Gatesman said. "Hold on a minute and let me see if there's a car nearby."

Thirty seconds later he told her, "I'm already on my way, so it looks like I can be there sooner than anybody else. Do you have your car doors locked?"

"Yes," she said.

"Do you have anything to defend yourself with if he comes after you? Pepper spray, a screwdriver, anything at all?"

"Please hurry, Marcus," she said.

She heard the siren well before Gatesman's car made a squealing turn into the Rankins' driveway. The siren died abruptly; he killed the engine and climbed out. Charlotte popped open her car door and turned in the seat.

"You all right?" he asked.

"I am now."

"He's still in there?"

"He left about three minutes ago."

Gatesman turned back toward his car. "Is he still driving that red pickup truck?"

"He took Livvie's car. The Datsun. I had him blocked in, so he tore off through the yard to get around me."

Gatesman looked at the yard now and saw the tread marks and the torn-up grass. "Which direction?" he said.

"Back the same way you came."

"I never saw him. Of course, I wasn't watching for a Dat
But I still don't think I passed him. He must've heard t
and pulled off somewhere."

He pulled open his car door and reached inside for the radio. Before he called the dispatcher, he said to Charlotte, “You want to go inside now and see if you can find your keys?”

“That’s a good idea,” she said, and slipped the keys into her side pocket before she climbed out.

46

At the farmhouse, Gatesman sat in his car for a while before going inside. He wrote a few things on a clipboard and told himself that he wanted to give Charlotte time to wake Livvie and explain things to her. Charlotte could do a better job than him, than any man could, in convincing Livvie that the right thing to do was to file charges against her husband. That no woman should ever put up with the kind of things Denny Rankin did. Gatesman had no time for cowards, and to his mind, men who bullied women or children were the worst kind of cowards.

And as he sat there in the car looking up at the porch, he could not help but remember Charlotte sitting on the swing with her face in her hands, sobbing after he had asked her out for sushi. She had run from him in tears, yet she had used his private number when she needed help. Women confounded him.

After maybe fifteen minutes, Charlotte appeared in the doorway and motioned for him to come inside. She met him in the foyer. "She's still fairly groggy," she told him. "I gave her a Vicodin less than an hour ago."

"I can't take her statement if she's out of it," Gatesman said.

"She's groggy but coherent," Charlotte said. "We're in the living room. Coffee or tea?"

"Whatever's easiest," he said.

"Same difference."

"Coffee, then. Black."

"I remember," she said, and walked away from him.

He watched her go down the short corridor and into the kitchen. *Little things like that,* he thought. *She remembers how I take my coffee. Does that mean anything or not?*

Livvie was in the living room holding a mug of tea with both hands, one foot tucked up under the opposite knee as she leaned into the corner of the sofa. He stepped into the room quietly, not yet in her range of vision as he considered the layout. If he were alone with Livvie, he would sit on the sofa beside her, but in this case, he thought he should leave that space for Charlotte and take the recliner for himself. In this case, Livvie would be more comfortable with another woman at her side.

He cleared his throat softly so that he did not surprise her, then he came into the room and crossed to the recliner. He sat on the edge of the cushion and said, "You doing okay?"

She smiled over the rim of her mug. "I was sleeping."

"I know. I'm sorry we had to wake you. Are you okay to talk about this now?"

She blinked once and continued to smile. "I was sitting here thinking about how quickly things change," she said.

"In the blink of an eye sometimes."

"You live your life day after day, just hoping for a change.

Then when it comes, you wish things could be the way they were."

"Some things are hard in the beginning," he told her. "But over time . . ." He stopped himself because he realized then that he was thinking about the change in her relationship with her husband, while she might be thinking about her son.

He leaned forward and set a little tape recorder on the coffee table. He pressed the record button, and then, just as he had done twenty minutes earlier with Charlotte, stated the date and time and the individuals present. Then he leaned back and smiled at her. "Ready to start, Livvie?"

She nodded.

He said, "Can you tell me how you got that split lip and that bruise on your face?"

Her own smile did not fade. He recognized it as the same kind of smile that came to his own mouth when he gazed into the distance and thought about the lake, the red canoe, the little girl on the dock.

"Denny," she said.

"How many times did he hit you?"

"You mean this last time? Last night?"

"Yes," Gatesman said.

"Four or five probably."

"Did he use his open hand or a fist?"

"Oh . . . I guess I'd have to say both. Punched and slapped and pushed, you know?"

"And this wasn't the first time he assaulted you?"

"The first this week maybe."

"So it's been a regular thing?"

"It's not usually so . . . I don't know," she said. "He grabs me and shoves me, he pushes me around. It's always been like that."

"So it's long past time it stopped," Gatesman said. "Would you agree?"

He waited at least ten seconds for Livvie's response. She answered with a nod.

"Would you mind responding orally," he said. "The recorder can't—"

"Yes," Livvie said. "The answer is yes."

"Your husband assaulted you and you wish to file a charge of assault. Is that correct?"

"Yes," she said. "Except that he isn't my husband."

Charlotte came into the room then, handed him the cup of coffee, then stood there beside his chair. He questioned Charlotte with his eyes, and she answered with her own look of surprise.

To Livvie he said, "Could you explain that statement please? Denny Rankin is not your husband?"

"I just mean that we never got married. We never had a ceremony or anything. Never got a license."

"So," he said, "the wedding band you wear . . ."

She looked at her hand, shifted the mug to her left hand, then worked the ring off her finger and laid it on the opposite edge of the coffee table. "He said it's white gold but I know it's not."

Gatesman did not know what more to say or do. Sometimes, he knew, comfort is impossible. Sometimes it is better to say nothing.

He looked up at Charlotte still standing beside his chair. "It would be good to get some photographs of both of you. The sooner the better. I hate to ask you to come into the courthouse now, but . . ."

"I have a camera here," she told him. "You can take the memory card with you. Would that work?"

"As long as I'm the one taking the photos," he said.

She said, "The kitchen has the brightest lights."

He remembered the tape recorder then and shut it off.

In the kitchen he was uncomfortable with having them stand against the white wall, with asking them to turn this way and that way, with asking Charlotte to pull the top of her bra a little lower to expose the entire scratch. He kept apologizing and told them, "I should really have a female deputy doing this," but Charlotte said, "It's all right, Marcus. Livvie and I are here together. We trust you."

Afterward he had them sign three separate sheets of paper each. Charlotte handed him the memory card from the camera. He slipped it into his shirt pocket and buttoned the pocket and then stood there uncomfortably.

He was finished doing what he had to do, yet he felt there was more to be done, though he had no idea what it might be. "I know how hard this must be for you," he told Livvie. She was seated now at the little kitchen table against the window, her arms crossed atop the table. "It's not, really," she said. "I just don't want him around me anymore." After a few seconds she leaned forward and laid her head atop her arms and closed her eyes.

Charlotte said, "Why don't I get her back into bed?"

Gatesman said, "I'll wait for you out on the porch."

He stood for a while on the edge of the porch looking off toward the mountains. The day had become clear and bright, a perfect spring day. *Except that there's no such thing as perfection,* he told himself. *Not as long as there's a human in the picture.*

He took his tape recorder and clipboard to his vehicle and placed them inside. Then he sat for a while on the car seat with the door open and his feet on the ground.

He thought, *This job would be a piece of cake if I just had a couple of switches inside my head I could shut off.*

When Charlotte came out onto the porch, he stood and crossed to the bottom of the steps. She had changed out of her torn blouse and now wore a dark blue knit shirt with long sleeves. He could see that she had been crying, and in his imagination he pictured the two women upstairs, Livvie lying in bed and Charlotte sitting beside her, holding her hand; Livvie sleeping peacefully because of the Vicodin and the soporific effects of trauma, Charlotte softly weeping on Livvie's behalf. He told himself that he could probably love this woman if only she would let him. He felt a powerful tenderness for Livvie as well, wished that he could enfold her in his arms and take away all of her pain, but for Charlotte there was something else as well, something whose name he had never learned.

"Well that was a surprise, wasn't it?" he said.

"That they were never married? I guess so."

He nodded, smiled, asked himself what else he should say.

"So what happens now?" Charlotte asked.

"Now I give my report to the DA; he swears out a warrant for Rankin's arrest. We keep looking for him until we find him."

"Does this . . ." she said, "I mean what he did to Livvie, and to me . . . this proclivity for violence . . . does it suggest to you that maybe he *is* responsible for the boy?"

Gatesman took a slow breath, released it through his mouth. "I wish I had an answer for that. For that and a lot of other things."

She studied his face, then smiled softly. "Did you ever think that maybe this isn't the right job for you?"

"Hourly," he said. "But nobody's offered to pay me to catch trout, so here I am."

She continued to stand there just outside the screen door. He pictured himself striding onto the porch, then abruptly stopped that image and made a small turn toward his car.

He said, “She’s probably going to want to go back to her own place as soon as she wakes up. In my opinion that wouldn’t be a very good idea.”

“I’ll keep her here,” Charlotte said.

“I’m sure you’ll take good care of her.”

“You don’t know Livvie. An hour from now she’ll be trying to take care of me.”

“Either way sounds good,” he said.

47

WHILE Livvie slept, Charlotte found little things to do and tried to keep her thoughts focused only on those activities, on mopping her muddy tracks off the kitchen and mudroom floors, on washing out the morning's tea and coffee mugs, drying them meticulously, setting them neatly in the cupboard, then rearranging the cups in a more orderly fashion. She swept the tiles in the foyer and her studio's hardwood floor and thought about running the vacuum in the living room but was afraid it would wake Livvie. She wanted Livvie to lie in the soft bed with the goose-down coverlet for as long as possible, to luxuriate in the warmth and softness and be unable to resist comparing it to the bed in her trailer, the tight quarters there, everything made of plastic or vinyl or molded fiberglass, a place where the windows frosted up so badly in winter that she couldn't see outside without scraping a circle in the frost, a place whose security was always at best tenuous, where the roof probably leaked and the propane tank heated unevenly and where the bedroom in the summer was a sweatbox. She wanted Livvie to awaken in the spacious perfumed bed and think, *This is the nicest bed I have ever been in.* She tried to put herself in Livvie's place and wondered if Livvie would feel the same envy and longing that she, Charlotte, would feel if their positions were reversed.

For the rest of the morning and into the afternoon, Charlotte's mind raced with such thoughts, even when she was thumbing through her cookbooks and especially when she was lying stretched out on the sofa and trying to concentrate on the soft music coming from the speakers, Taj Majal on continuous repeat, the soft Hawaiian vowels, *Lele, lele e nā manu . . . Paint my mailbox blue . . . Please take off your shoes, I slice me some sashimi . . .* And all the time her mind kept racing, racing, growling like an overheated engine, like the engine of a high-performance race car flying around the track at top speed, the throttle full-open, pedal to the floor. *How many more laps can it take at this speed?* she wondered. *How many more miles before the whole thing blows apart?*

It was midafternoon when Livvie finally stirred. Several hours beyond the time when Charlotte thought she would surely go mad with all this waiting. Charlotte's head had been throbbing so insistently that she feared another migraine might be coming, a real migraine this time like the ones she used to have in her hotel room in the weeks after leaving her husband, when every fear and worry was multiplied tenfold. But then she heard the toilet flush upstairs and she immediately leapt up from the sofa and turned the volume very low on the CD player and stood there listening. Water running in the lavatory. The soft scrape of feet.

Charlotte went to her desk in the corner of the room, sat down and jiggled the mouse to awaken the monitor. She opened her e-mail, and for several seconds after she heard Livvie at the threshold, she remained staring at the screen, pretending to be reading.

Then Livvie said, "Is it okay if I come in?"

Charlotte turned away from her desk. "Oh, hi. You're up. Come in, come in and sit down."

Livvie remained standing just inside the threshold. "Did I really sleep for five hours?"

"You really did."

"And it was this morning we talked to the sheriff? Not yesterday?"

"Same day," Charlotte said with a smile. The pounding inside her head had stopped. Livvie stood in the wide archway with the afternoon light from the kitchen filling the space behind her, and all around her, tiny motes of dust moved up and down in the yellow light, rising and falling in their unpredictable orbits.

"Thank you for everything," Livvie said.

"For what? I didn't do anything."

"It's a lot to me."

"Well . . . I'm glad to hear that. And you're very welcome."

Neither woman spoke for a while. Charlotte sat there smiling, watching Livvie, who appeared deep in thought. Then Livvie said, "Is that Hawaiian music?"

"By way of Beverly Hills," Charlotte said. "Hawaiian, calypso, a little reggae thrown in . . . Do you like it?"

"I do."

"I'll make you a copy."

Livvie smiled, but Charlotte could tell that the young woman's thoughts were already elsewhere. Then Livvie said, "I think I'll head back now and get things straightened up."

"You can't go back there," Charlotte said.

Livvie only looked at her.

Charlotte swung around fully in her chair. "Is the trailer in your name?"

"No," Livvie said. "Why?"

"You don't own it and you're not really married. So legally you have no rights there. Legally he could have you arrested for trespassing if he wants to." Charlotte knew that this was not wholly accurate, that Livvie and Denny's relationship could be considered a common-law marriage, but she saw no reason to discuss those points.

"But the sheriff said he'd put a thing out for him. An APB."

"That's just it," said Charlotte. "Let's say he slips back here and goes to the trailer and finds you there. Do you think he's going to be pleased to know that you filed charges against him?"

"But everything I own is back there."

Charlotte thought for a moment, then stood. "We'll go back together. You get everything you need, we come back here, and in a day or two, when we know he's in jail and not getting out, then maybe we can find some way to get you back into your trailer."

"I'm the one who paid for it," Livvie said. "I give Denny money every month."

"Wait a minute," Charlotte said. "You've been living there thirteen, fourteen years? And you're still paying on that trailer?"

"Denny had to borrow against it. When he bought his truck."

"That's what he told you?"

Livvie nodded. "The payments are three hundred dollars a month, he said."

Charlotte crossed to her and put her arms around her and

held her close in the yellow light. "We'll get it all straightened out," she said. Livvie stood with her hands at her sides but leaned her head close, and Charlotte laid a hand to Livvie's hair, pressed the side of her head against Livvie's. "Don't worry, okay? I'll get it all straightened out for you."

48

CHARLOTTE went into the trailer first, walked from the front to the back, and looked into every room. Then she returned to the front door, where Livvie stood waiting. "It's okay," Charlotte said.

The first thing Livvie did was clean up the bloody tissues she had left crumpled on the sofa. She carried them into the kitchen and put them in the trash. Then she noticed a dirty plate and cup and fork on the kitchen table. She put them in the sink and turned on the hot water and reached for the bottle of dish detergent. Charlotte stepped up beside her and took the bottle of orange liquid from her hand. "I'll clean up. You go pack your things."

Livvie stood motionless for a few moments, then turned away and started for the bedroom. Then she remembered something and came back to the kitchen and opened a cabinet. She took out a blue plastic cup, looked into it, and placed it back on the shelf.

"He took Jesse's lunch money," she said.

"How much?" Charlotte asked.

"It was only ten dollars or so. But if he took the rest . . ." She turned away and walked quickly toward the rear of the trailer. Charlotte shut off the water and dried her hands and followed.

When Charlotte came to the doorway of Jesse's room, Livvie already had the twin mattress lifted halfway off the bed. "Can you hold this up for me?" she asked. Charlotte put both hands on the mattress and lifted it higher. Livvie dropped to her knees, ran her hand back and forth over the top of the box spring mattress. Then she checked the bottom of the twin mattress to make sure nothing was sticking to it.

Charlotte asked, "What are you looking for?"

Livvie did not answer but went to the other side of the small bed. "You can let it down now," she said, and after Charlotte did so, Livvie raised the other side and looked between the mattresses. When she finally dropped the mattress into place again, she stayed on her knees and leaned her forehead against it.

Charlotte asked, "How much was it?"

Livvie leaned back a few inches but continued to stare at the mattress. "Four hundred and twenty."

"What were you saving for?"

Livvie shrugged. "Anything. Christmas, Jesse's birthday . . . He'll be a teenager this year. July seventeenth. I wanted to get him a really good art set."

A slowly twisting pain worked its point around inside Charlotte's chest. She felt the frame of the doorway closing in toward her, pushing the breath from her lungs. She knew she should excuse herself, say something like, *I'll wait out here while you gather up your things*, but she could not open her mouth or she would vomit, all the blackness would come spewing out, so she turned away, and with a hand to the wall, made her way back to the living room, back to the kitchen. She leaned against the sink and fumbled for the *Hot* lever and turned the water on, gushing into the basin. She leaned close to the water and sucked in the air and kept blinking and gasping until she could see the water and could feel it splashing against her face. And even after she smelled the heat and felt the sting of the tiny droplets, she remained in that position until certain she would not pass out, would not fall to her knees and start blubbering, would not bring what little was left of the world crumbling and crashing in a landslide atop her.

49

In the bedroom directly across the hall from Charlotte's, they deposited Livvie's clothes and the bags and one suitcase she had packed at the trailer. "This is actually the biggest bedroom," Charlotte told her. "I only picked the other one because I like the sun in the morning. But you can sleep late in this one. And it gets the afternoon sun, so it will always be nice and warm when you come to bed."

Livvie nodded and offered a small smile but said nothing. She had spoken very little at the trailer or on the ride back to Charlotte's house. Now, after emptying her hands, she stood nearly motionless. Across the bed lay a dozen pieces of clothing on wire hangers, two grocery bags full of shoes and socks and underwear, and a small, brown pasteboard suitcase.

"Can I help you put things away?" Charlotte asked.

Livvie turned to look at her. "I was supposed to be at Mrs. Shaner's at one o'clock. I should call her and apologize."

"Let me call her," Charlotte said. "What's her first name? I'll look up the number."

"It's seven-four-two-two," Livvie said. "Rosemary. Tell her I'm sorry, tell her I . . ."

"Don't worry," Charlotte said. "I'll take care of it."

She started toward the door, but stopped when Livvie said, "He took my car."

"Yes, he did."

"I have to work tonight. I need to call somebody, see if I can get a ride."

Charlotte moved close again and put both hands on Livvie's shoulders. "You cannot work tonight," she said. "It's impossible. You get sick days, right?"

Livvie nodded.

Charlotte asked, "Who do I call?"

"I don't know for sure, I never took off."

"You've never taken a sick day?"

"I can't afford to."

"This time you will," Charlotte said. "Tell you what. There's a very comfortable chair right over there. Go sit by the window and get your breath back. I'll make the phone calls, then I'll be back to put your things away, okay?"

Livvie's eyes were frightened, her face without expression. "I feel so out of it," she said.

Charlotte said, "I'll bring you something to help you relax."

50

LIVVIE ignored her clothes and opened the little suitcase. From the suitcase she took a child's backpack, a plastic picture of four turtles dressed like martial arts warriors on it. She zipped open the backpack and removed items one at a time and arranged them atop the heavy cherrywood dresser. A bendable Superman doll and a GI Joe. Four colorful, shiny miniature pickup trucks, all of them red. Two unopened packs of Topps baseball cards. One scuffed and dirtied baseball. A yellow miniature Tonka dump truck. A spiral pocket notebook.

Against the dresser's mirror she leaned a handmade valentine and a handmade Mother's Day card, one at each end of the dresser. Between them she set a framed picture of Jesse, a copy of the same five-by-seven school photo used at the candlelight vigil. She set the empty backpack in the corner nearest the bed.

From the bottom of the suitcase she removed several loose sheets of paper, the same four drawings from the corkboard plus five others. She picked them out of the suitcase one at a time, held each for several seconds as she gazed at it, smiling, then laid it atop her pile of clothing. The last item in the suitcase was a sketch pad. She lifted this out, looked at each of the first three pages, the only pages used, then laid the sketch pad atop the nightstand. Now she returned the loose sheets to the little suitcase, with its lid standing open, on the floor beside the backpack.

Charlotte was fully inside the room, a bottle of Evian in one hand, an Ambien in the other, before her eyes fell on the dresser. The breath caught in her chest, and she turned away from it quickly, said "Here you go" to Livvie, and handed the water and Ambien across the bed to her.

"Is this the same thing you gave me before?" Livvie asked. "'Cause I still feel really spacey."

"It's just a mild sleeping pill if you need it. But if your cheek hurts, or your lip . . . the Vicodin is for pain. Would you like another one of those?"

"No, thank you," Livvie said. She set the water and Ambien on the nightstand.

Charlotte reached for the first hanger on the bed, which held a pair of black chinos, and hung it in the closet. She wished she could stand there and gaze into the closet instead of having to look at the rest of the room.

Livvie said, "I know I'm only going to be here for tonight, but I wanted to put my things out anyway. Jesse's things. I don't think I could relax without them."

"It's okay," Charlotte said. She turned toward the bed and reached for the next hanger and took her time placing it inside the closet.

Livvie said, "I did something I'm not sure about now."

Charlotte found that if she kept her gaze low, sweeping across the floor, she could still turn to the bed to retrieve the hangers one at a time. "What did you do?" she asked.

"I left a note for Jesse. On his pillow. Telling him where I am."

Charlotte picked up a hanger, felt the weight of the clothing but could not identify it, kept looking at the floor as she turned, and the piece of clothing swung slightly with the movement. She placed the hanger on the rail but left her hand there, held to the rail because she thought her knees might give out, thought the darkness deeper inside the closet might pull her in. She asked, "What aren't you sure about?"

"I mean, what if Denny comes back? I wouldn't want him coming here to get me."

Charlotte's chest ached. Her throat felt clogged. She wanted to run to the bathroom and throw up, but she doubted she had the strength to do so. When she spoke, she thought her voice sounded odd, dusky and thick. "Denny won't dare come to my house. He's surely not that stupid, is he?"

Charlotte waited for the answer, but there was none. Instead she heard or maybe only felt Livvie approaching, felt her standing there behind her. Now Charlotte turned away from the closet, and there was Livvie with a wistful, small smile, a still-crooked smile from the swelling that had not gone all the way down. She had the little spiral notebook in her hand. "Can I show you this?" she said. "It's one of those flip books, you know? Just peel back the bottom corner and riffle through the pages."

Charlotte's hand was shaking when she took the notebook, so she moved quickly, hoping Livvie wouldn't notice the trembling. She held the notebook in the palm of her left hand, used her right thumb to expose the sketches in the pages' corners.

"Isn't that clever?" Livvie said. "That's supposed to be me hanging up clothes on the clothesline."

"He's got the laundry basket, the clothespins, and everything," Charlotte said.

"He was always making things like that for me. I only brought a few of the things back with me."

Charlotte looked at her and smiled and felt sick to her stomach. She handed the notebook back to Livvie, who returned it to its place atop the dresser.

"You don't think that if Denny does come back," Livvie said, "he'll destroy the things I left there, do you? Just out of spite? I mean, all of our clothes are still there. All of Jesse's clothes and most of mine."

"If you want to," Charlotte said, though even as she heard the words she knew they were a mistake, "we can go back tomorrow and get everything. This dresser is still empty, right? There's plenty of room. And there's a whole other bedroom."

"I probably would if I was going to stay longer."

"Maybe you should consider it," Charlotte said, though the sense of having made a mistake grew stronger with every word, the confusion in the repetition she heard inside her head, the voice asking, *What are you doing here, Charlotte? What are you doing?* She blinked and looked at the far wall, and everything looked strange to her then, familiar yet not at all, the pale green paint on the walls and the corner of the lace curtain. She slid her gaze to the right and looked out the window below the half-raised blind, saw her backyard extending out to Mike Verner's field, the clothesline stretched across the sky. From where she stood, she could not see the barn or, just beyond it, the other leg of the *L*-shaped field, but she knew they were out there, always out there. Past the barn and the field were the trees where the crows roosted. It never changed, never would. The scene was the scene, she could not paint over it. Put a new blank canvas on the easel and the old picture would bleed through. That's why she couldn't paint, she realized. Because no amount of paint could ever cover the old picture. That constant scene. That one irredeemable moment.

She turned and looked at Livvie, who was standing there now, hanging up the rest of her clothing. She watched Livvie place the last hanger on the rail and then turn to her, smiling, and Charlotte felt the tightness in her neck and at the base of her skull, and all she wanted was to call Livvie to the window and have her look out, have her see what Charlotte always saw out there . . . have what must happen happen . . . let everything come to its end.

And Livvie told her, "This is the nicest bedroom, Charlotte. I can't believe how nice it is."

"I'm glad you like it," was as much as Charlotte could manage.

51

WHAT were you thinking? Charlotte asked herself again. It was the same question she had been asking all through the evening, during the light supper of canned soup they shared, during the clean-up and awkwardness of silence that followed. They had tried to watch television for a while, but the bottle of wine did nothing to calm Charlotte, only made her more restless and anxious, so that at not yet nine, she went into the powder room and switched on the mirror light and looked at herself in the glass, wondered how all that frenetic activity beneath her skin and inside her skull could not be visible somehow. She felt as if every cell in her body was racing around aimlessly, drunk with fear. Her skull felt as if it must soon burst apart from the pressure. Yet in the mirror Charlotte appeared calm, still, so self-contained. Charlotte looked at that woman and asked, a whisper, "What were you thinking?"

She returned to the living room and opened her hands to

Livvie. Two Ambiens lay in her right palm, a Vicodin in her left. "Take your pick," Charlotte said.

Livvie touched the Vicodin. "This is the one that made me feel so spacey?"

"Right," said Charlotte. "The other ones will help you sleep."

"I feel like I've been sleeping all day," Livvie said.

"I know, but trust me. You don't want to lie awake all night. You'll just lie there in the darkness and relive everything."

Livvie picked the Ambiens out of Charlotte's hand.

Charlotte popped the Vicodin, on top of the Ambiens she had already taken in the powder room, then lifted her wineglass to Livvie and toasted, "Chin-chin."

52

AND now, alone in her bed at half past eleven, the house quiet but for the usual ticks and creaks, the occasional hum of the furnace blower, Charlotte felt a pleasant heaviness in her body but no sleepiness. Her cells, at least, had ceased their mad racing about, and she felt the peculiar sense that her body had lapsed into a coma, her limbs motionless and content to remain that way while her mind continued to grind on, though without the anxiety now, in a kind of reconciled acceptance of the sadness of its thoughts.

Charlotte understood now what Livvie's son had meant to her. How she must have clung to his every smile and kindness, and how he must have clung to hers. They had been alone in a world filled with malice and threat. But at least they had been alone together. But now . . .

Ever since the candlelight vigil, Charlotte had been struggling to adjust to her jarred perception of the boy. Until she saw his sketches, she had been able, most times, to think of him as just a nasty little boy, sullen and angry, destined to perpetuate life's misery. But when she had been forced to see his talent, his sullenness took on a different hue. Maybe, she thought, he was sullen because he felt different from his peers, different from those rough-and-tumble boys who only want to fight and play football. Jesse wanted to draw pictures. And now Charlotte had met his mother too—*Had brought her here, for God's sake! Charlotte, what were you thinking?*—a woman who was sad, yes, but sweet to the bone, and with such a mother, Jesse surely must have dropped his mask of sullenness. Maybe, to a lesser degree, with his art teacher too—the woman who had organized the candlelight vigil and had put his pictures on display. *Had he been sweet with her, his teacher?* Charlotte wondered. *Had he trusted her? Had he smiled at her with no trace of anger in his eyes?*

Had Jesse and his mother snuggled together in their tight little trailer? Charlotte wondered. *Had they played Yahtzee, worked on his homework at the kitchen table?*

Had Jesse been the one to comfort her in the wake of her husband's violence, the one to take her hand and stroke her hair, to soothe her as she no doubt soothed him after his own beatings?

It must have been so, Charlotte told herself. *They had each other, whereas you . . . You had your art, or so you thought. You had color and light.*

And do they comfort you now, Charlotte? Do they give you what you need?

53

CHARLOTTE dreamed that the man made of shadow came toward her in her backyard. He came close enough that she could see him motioning with his hand, telling her to come with him, follow him. She rose out of her lawn chair and walked behind him through the darkness. They walked past the barn and into the field, and as they walked she could hear more and more clearly the woofing of the vultures. Just after the man entered the trees with Charlotte close behind him, she looked up and saw the branches heavy with crows, and she wondered, *How is it possible that I can see them so well in the darkness?* There were so many crows that they completely obliterated the sky, yet she could see each crow distinctly, the oily, blue-black feathers, the shining yellow eyes. Then she smelled the carcass, the dead opossum, and the scent was overpowering, sickening and palpable, greasy on her skin. The man said, "Here," and she looked at him and saw that he was smiling. She could feel the vultures milling about her feet, their long feathers dragging through the leaves, their red-skinned heads brushing against her legs. "Here," he said again, and nodded toward the ground. But she would not look down because she knew that she should not. "Just let me look at the crows," she told him. The man's smile faded then, and he backed away from her, and one of the vultures walked between her legs, and because her legs were naked now, because she was suddenly naked, the scrape of its feathers startled her so that her body went rigid, and she wanted to scream but could not, she wanted to run but could not, and when she awoke suddenly, gasping and sitting up, the scent and the taste of the rotting opossum still filled every breath, so that she rolled off the bed quickly and grabbed the little trash container beside her bed and knelt there heaving with the dawn's light falling in through the window and onto her back.

54

AFTER she had emptied the trash container into the toilet, had flushed the toilet and rinsed out the trash container in the tub, after she had rinsed out her mouth and gargled and returned the trash container to its place beside her bed, she sat on the edge of the bed for a while and wondered if she should climb back beneath the covers or whether she should get up. *If you get up,* she told herself, *what are you going to do? Should you make breakfast?*

You have to get her out of your house, she thought. *You have to get her away from here.*

She rose quietly and put on a pair of jeans, a pink T-shirt, and a long-sleeved Nautica shirt that she left unbuttoned. She put on clean socks, the thick, heather-colored Ralph Laurens that kept her feet warm. *You should take her out to breakfast somewhere,* Charlotte thought. *Then stop by the trailer on the way back. And maybe she'll want to stay. You can bring up her work, the people in town she cleans for. The generating plant. Talk about how important it is to keep busy. To keep ourselves occupied. You can lend her the Jeep if necessary. If necessary, you can buy her a car.*

Once she had made up her mind about how the day would progress, Charlotte felt better. The dream still lingered, but she told herself, *It was only a dream*. The morning was cool but already bright at just after seven. The grass was damp and a vivid green, and this morning, the sound of the crows waking each other in the trees did not fill her with grief.

She reminded herself of what June always said. What is, is. If you can't accept what is, you can't move on.

She washed her face and brushed her teeth and ran the brush through her hair. She made little attempt to be quiet and, in fact, hoped that her actions would wake Livvie. As soon as she heard Livvie stirring, she would go to her room and say, "I'm really hungry for waffles this morning. Let's go up to Carlisle to the IHOP."

But no sounds emanated from Livvie's room. Charlotte stood outside the closed door, held her own breath, and listened.

She put her hand to the knob. A slow half-twist. The latch clicked out of the strike plate. She eased the door open, winced at the creak of hinges.

The bed was empty. Neatly made.

Immediately Charlotte's heart began to race. "Livvie?" she said, then pushed open the door. The room was empty.

Charlotte hurried downstairs. "Livvie?" she said.

She checked every room. Every room was empty. She stood in the kitchen between the counter and the table, her heart beating wildly now. *You wanted her gone,* she told herself, *but this is different. Her things are still here. But where did she go?*

She could feel the window behind her, the light on the window that looked out on her backyard. She turned and stood with her hands on the edge of the little table. *What if she went out there?* she asked herself. *What if she's out there?*

And the longer she stood there looking out, the more she convinced herself that Livvie had awakened early, had lain awake in her bed and listened to the darkness talking to her. Maybe the man made of shadow had come to her last night after he walked away, disappointed with Charlotte. Disappointed because she had been afraid to look down to see what the vultures were squabbling over. So the man had gone to Livvie instead. And now she was out there in the back where he had told her to go.

Charlotte told herself, *If the back door is unlocked, that's where she is.*

She went into the mudroom and put her hand to the door and tried to jerk it open, but the door remained locked. *Okay,* she told herself, *but you can lock it from the outside too. You can press the little button and then step outside and pull the door shut behind you and it will be locked. So whether it's locked or not doesn't mean a thing, does it?*

Charlotte slipped her feet into the Timberlands. She looked down at the loose laces and told herself that she should tie them, but then she asked herself, *Why bother? What difference does any of it make now?*

She knew what was coming now and what had been coming all along, and she knew that she had no choice but to accept it. *What is, is,* she told herself. *Accept what you cannot change.*

She went out onto the back patio and stood there looking across her yard. *How I loved this place,* she thought. *Not another house in sight. I thought everything was perfect here.*

She went out onto the grass and started walking toward the barn, where she knew Livvie must be. It was only natural that

Livvie would be drawn there. A mother's instincts. A mother's intuition.

You should have had children, Charlotte told herself as she walked. *You wouldn't be here now if you had had a child of your own. None of this would have happened.*

Her chest was aching now, made sore with every breath. She could feel her shoelaces dragging, could feel the way they pulled at her. *Why didn't you have children?* she thought.

Her face was wet with tears by the time she reached the corner of the barn. Her eyes stung and she sucked hard with every breath, but her lungs felt empty. She moved like an old woman now, bent forward and hollowed out, brittle with sorrow. Every exhalation carried a small whimper of regret. *It hurts too much,* she told herself. *It hurts too much to live.*

When she saw the fenced-in pasture behind the barn, she knew she could go no farther. There was no strength in her legs, no air to breathe. She saw the tall grass, the weeds on the other side of the fence, and she told herself, *That's where you fell down.*

And she remembered the feeling then, the feeling of crushing disbelief that had dropped her in the weeds, the sear of astonishment that had brought to an end her mad race for something like escape.

"Livvie!" she tried to cry out now, but it was little more than a grunt, an exclamation of pain as sharp and senseless as the caw of a crow. All she wanted was to fall into Livvie's arms now, but Livvie did not come running, nobody heard or answered her cry, and she dropped to her knees in the short grass and then fell forward onto her hands, still gasping and trying to call out, "Livvie! Livvie!" as all the colors ran dark and the light was extinguished.

55

SHE awoke to a clanking sound and also a chuffing, as if a little boy were pulling his wagon and pretending to be a train coming toward her. Above was blue sky, a vast, far emptiness. She rolled her head to the side and saw two men in blue scrubs jogging toward her, a gurney in tow. One man, the bearded one, was overweight and puffing loudly.

She tried to sit up but a hand pushed her down. "Lie still," Livvie said. "Just lie still and wait."

Charlotte looked up at her. "I went looking for you," she said.

"I just went home, is all. I forgot my toothbrush."

The paramedics took over then. They moved Livvie out of the way, took Charlotte's blood pressure, and listened to her heart. The bearded one laid his hands on both sides of her neck, held her neck as if to choke her, but, leaning close, asked, "Do you feel any pain anywhere? Did you fall or lay down on your own?"

She could smell his breath when he spoke, coffee and cigarettes, but she watched only Livvie; Livvie standing three feet away, one hand to her chest, the other hand kneading the knuckles. "I'm sorry," Charlotte said.

Livvie held up both hands. "Shhh, lie still. Just let them check you out."

"Is she on any medication?" one of the paramedics asked.

Livvie told him, "Sleeping pills last night. And a Vicodin, I think. I don't know what this morning."

"I was coming to see you in the barn," Charlotte said.

Livvie said, "Shhh," and moved closer, stretched out an arm past the paramedic, and squeezed Charlotte's hand. "I wasn't in the barn. I went home to get my toothbrush."

A brace was placed around her neck, and she was looking at sky again. She was staring straight up into the center of it but she could see the way it curved out on the edges of her vision, could see it curving down to enclose them.

At the same time the paramedics lifted her onto the gurney, a crow cried out from the trees and Charlotte sucked in a breath and began to tremble. She felt the straps tighten and she could not stop shivering. Livvie walked beside the gurney and held on to Charlotte's hand and looked down at her and tried to smile, and Charlotte kept her eyes on Livvie all the way to the ambulance in the driveway, and all the way there she could see blue sky rolling past behind Livvie's head, could see the sky turning all around them as if they were inside a bubble, motionless, while the shimmering surface of the bubble itself kept slowly revolving.

56

CHARLOTTE did not see Livvie again until the doctor in the emergency room was through scolding her, warning that she could do irreparable harm to her organs if she wasn't careful, that dehydration was a serious matter. "Wine is not a good substitute for water," the doctor said. Charlotte smiled up at her and asked, "Then why did Jesus turn water into wine and not the other way around?"

The doctor was a tall woman with thick, black hair and dark eyes that seemed to catch the light when she smiled. She said, "Listen, young lady. I like a glass or two of Lambrusco myself every night, but the organs need water."

"Turn me loose and I'll drink a gallon of water," Charlotte said.

The doctor told her, "Ask me again tomorrow." She turned and grasped the blue curtain and drew it open.

In the lounge, the doctor spoke with Livvie for a few moments, told her that Charlotte was being moved to room 217 and Livvie could see her there. Livvie took the elevator to the second floor, then stood by the window in the empty room, and looked down on the parking lot. She was still there when the sheriff's car pulled into the lot and Marcus Gatesman climbed out and crossed to the entrance.

A few minutes later Gatesman appeared in the doorway. He looked at Livvie standing with her back to the window now, looked at the empty bed. Livvie told him, "They should be bringing her up any minute now."

He said, "I heard it on the scanner. I didn't know if it was you or Charlotte."

"The doctor said she's dehydrated and malnourished. They want to keep her overnight and give her more of that glucose drip, get her electrolytes back to where they ought to be."

"It said on the scanner she passed out in the yard. A woman unconscious on the ground is actually what they said. I take it you called it in?"

She told him how she had left the house in the gray of dawn, went back to her trailer and gathered up a few small things, then walked back to the farmhouse through the trees when the light was full. How she had seen a body on the ground behind the barn and had run to it as quickly as she could. She did not tell him how her own heart had suddenly raced at the sight of that crumpled body and how breathlessly she had sprinted toward it, only to slow, disappointed, instantly drained of hope, and then pushed herself forward again. She said none of that, yet somehow, he knew.

"You thought it was Jesse," he said.

"At first I did." She looked away then, stepped up to the bed, picked up the pillow, turned it over, and laid it back down. Then stood there looking down at it, unable to meet his gaze.

He told her, "It's nothing to be ashamed of. I understand exactly how you must have felt."

She looked up at him then, saw that he was smiling. She smiled in return.

"After the accident with Patrice and Chelsea," he said, "I can't tell you how many times I thought I saw them in a crowd somewhere. How many times I went chasing after some woman with a baby in her arms. It was totally irrational of me," he told her. "But totally natural too."

She nodded.

He said, "Anyway, I'll go hang out in the lounge for a few minutes."

She said, "I should probably step out of the way too. Let them bring her in and get her settled first."

"There's a coffee machine in the lounge, if you're interested. My treat."

"You keep it up," she said as she crossed toward him, "you're going to end up in here too. You people and your caffeine all the time."

"You want me to drink water this early in the morning?"

"Don't ask me," she said. "Ask your kidneys."

57

By the time they returned to Charlotte's room, a half hour had passed. She was dressed now in a hospital gown and had a glucose drip feeding into her left arm. Livvie appeared first in the doorway, and then close beside her, Marcus Gatesman. Each held a bottle of water from the vending machine. Livvie looked in at Charlotte and smiled, then said to Gatesman, "I'm going to step into the ladies' room. You go ahead and say hello."

Gatesman walked in smiling. "I never took you for a pagan," he said.

"Excuse me?"

"I had just gotten onto I-81 when it came over the scanner. Beautiful woman, facedown in the grass. That's part of your morning ritual, I take it?"

The word *beautiful* did not escape her attention. How long since any man had referred to her as beautiful? She felt a flush of heat in her face. "Only when there are no virgins to sacrifice," she said.

"Which must be most of the time these days."

"They're getting harder and harder to find," she said.

He stood beside the bed, smiled down at her. *So calm,* she thought. *So still.* She envied his stillness and wondered how he had managed it. Could he teach it to her?

"So from what I hear," he said, "you've not been taking very good care of yourself."

"Is that what you hear?"

"It's all over the hospital."

"Vicious rumors," she said, "nothing more."

He stood there smiling. She nodded at the bottle of water in his hand. "So what is this, some kind of conspiracy? I saw Livvie had one too."

"Apparently she's the only one between the three of us who has any sense."

He seemed a different man now than the one who had stood at her porch steps like an awkward teenage boy. The one who, when she had broken into sobs, had been so tentative and uncertain. She could tell from his smile that he knew nothing of her morning but what Livvie had told him, and that Livvie knew nothing but what she had seen. No one had been able to see into her heart and her mind. Her thoughts and her fears were still hers alone, and the latter were somewhat abated now, as if the flood of panic had washed away the debris, leaving behind only a small, still pool of fear. In this relative tranquility she allowed herself to see Gatesman not as an enemy in waiting but as the opposite.

"Where were you headed on 81?" she asked.

"Harrisburg," he said.

"Ah, yes. Harrisburg."

"My meeting's not till one, though. I'll still make it. I only left so early because there's this place I was going to stop for lunch."

"The sushi place?"

"Naw, I'm saving the sushi for later."

"I'm envious," she said.

He smiled and said nothing for a while, and she could see him thinking. And she told herself, *Maybe it's the glucose, I don't know. But maybe I could. I mean, why shouldn't I if he asks?*

She looked at him and felt his calmness, felt that slow, deep stillness that he had somehow achieved. She wondered what it would be like to have such a man lay his hands on her. She could not imagine that he would be in a rush, no matter how long it had been for him. In fact because it had been so long, he would take his time and savor every minute, she was sure of it. She imagined that he would put his hands to her face first, he would lean close but not yet try to kiss her. First he would lean close enough to smell her hair, allow his cheek to graze hers. One hand would slide from her cheek to her neck, and then very slowly, that hand would come down over her breasts, and probably he would turn now and kiss her neck, and stand in just that position, his mouth motionless against her skin, as his other hand made its way over her shoulder and so slowly down her back . . .

It was then, Livvie returned to the room. She said, "You're getting your color back. That's good to see."

She stood at the foot of the bed.

Gatesman looked at her and smiled. To Charlotte, he said, "Would you believe that she's never tasted sushi?"

Charlotte looked from Gatesman to Livvie. She said, "You should take her to Harrisburg with you."

A few moments passed. Then he said, "That's been discussed already. Motion vetoed."

Charlotte turned her gaze to Livvie. "Why wouldn't you go?"

"I plan to stay here and keep you company. Make sure you do what the doctor says."

Charlotte saw a sheepishness in Gatesman's smile now, and she thought it distasteful. She told Livvie, "I appreciate your concern for me, I really do. But to be honest I'd prefer to be alone for a while. As alone as a person can be in a place like this."

"Oh," Livvie said. She lifted a hand off the foot rail. "Okay."

Charlotte looked up at Gatesman. "Is there a museum or a mall or something near where you're having your meeting? Some place she can hang out and be comfortable?"

"Dozens of places," he said.

"Then you'd better get going. Don't let her tell you no."

Now Charlotte looked to Livvie. "Did you drive the Jeep here?"

"Yes," Livvie said.

"Leave me the keys, okay? I doubt very much I'm going to spend the night here. I'll see you when you get back."

Gatesman said, "We'll bring you some sushi."

She reached for the TV remote beside her pillow, aimed it at the TV mounted on a shelf near the ceiling, depressed the power button. "Have fun," she said.

58

ONE glucose bag emptied, another attached.

You fraud, Charlotte told herself. *You despicable fraud.*

In the afternoon, a nurse drew blood. An hour later she returned with another bag of glucose. "We're getting there," she said.

"Where is 'there'?" Charlotte asked.

"Where everything looks good again."

"Trust me," Charlotte told her, "we're not even close."

59

At half past six, with the light in the window turning gray, Charlotte could lie still no longer. She climbed out of bed and found her clothing in the little cabinet, took it into the bathroom and changed. Ten minutes later she appeared at the nurse's station. "Do you have something for me to sign?" she said. "I'm going home."

"You can't go home until the doctor releases you," the nurse said.

"Good night," Charlotte said, and turned toward the elevator.

60

SHE was in her bed but awake when the headlights filled her window. She heard the slow crunch of gravel, then heard it stop, heard the engine fall silent. *There should be two car doors,* she told herself. *He'll at least walk her to the door.*

One door closed, a soft thud, followed by another. She looked at the clock on the nightstand. 10:19. *Long dinner,* she thought.

Two voices whispering in the foyer. First hers, then his. Her footsteps light and graceful on the steps. Charlotte's bedroom door squeaked open. "We're home," Livvie whispered. "Are you awake?"

Charlotte said nothing. She stared at the darkness that now filled the window.

"Good night," Livvie whispered, and eased the door shut.

Voices in the kitchen. Murmurs, soft laughter.

Charlotte told herself it did not matter. She told herself she was happy for Livvie, happy for Gatesman.

She told herself, *You reap what you sow.*

61

EMPTINESS everywhere, darkness and dreams. She awoke to the sense of somebody in the room, though it was not Livvie, of that she was sure. She lay listening, alert, waiting for a sound. "I'm not afraid of you," she said, though she was.

After a few minutes she rolled to the side, reached out to the lamp on the nightstand. Turned on the light, looked from corner to corner. No shadow but her own.

She sat in the chair by the window for a while. The light from her room lay in a trapezoid on her lawn. She kept waiting for a figure to step into the light and look up at her. *Are you coming out?* he would ask. *Or should I come up?*

But the minutes passed—fifteen, then thirty—and no one appeared. She sat there and shivered and felt she had never been so cold. She climbed back into bed but could not get warm. *What's wrong with me?* she wondered. *Why can't I stop shivering?*

She decided that she needed something to help her sleep,

something to quiet her nerves. It did not matter what the doctor had said. The doctor did not know. She went into the bathroom, and without turning on the light, she found the bottle she needed and shook two tablets out into her hand. She put them in her mouth, took a swallow of water. Yet still she shivered. So empty, so cold.

62

THAT night, for the first time, she dreamed of Jesse. Jesse walking the tree line just off the lane, heading home. In her dark sleep, Charlotte steps off her rear patio and walks out to meet him. He sees her coming and turns back into the woods, disappears into the dark branches. But Charlotte knows where to find him, and he is there waiting, sitting on the fallen tree, unafraid and still. The tree trunks are black with a recent rain and the ground is shiny-wet. The rain falls from the canopy in heavy drops that thump against her head and shoulders but make no sound. The crows sit overhead, silent, too, waiting for a gunshot. And Jesse sits there with the shotgun standing between his legs, his small, wet hands on the black, wet barrel. Charlotte's footsteps make the only sound in this dream. The soft, wet crunch of leaves beneath her boots. She is so very cold in this dream, she is shivering, unable to control the violence of her shivers, rattling like a skeleton. She moves close to him, needing warmth. He watches silently with a strange, crooked smile on his mouth. His eyes are the darkest things in the woods, blacker than the crows. Charlotte wants to speak, wants to break the woods's silence, but she can only shiver. She feels the strangle of words in her throat, but when she opens her mouth, nothing but a raspy grunt is possible. Jesse blinks a slow, sleepy blink and his crooked smile widens just a bit. Then he looks up into the trees, and with that, the crows come down off the branches. They just step forward and come down with wings spread, drifting down in a beautifully slow and silent descent. They land at Charlotte's feet until they completely blanket the ground. Others follow from the treetops to land on her shoulders. Their weight is peculiarly soft but heavy. More and more crows descend to land atop her and pile up at her feet. The ones at her feet sit motionless while looking up at her, hundreds of small, bright eyes. Soon there are too many on her shoulders, and she is leaning forward from the weight, yet they descend, they settle on her back now, driving her lower. Then she is on her knees, yet more crows drift down, as many as the leaves themselves, and she realizes suddenly that the leaves are falling and turning into crows as they fall. She is pushed onto her hands and knees, struggles to hold her head up. Jesse isn't even watching now; he is staring up into the canopy, up through all those black, denuded branches to where a pink glow rises, the first blush of morning. Charlotte watches all this in a kind of slow motion as one elbow collapses from the weight on her back and she falls to the side. Now she turns her head skyward, and all she can see is a beautiful, graceful cloud of black wings descending, and then everything is a soft, fragrant black atop her, fragrant with the scent of a misty night sky.

It is not a frightening dream, but so crushingly sad. The weight of the crows as they cover her is the weight of sadness. Breathing becomes more and more difficult, but she does not panic; this is what she wants, to be subsumed by the blackness.

The only unpleasantness is the chill. *The crows should be warm,* she thinks. *The bodies should be warmed.* And now that her consciousness has turned to the chill, the chill becomes everything, the only sensation. The chills and the breathlessness, the suffocating sadness. She cannot breathe, but she is shivering violently, her bones like ice, body rattling in the wet leaves. *Christ, the cold, the cold,* she thinks, *I can't stand the cold . . .*

63

SHE awoke gasping for air, her body curled tight beneath the comforter but covered with goose bumps, the comforter pulled over her head and down over her face. She exposed her head and sucked in the air, but she could not stop shivering. She told herself, *You're freezing to death. What is wrong with you?*

There were more blankets in the empty bedroom down the hall, so she switched on the lamp on the nightstand, climbed out of bed, and made her way to the door. Her bare feet felt numb on the hardwood, toes curled and stiff as if she were walking on ice.

Stepping out of her own room, she faced Livvie's. The door was only partially closed. Charlotte moved closer, peered through the opening. The sibilance of breath, regular and warm. She eased the door open wider, a slow, soft creak that did not disturb the rhythm of Livvie's breaths. The light from Charlotte's room flowed softly into Livvie's.

Charlotte moved closer, walked lightly on her heels, and came to stand beside the bed. Livvie lay sleeping on her side, her body open and facing Charlotte, knees slightly bent, one ankle atop the other. She lay uncovered in pink pajamas, faded flannel in the shape of her body. *How can she sleep like that, uncovered?* Charlotte wondered. *She must be warm, she must be so warm.*

Livvie's lips were parted just slightly, and Charlotte could hear each breath escaping, a whispered *shhhh*, a mother's *shhhh*. The sound itself was warming, the warmest thing she knew. Charlotte sat on the edge of the bed as delicately as she could, moved only an inch at a time, measured her own breaths against Livvie's. Finally she lay beside Livvie and brought her legs up, leaned so close that her toes touched a flannel pant leg. She could feel the breath from Livvie's mouth now and moved her own face even closer, wanting to breathe Livvie's breath, wanting the warmth and life in her. And when the breaths alone were not enough to warm Charlotte, when still she shivered, she moved closer still, hands reaching softly, feet reaching for Livvie's feet.

Livvie inhaled and drew back when Charlotte touched her mouth—not a sudden movement but sufficient to wake Livvie. She saw Charlotte's face so close and drew back farther, blinked, coming alert. Her eyes opened wider, and only then, in the look that came into Livvie's eyes then, only then did Charlotte realize what she had done, see where she was, and feel the coldness return.

"No," Charlotte said pulling away, pushed away by the look in Livvie's eyes, "it's not . . . I was so cold . . . I've been so cold."

Livvie said nothing. Then looked away. And reached to the foot of the bed, pulled the comforter up, covered her body, and turned toward the window, curled and covered on the edge of the bed.

Charlotte turned in the opposite direction, put her feet to the floor. She hurried across the ice to her own room, the sheets cold, and cocooned herself in the comforter, too cold to move again, too cold to reach out and extinguish the light.

64

NEXT morning a misty dawn. Charlotte lay still cocooned, listening as Livvie packed up her things. Footsteps on the stairway, three trips up and down to carry everything onto the porch. *How will she carry it all home?* Charlotte wondered. But then she heard a car arriving, again the slow crunch of gravel. She climbed out of bed with the comforter still wrapped around her shoulders and went to the window. There was Gatesman's brown sedan at the end of the driveway, the engine idling. Waves of heat rose off the hood. He climbed out and came toward the house and disappeared from Charlotte's view. His voice was low, a few whispered words. And soon he reappeared on his way back to the car, Livvie's suitcase in one hand, a grocery bag in the other. He opened the rear door and set them inside on the seat.

Charlotte held the comforter tight around her as she hurried down the stairs. At the foyer she stood behind the screen door, looked out onto the porch, saw Livvie handing Gatesman the final overstuffed grocery bag. Livvie stood there for a moment, watching Gatesman, then said in a soft voice, "I'll be right back." When she turned to the door, she saw Charlotte looking out.

Livvie said, "I was coming up to say good-bye."

"You don't need to do this," Charlotte said. "It wasn't what you think last night."

Livvie came close to the screen but did not reach for the door. "I just think this is better," she said. "I want to be back at the trailer anyway. I mean, if Jesse comes back . . ."

"I was just feeling lonely is all. I just . . ."

"I know," Livvie said.

And Charlotte thought, *But you don't.*

Livvie said, "I can't thank you enough for everything you've done."

"What about getting back and forth to work? You can use my Jeep, I'll get you the keys."

"It's okay. Mark is going to go to the bank with me today. He says he can get them to give me a loan."

"I'm sure he can," Charlotte said. Then, "What if Denny comes back?"

"We don't think he will."

We? Charlotte thought. *It's* we *already.*

And why not? she asked herself later. She had gone to the Windsor chair in her studio, sat wrapped in the goose-down comforter while the orange glow of morning slowly turned the window and curtains into a portrait of light. *Why should it not be* we *already?* she thought. *They're entitled,* she told herself. *They're deserving.*

Unlike you, she told herself. *Who deserves only you.*

65

THE passing of days, each one a bit warmer. Sometimes it rained, and if it happened in the afternoon, the yard would seem to steam afterward, the grass brilliant green in the sunlight, and the Credence Clearwater song would come into her mind then and play over and over, *Have you ever seen the rain comin' down on a sunny day?*

She took to walking again because it was a good way to pass the time. But she carried no camera now, no little sketch pad tucked into a pocket. She kept to abandoned logging trails now, where she knew she would encounter no one, only chipmunks and squirrels, a fat groundhog waddling across her path.

If she saw buzzards or crows, she always paused to consider them, watched them in flight or studied them while they, from a high branch, studied her. She had read that crows like shiny things, that they are monogamous birds who will gather bits of shiny things to decorate their nests, pop-can ring-tops, cellophane, and foil. So for a week she went into the woods at midmorning, after the crows had departed for the day, and on a stump near their roost, she laid a piece of jewelry small enough for their beaks—an earring, a broken silver clasp—and on every subsequent day the item was gone, so she replaced it with another. On the seventh day she gave them the Tiffany diamond, the Christmas ring she had always resented.

From time to time, in no set pattern—sometimes in the middle of the day when she was reading, sometimes as she lay awake at night listening to the rain—she would be convulsed with sobs that struck her from out of nowhere, that left her breathless and weak and feeling kicked in the stomach.

She answered none of the phone calls or e-mails, kept her doors locked, ignored the knocks on her door. One time Livvie came and knocked on the door, then sat on the porch swing for an hour before finally driving away in the car she had driven there, a used beige Corolla with a dent in one fender.

Charlotte bought her groceries at a convenience store in Andersonburg, well south of Belinda, well east of Carlisle. She ordered her medications online.

66

Four days before May, on a warm pleasant evening in the hour of magic light, Charlotte could not resist the scent of the air, the perennials poking up in little splashes of color, the lemony glow she loved only second-best to the light of morning, and she sat on the porch swing, rocking slowly back and forth. On that peculiarly peaceful evening, two things happened that caused her to understand that the interlude was over, that the days of quietude, as she had always known they would, had come to an end.

Had she not been looking out across the porch at the copse of birches that hid the blueberry patch, she might have had time, just as the shiny, black pickup truck turned into her driveway, to scurry inside and lock the door. But not even the sound of the vehicle's approach registered on her until it was close enough that, turning abruptly to look, she could see Rex through the windshield, could see his smile as he lifted his hand in a wave.

Oh God, she thought, and wanted to run but held to her seat and only stopped the swing from moving.

He climbed out of his truck and crossed to her with a shuffling, lumbering stride. His cheeks and skull were freshly shaved and gleaming, his smile sheepish. It was the first time Charlotte had ever seen him in anything other than his bloody smock and apron, and just the sight of him now in his tan guayabera shirt over chocolate khakis, his chest and shoulders and stomach huge, filled her with a sudden sadness and made the lemon light go gray. Worst of all, he shuffled toward the porch with a Whitman's Sampler in one hand, a spray of daffodils and baby's breath in the other. She thought, *Such a sad cliché,* and immediately despised herself for the thought.

He remained at the bottom of the stairs, just as Gatesman had done. Charlotte felt her sinuses thicken, felt the bruise return to her chest.

He said, "Nobody's seen you around for a while."

"Working," she told him. "Just . . . always too much to do."

"Cindy figured you had enough of us hicks as you could stand and moved back to the city. I'm glad to see you didn't."

"Still here," she told him. And told herself, as she watched him smile and nod, *He's going to come closer now, going to put one foot up on the step.*

Ten seconds later, he did. "I was thinking," he said.

"Rex," she said, and leaned forward on the swing, put both hands atop her knees, and shook her head. "I'm sorry," she said.

"Well," he said, and looked off to the right for a while, then turned his gaze to her again. She thought, *You can't blame a man—*

"—for trying," he said.

"I'm flattered," she told him. "I truly am. And if things were different . . ."

"What things would that be?"

"Me, actually. If I were different."

"It's not a different you I'm interested in."

"I'm sorry," she told him. "I truly am."

He nodded again and stared at the edge of the porch. Then he leaned forward to set the box of candy and flowers on the boards.

"Rex, no," she told him. "Please don't."

But he was already moving away. A blush of blood reddened the back of his neck and spread upward, until finally every inch of his lovely round head looked inflamed.

Long after the sound of his truck had faded, she remained motionless on the porch swing. She sat leaning forward, hollowed out. Every now and then she looked to the things he had left behind. The box of candy struck her as tragicomic. But the flowers looked funereal, like something stolen from a baby's grave.

67

THE second incident occurred just before ten the same evening. Her cell phone vibrated atop her desk, four rings until it switched to voice mail. A minute later, a single vibration. She considered ignoring the message until morning, but finally crossed to her desk, picked up the phone, and listened to the message.

"Hey, beautiful," Mike Verner said, "where the hell have you been keeping yourself? How am I going to keep Claudia on her toes if you're not around for me to flirt with? Anyway . . . I just wanted to give you a heads-up. I hope you love country life as much as you claim you do, 'cause you're about to be getting a nose full of it. Two weeks from now there's an auction up near Lewistown, and if all goes the way I hope it does, I'll be coming back from it with ten head of Belted Galloways. Those are the ones people call Oreo-cookie cows? Black on each end and white in the middle? Anyway, I'll be unloading them over there in the pasture behind the barn. In fact, I'll be keeping them there until

I can fatten them up enough to sell off again. So you're going to have some company, is what I'm saying. I apologize for this. I mean, I know how much your peace and quiet means to you. But it's not going to be as bad as you might think, I promise. Hell, you might end up being the Van Gogh of Oreo cows, make all of us famous . . ."

The message lasted another ten seconds or more, but none of it registered on her, none of it mattered. She clicked the phone shut and laid it on the desk and stood there motionless, barely breathing. She knew that if she moved, everything would come crashing down at once, everything that had loomed over her the entire month, all of life balanced like a teetering boulder just above her head.

Eventually she made her way back to the recliner, sat down, and stared at the black face of the television set. After a while she closed her eyes. Every breath made a sound when it left her, a syllable of pain, as distant yet as near as the crow-black trees.

And there on the recliner in the darkness of her house she saw herself for what she was, what she had become in the space of a month, less than a month, a creature composed now of nothing but fear and a constant, desperate need. This house that had been her blessing, this luxurious solitude and the peace that came with it—it had become nothing more than a place in which to hide, windows to cower behind, doors to keep locked. And the thing that her work had given her, that glorious ineffable thing, that brilliant glow of creation she had imagined herself surrounded in as she stood at her easel each morning, it was all gone now, shriveled away. No, worse than shriveled; rotted away. Rotted away like a once-lovely piece of fruit. Consequently she was old and empty, made brittle by fear. *You don't even have the strength to climb the stairs,* she told herself.

You don't even have the strength to brush your hair.

And she told herself, *You cannot live like this.*

She had to hear it only once to know that it was true.

68

As Gatesman drove toward Charlotte's driveway at a few minutes past seven in the morning, with a thin, damp fog hugging the fields and muting the spring colors, with the weak light only now opening up to reveal the distant, rounded hills, he was not yet aware of any sense of urgency, no need to rush through those last minutes of stillness before the sun cleared the treetops and the school buses rumbled. She was probably already gone, off to wherever. "I have to meet with someone soon and likely won't be around when you get here," her note had said, "but it's important to me that you and only you pick up the package at your earliest convenience."

He was curious, of course, as to the nature of the package and why she had chosen him to retrieve it, and for what purpose. Her short note had been written on the blank interior of a small thank-you card whose artwork, a simple rendering of a leafy branch with a few ripe cherries hanging from it, seemed to him vaguely Japanese. According to its time stamp, the envelope had been processed in Belinda on Saturday morning and did not land on his desk until Monday night. Separating the afternoon mail was usually the last thing Tina did every night. And there it had been this morning, Tuesday, May first, laid smack in the center of his desk blotter on top of his empty coffee mug—Tina's way of letting him know that she had seen the feminine handwriting and knew that he had received either a thank-you card or an invitation from a woman, and that Tina would not rest until he revealed the contents to her.

That was one of the reasons he had slipped out before Tina arrived. The moment he saw that the note was from Charlotte, after he hurriedly checked the other mail and listened to his phone messages, none of any urgency, he decided to take care of this matter first, this private and as-yet-unknown matter. The note neither identified the package nor included any instruction as to what to do with the package after he had picked it up, but he felt certain there would be another note of some kind at the house. A small part of him resented Charlotte's assumption that the county sheriff had nothing better to do first thing in the morning than to respond to her summons, but another part of him, the larger part, was amused and flattered by the trust implied by her request.

But why now? he wondered. Their contact in the past month had been negligible. In fact, not a single word had passed between them since that morning in the hospital. A couple of times he had suggested to Livvie that one or both of them should call on her, but Livvie had cautioned, "Let's just give her some space." He knew that something had passed between the two women, but Livvie would provide no details, would say only, "It wasn't even an argument, just a feeling, is all. She needed her own space and I needed mine. Let's just leave it at that." But on those occasions he had not failed to notice the look that came into Livvie's eyes, what seemed to him like a passing cloud of sadness. But he never tried to probe the secrets they shared. Women had always been a mystery to him, and he saw no reason to assume that that would change.

"I'll leave it on the secretary in the foyer," Charlotte had written. "I'll put a key under the mat on the front porch. Just let yourself in."

He reasoned that it was a matter of trust and nothing more. Charlotte trusted him, it was as simple as that. There was a time when he had hoped for more than trust from her, but he was satisfied now with the way things had worked out, and he considered himself a man who knew enough to count his blessings.

This fine spring morning, for example. Within an hour or so, the fog would all be burned away, the air clear and cool and the new leaves flicking like little green tongues whenever a small breeze stirred. So after he parked and climbed out and crossed the yard to her porch, after he laid back the corner of the welcome mat and recovered the key and inserted the key in the lock and eased open the door, he paused to look again at the line of trees beyond the garage, the barn and the field, to enjoy, just a few moments longer, the look and feel and scent of a hushed morning soon to fade.

Sfumato, she had called it once. The effect of the fog as it smokes and blurs the trees. A painter's technique. A story about da Vinci, he remembered. Yes, right there on that porch swing, that's where she had told it to him, da Vinci and *The Last Supper.* Or had it been in the kitchen? He couldn't quite remember where that particular conversation had taken place, couldn't remember the exact circumstances. Not that it mattered.

"Sfu-mato," he said aloud now, then smiled at the peculiarity of the word. A peculiar word for such a lovely morning. Leave it to Charlotte to even know such a word.

He pushed open the door then and stepped inside. The house was cool and dark and silent. He had hoped to smell coffee but instead detected the scent of wet ashes. She had probably made a fire recently, then closed the screen and gone to bed and allowed the fire to burn itself out, without ever remembering to close the flue. *A lot of BTUs going up the chimney now,* he thought. He told himself that he would close the flue before leaving, save her a few dollars on her gas bill.

Maybe it was only the stillness of the house that quieted him. He knew that he was alone in the house, no need for stealth or any attempt to maintain the silence, yet he found himself moving with a deliberate, even delicate step across the foyer. He didn't bother to turn on the hall light because he could already see the secretary against the wall, could see it well enough to make out the only item atop the slender shelf. It was a book of some kind, a slender, oversize book with a plain canvas cover. *Dark green,* he thought, though he would have to carry it outside to see the color clearly. Stuck to the cover was a Post-It note whose message in the dimness he could not read.

He stepped back to the doorway, held the book in the light.

For you, Marcus. Thank you.

That's it? he thought. *Does she mean it's a gift for me? Or does she expect me to do something else with it?*

He opened the cover to the first page and saw that the book was a journal of some kind. It was, in fact, a sketchbook, but he had never seen one of those before and so assumed that the writing, a tight, cursive script in blue ink, with lines that slanted slightly downward across the page, defined the object. The first words were, *The morning of April third . . .*

He stopped reading and looked up, looked out through the screen. He knew that date. How could he not? And suddenly there came a shortness of breath, a flush of heat. "God, no," he said.

And then, another thought. He turned abruptly, looked up the stairs. "Charlotte?" he called. No answer. He laid the journal on the secretary and raced up the stairs, yanked himself forward with his hand on the banister rail. He found her bedroom quickly, knew in an instant that it was hers, but was relieved to see the bed empty and neatly made, relieved to see the dresser and nightstands and all else looking perfectly normal.

He then checked each of the other rooms but found nothing amiss. Went downstairs then and made a quick check of the house, glanced into every room, no sign of Charlotte. "So okay," he told himself. "You're jumping to conclusions here. Now calm down."

Yet his heart would not quit racing. He returned to the foyer, retrieved the journal, and stepped onto the porch.

He was reluctant to open the journal again but knew he had to do so. On the edge of the porch, he stood for a moment to look out across the yard. His morning, in the past two minutes, had taken on a quality of strangeness. He had always considered Charlotte Dunleavy an unconventional woman, and that was part of the attraction, but this was something more, an incongruency of actions that troubled him. The edges did not line up.

The rumble of a school bus came into his consciousness only after he saw the bus out on the highway, bus number seven, long and yellow and lumbering toward the middle school. Then the bus passed and the morning was quiet again, but the strangeness remained.

He looked down at the journal.

For you, Marcus, the note said.

He needed a few moments to think. He needed to sit and catch his breath. He turned, considered the porch swing.

The one time he and Charlotte had sat together on that swing now seemed impossibly distant to him. In fact, he was not even certain that they had ever sat side-by-side on the swing. *Wasn't I in the wicker chair?* he asked himself.

He remembered words and looks that had passed between them and many things that had been left unsaid. He had to admit that the feelings from that time were still tangible, not as raw or clumsy as they had originally been, not as bruising, but still there nonetheless. The feelings as they returned to him now made the morning seem to shrink even tighter around him, made a kind of cloudiness fill his mind so that nothing seemed clear.

"Sfumato," he said again.

The morning was still cool, though the day promised to be warm. In the distance beyond the highway, a line of blue hills was rising to the sky, seeming to grow minute by minute out of the evanescing fog. "The Tuscarora Mountains," he said.

At his back, in the trees behind the cornfield, a crow cawed. In front of him, wisps of fog rose off the lawn. He could smell the wet grass. The sky was brightening in the east. In an hour the yard and the porch would be filled with light. Sunlight would stream in through the windows. But for now the porch was cool and dim and the house was quiet and smelled of ash. The crows were awakening in the treetops, beginning their noisy aria to morning.

He crossed to the swing and sat down in the center of the slatted wooden seat. The chains creaked with his weight. He laid the journal on his lap, he laid back the cover, and he read.

69

THE morning of April third was a soft, damp morning but one that smelled pink with promise. I awoke before dawn and sat in the darkness of my studio with the curtains open and a mug of green tea in my hands. By degrees the night slowly faded away, and after a while I was able to see a mist of rain coming down outside, a mist so soft that it made no sound on the roof or against the window. Only when I stood close to the glass could I hear a gurgle in the rainspout and see the gentle bubbling in a shallow puddle in the driveway.

When the morning was nearly light enough, I went to my easel, lifted off the sheet, and looked at the painting in progress, the Amish children standing in a yard as a buggy and a Harley pass in front of them.

I never finished that painting, but to this day I can see the finished work inside my head. I can see other paintings too, other scenes I will never paint, all of them complete here inside my head, each one of them a mockery of who I thought I was and would be.

Anyway, that morning. I stood there looking at my painting, sipping my tea, and feeling very pleased with how things were going. That misty rain and cat-footed dawn were quieting and made me tranquil. It wasn't exactly an overcast morning, the sun was softly veiled. I would call it instead a luminous morning. The line of fog across the horizon did not block the sunlight but diffused it. I remember thinking of it as a tempera wash. The important thing here is this: Thanks to the morning or my painting or whatever, I felt—and my phrasing is inadequate, I'm sure—quietly jubilant. I felt on the verge of something.

And I was, I surely was. My mistake was in thinking it would be something wonderful.

Anyway, when the light was sufficient, I opened up my paints, prepared my palette, dried off the brushes. I sipped the last of my tea and set the mug aside. And within minutes I was utterly lost inside the painting. By which I mean that I was simultaneously in it and outside of it. That's the strange thing that happened to me sometimes, the way I separated and became the unemotional artist wielding the brush, conscious of the length of stroke and the heaviness of the pigment and the degree of light that emanates from it, yet I became a part of the imagined scene as well. That second me was standing at the roadside, just outside the frame of the picture, watching as the biker and buggy passed each other. I could smell the cut grass as it flew up in little green splinters behind the whirring blades. I could smell the horse as it gamboled by and could feel the heat rising from its muscled flanks. I could feel the rumble of the Harley's engine vibrating my eardrums and feel the heat coming off its flared exhaust pipes. It was a moment frozen, yet alive and dynamic, with everything slowed down and stretched out so that all the details and undercurrents were exquisitely vivid to me. It was one of those moments that just happened sometimes. One of those wonderful moments.

The gunshot exploded as if it had been fired past my ear. I swear the room shook with it. I gasped and staggered backward and felt physically knocked away from my painting, literally yanked out of it. Then came three more shots. *Bam! Bam! Bam!* By the fourth one I was standing at the window, trembling and rigid while the paint dripped down the brush and onto my fingers. Twenty, maybe thirty crows were in frantic flight away from the trees. And me . . . It is no exaggeration to say that I felt assaulted. My head was suddenly throbbing, my blood pressure sky-high. And moment by moment my fury grew.

I ran to the kitchen as fast as I could. I don't remember now if a plan of action had occurred to me or not. If so, I didn't pause to think it out beyond the first step or two. When I try to recreate those moments in my memory, all I see is a furious, red-faced woman with her face made ugly by rage.

On a shelf on the wall beside the door leading into the mudroom I kept a pistol. Before I left New York, June had insisted—make that *ordered* me to buy one. "A woman living alone in the country needs to protect herself," she said. But I fooled her and only bought an air pistol, a pellet gun that to an untrained eye looked exactly like a real gun. And I kept this pistol in the mudroom because it had already come in handy several times for chasing raccoons out of my garbage cans.

So there it was on the shelf that morning, my tranquil morning shattered yet again. I jammed the pistol down into my waistband of my baggy jeans and shoved my feet into my boots. And this time I laced them up—not like the first time I had confronted Jesse out there. Yes, this was the second time. The first time, despite my anger, I had tried to be pleasant, tried to reason with him, but he had treated me with such contempt that . . . I don't know, but maybe that had something to do with why I was furious now, because of the way he had already humiliated me. I felt in no hurry this time, furious but strangely calm and deliberate. Every little thing I did, right down to pulling my old gardening hat off the hook and jamming it onto my head, felt ordained.

As if I were my own painting come to life, I watched myself march outside and across the wet yard. In fact I can still see those moments in exquisite detail. The grass was glistening and jewel-like. With every step I sent tiny diamonds of moisture flying. I was wearing my Timberlands, baggy jeans, and a loose blue shirt with short sleeves and a V-neck. And I wasn't wearing a bra. I never wore a bra when I was working. It was one of those silly little superstitions artists have, I suppose, but I always wanted my work to be unfettered, unrestrained, and going braless helped me to feel that way. I remember the way the shirt rubbed up and down over my nipples as I marched across the field that morning. And the air was chilly, so my nipples were hard. It was a good feeling. I'm ashamed to admit that now, but it was. I felt predatory. Like a big game hunter with a nipple erection.

When I entered the woods I became very deliberate in my movements. I wanted to sneak up on the boy, throw a good scare into him. I felt confident he would be sitting near the same fallen tree where I had found him the first time. That seat gave him a nice clean shot into the crows' roost. And sure enough, there he was.

He was sitting there with the shotgun resting beside him, propped against the log. The roost was empty and he sat staring off into the dimness of the woods. Maybe he was waiting for the crows to return or for an unlucky bushy-tail to happen by, I don't know. Maybe he was pondering life's mysteries. In any case, he was just sitting there, as still as a mushroom. He was capless, wearing one of those tan duck-cloth hunting coats, jeans, and muddy, old boots. The coat was way too big for him, a man's coat, and it made him look even smaller than he was.

I circled around behind him. The ground was sodden and muted my steps. Rain was still dripping from the canopy, *plop-plop-plopp*ing onto the soft ground, plopping onto my old hat and then rolling around to the rear of the brim to drip down my shirt. It felt like little icy pellets trickling down my spine. Even so, I was in no hurry. I had the patience and resolve and the blind, stupid wrath of Jehovah in my blood. I stood and watched and waited for the perfect plan of revenge to come to me.

I remember now how it amazed me that Jesse did not turn or even cock an ear as I crept up behind him in the woods. Every crunch of damp leaf beneath my boots sounded loud to me, every scraping scuff of my heels. Jesus, I can even *smell* those woods again. That damp, chill, rich, rotting leaf smell: I used to love it, used to revel in it—no more concrete and exhaust fumes! No more clamorous, crowded, stinking congestion of people! I remember reveling in all that every time I went into the woods, exulting in it. Even as I sneaked up on Jesse. The woodsy scent was the scent of my freedom, what I thought of as my hard-won, well-deserved freedom, and I was inhaling it with every breath, cherishing it even as the outrage built inside me that somebody, a little boy for God's sake, had the audacity to intrude upon it.

Jesse never heard me coming, never flinched. He was in his own world, I suppose, dreaming his twelve-year-old dreams. But when I spoke, he jerked upright so abruptly that he slid right off the log and landed on his butt, facing me. I didn't even try to keep the evil grin off my face.

To feel such animosity toward a child—me, a grown adult, a compassionate person—it burns my face with shame.

"Kill anything today?" I said.

He sat there and blinked at me. More accurately, at the black pistol I held leveled at his chest. He didn't answer. Didn't so much as breathe.

"How does this make you feel?" I asked. "You like being on this end of a gun for a change?"

He said, "All I was doing was shooting at crows."

And at that moment, I swear to God, something snapped inside of me, some part of me saw him exactly as he was, just a boy, just a lonely little boy. And my heart ballooned with love for him. I looked at him with his raven hair all slicked down by the misting rain, his dark eyes like polished onyx, him sitting there on the sodden ground, a child who found more solace in the damp woods than in a schoolroom, and something trembled all the way through me. Something quivered in my soul.

My chest felt heavy all of a sudden, as if I couldn't get any oxygen into my lungs, just a lot of sterile air. I saw myself standing there like a bully, and I saw myself as I truly was, weak and selfish and ridiculous. All I wanted at that moment was to go to the boy and kneel down beside him and gather him into my arms, apologize for frightening him, lay his head against my shoulder, hold him as tightly as I could.

I wonder how many people have experienced such a total inversion of emotions. How many people have looked at somebody else, somebody not their own flesh and blood, a stranger even, and suddenly felt themselves drowning in love for that person? I don't know, maybe I'm making too much of it. Maybe it was just my maternal instinct kicking in, my unfulfilled longing for a child of my own. June once suggested—this was a few months after Mark and I split up—that I should make a withdrawal from the sperm bank and cook up a little honey bun in my Susie Homemaker oven. But by then I was building a different kind of fantasy, one I hadn't even shared yet with June. I was thinking that maybe I could make like O'Keeffe, that my peace and fulfillment (and maybe a new man) lay west of New York City. Pennsylvania was no Abiquiu, and Mark was sure as hell no Steiglitz, but, let's face it now, I was no O'Keeffe. But if I could do even in miniature what she had done . . .

So I'll concede maternal instinct for part of what I felt for Jesse that day, but not for all of it. Something about the sudden feeling that surged through me when I looked at him sitting there on the wet ground, something about that tableau, for just a few pure moments, made me . . . I don't know. I don't know how to express it. I felt so connected to that instant in time. And, therefore, connected to Jesse. Bound, soul to soul. And the truth is, funny as it might seem to others, I still feel connected to him. Even as I write this, I can feel that connection pulling at me, trying to take me somewhere.

As for the boy, after he sat there on the ground and blinked at me for half a minute or so, I told him, "You ever stop to think how the crows feel about being shot at? You ever think about how it feels when you hit one of them?" The moment I said that my voice quavered and I almost broke into tears, because I ached for the crows too. This was the moment when I was bursting with yearning or agape or whatever the heck it was, so I was aching, truly aching inside, for everybody and everything.

I remember so vividly the moment that feeling peaked. But how to describe something that words can't capture?

There's an old movie from the forties or so, Van Johnson is the star, I think. He's a test pilot for some little company struggling to stay afloat, trying to get a fat government contract, so he's desperate to break a high-altitude record in his new little plane. So he puts it into a steep climb and starts slicing up through the clouds. Then he's above the clouds and everything is clear and still and perfect, and he's still climbing. This was me getting high on agape. He's only three thousand feet from a new altitude record, but now the little plane is starting to strain from the effort. Now two thousand feet, and the cockpit is starting to rattle. Now, only a thousand feet to go, but the engines are screaming, rivets are popping, and the experience is so heady, so intoxicating and euphoric, that poor Van's skull feels like Vesuvius about to blow. Then the altimeter crosses over into that magical realm of untouched altitude, and Van's partner down on the ground is screaming into the radio that enough is enough, but Van is so fucking *high* that he just keeps pushing it. And, of course, the engines flame out. The plane stalls. Starts to fall back to Earth. Flips nose down. And goes into a deadly, maniacal spin, down down down through a deathly blue silence.

That was me on agape. After the peak, the plummet.

The chill that seized me then, it was terrifying. All of the warming love and sense of connection simply vanished, and in that absence, a cold, icy wind washed through my veins and into my heart. A chilling, freezing sadness. How did Neil Young put it? *Out of the blue and into the black.*

I stood there shivering with cold. My hand was trembling and so was the black pistol it held.

The boy noticed it too. Something shifted in his eyes then, a turning of the light, the disappearance of fear. The cocky lilt returned to his mouth. Without moving his head he looked to his right where his shotgun still rested against the fallen log. I jerked the pellet gun at him, which had the desired effect of making him flinch, and in the next instant I strode forward and grabbed the shotgun low on the barrel and pulled it out of his reach. It was a stupid thing to do, I know. Not what I did but how I did it, yanking it away from the boy like that. Had the trigger snagged on a spike of bark or twig, had the boy lunged for it and gotten a hand on it, I might have blown my own head off. I can't tell you how many dozens of times I have played that possible ending over and over in my imagination.

Obviously, it never happened. The boy made a grab for his shotgun, but I was too close, I had only to reach out for it, and his fingers never touched it.

I've never seen such fearlessness in a person so young. Where does that capacity come from? By now I'm standing there with his shotgun in my left hand, my pistol in the right. I'm breathing hard and shivering and I've got a tunnel vision that has thrown the surrounding woods in deep shadow. There's just me and Jesse and the empty space between us. And I'm feeling *strange*. I'm a little bit nauseated, a little bit dizzy now that all the Gaia goofiness has drained out of me. I feel disembodied. Like I'm up there on one of those branches and looking down at a crazy woman below.

From that perspective I watched Jesse climb to his feet in no hurry at all. He brushed some dirt off the palms of his hands, pushed that long, wet hair off his forehead, and gave me a smirk. "These ain't your woods, lady," he said.

The crazy lady tried to grin at him, but she was sucking darkness with every breath, not a whiff of oxygen in any of it. She said, "And those ain't your crows."

His answer was a tiny snort of disdain. Then, "I need my shotgun back."

"Do you? Well guess what. You can't have it."

"That's my dad's shotgun. You can't keep it."

"So tell your dad to come to my house and pick it up. I'd like to have a little talk with him."

He held that smirk awhile longer. Then his eyes went sleepy and hooded. And then he dismissed me utterly, he turned away as if he were the one holding a weapon in each hand, me the defenseless one, and started walking toward the edge of the woods.

How many times had Mark done that to me? How many times had he dismissed me with a smirk, then nonchalantly walked away, just to show me how meaningless I was, how insignificant? And now a child was treating me the same way, a boy barely half my size. I couldn't let him get away with it.

"Isn't this a school day?" I said as I followed him out of the woods. Rain dripped down from the canopy, big heavy drops on my shoulders and the brim of my floppy hat. Each one felt like an icy stab. "Why aren't you in school instead of out here killing harmless birds?"

He just kept walking, almost leisurely, as if I were of no concern whatsoever. As if I didn't even exist. For me the situation was becoming increasingly dreamlike, the kind of nightmare when you are trying and trying and trying to remember the combination to your school locker but the halls are emptying and the classroom doors are slamming shut and you still can't get your locker open, and maybe this isn't your locker after all—is this the right locker, is this the right school?

"Just tell me why you feel the need to shoot birds," I demanded. "Explain it to me so that I can understand."

Out in the field now, he turned left and followed the tree line toward Metcalf Road. Way out on the horizon, the sun was poking up out of the fog bank that hugged the ridges, and it had turned the fog a pale orange, a beautiful, soft pastel orange that for some reason, I can't explain why, made me inexpressibly, overwhelmingly sad. The beauty of it was like a cold slap that brought me up short. The misting rain had all but stopped by now, and the wash of sunrise made every other color more vibrant too, the dark, wet bark of the trees and the short, stiff stubble of cornstalks in the field and even the chalky white clapboards of my house. And now, seeing my house, I had the feeling that I was standing way over there behind my window and watching Jesse walking toward the road with some loony woman hurrying after him. The old bat had a shotgun in one hand and a shiny black pistol in the other.

"Why don't you just stop for a minute and look at that sunrise?" I demanded. My voice sounded shrill and desperate.

He snorted again, made that dismissive sound that's like a suppressed laugh but isn't suppressed at all, a sound so resonant with contempt.

That snort of his set something off in me. I took one long stride and came up behind him a lot harder than I intended. And with my right hand, the one holding the pellet pistol, I grabbed hold of the collar of his jacket, that too-large, heavy duck-cloth coat, and I jerked him away from the woods and shoved him straight across the field.

I didn't mean for the barrel of the pistol to slap up against his cheek when I grabbed him, but it did, and it must have felt so icy-cold against his skin. I remember that he walked with his head cocked to the side a little, not wanting the barrel to touch him. And I'm ashamed to admit it, but I took a malicious glee from that observation.

"What's the matter? You afraid of a little pistol? Afraid it might go off?"

He was afraid, I could feel it. And I am so, so ashamed of the pleasure I derived from that. I liked that he was afraid of me. I liked it very much.

I think I kept harping at him as I shoved him across that field, but I see that part of the scene from a distance, as if I'm back home behind my window. I can see my mouth moving, I see his hunched-up shoulders and our awkward little march. I held tight to his collar and gloated every time the cold metal touched his cheek and he twisted away from it.

I pushed him toward the house, but as we came into the yard I knew I didn't want to go inside yet, didn't want this to fizzle out with a telephone call to his mother. Didn't want that dark scowl of his spreading like soot throughout my sunny rooms. So instead I pushed him toward the barn.

"Slide open the door," I told him.

"What for?" he asked, and now it was his voice that sounded small and frightened, and God, how I reveled in that!

"Open it!" I said.

He slid the door open and I shoved him inside. The room was cavernous and dim and smelled of last year's hay, hundreds of bales of it still stacked in the loft and in the rear corner of the main floor. Mike will come over with his wagon every now and then and load it up and take the hay back to his cattle, and sometimes on sunny days I stand in the corner of the porch and watch, and I see the motes of dust glinting like mica in the sunlight, and I remember how I used to love the raw, clean, dry, earthy scent of hay. I used to love the barn.

I have no idea why I took Jesse there. But as my eyes grew accustomed to the dimness, I noticed the stairs leading to the lower floor, so I pushed him toward them. I can't account for any of my actions, why I did what I did. After his snort of derision I seemed to be moving in a dark dream, kind of jumping jerkily from one piece of action to the next, illuminated only by a flashing strobe light. When a thought occurred to me, it was only a piece of a thought, nothing whole or coherent, a mere splinter of light in a fuzzy room. *Downstairs!* I thought when I saw the stairway. So I shoved him toward the stairs.

The lower floor contains several stalls plus a wide corridor for when the cows were let out to pasture. There's no wooden floor, just trampled earth pounded rock-hard under decades of hooves. And unlike the main floor, this area is relatively bright, if cobwebby, and aerated by lots of missing boards. So it's damper, too, and has a vaguely cloying funk to it of steaming hides and old manure and mildew.

"What are we down here for?" Jesse wanted to know.

I shoved him into the corner stall, pushed him toward the wall. He stumbled forward a few steps, then turned to look at me.

For a moment I just smiled at him. He pushed the hair off his forehead. "So?" he finally said. "Now what?"

His bravado had returned, and I didn't like it one bit. I wanted to squelch it again. "Now you find out what it feels like to be shot at," I told him.

I waited for the fear to return to his eyes, but it didn't. His eyes narrowed and his jaw went tight. He even lifted his chin a little and looked down his nose at me. If only he had reacted differently, if only he had let his lip quiver, or if his eyes had shone with tears. If just for a few moments he had acted like a frightened little boy . . .

He didn't, though. He looked like Mark looking at me from across the lobby, the day I walked away from that life. That beautiful face of his with the fuck-you smirk.

Above Jesse and to his left, a board was missing from the rear wall. A beam of pale morning light lay across his shoulder. But then he raised a hand and shoved the wet hair off his forehead, and in doing so, he moved a few inches to the side, and the beam of light lit up the left side of his face. But the other half remained in shadow, so his handsome little face looked asymmetrical and misshapen, and that smirk looked so evil to me, and a sudden dizzy fear shot through me.

"You're not going to do anything," he said. He was so damn sure of himself. Where does such confidence come from? In my entire life, I doubt I ever once felt such confidence. So, of course, I couldn't abide it in a child.

I propped his shotgun against the wall, then leveled the pistol at his chest.

"Yeah," he said. "Like you're going to do it."

I tried to match my sneer to his, but inside I felt on the verge of tears. On the verge of hysterical collapse. But I just couldn't let it happen again. Not again, damn it! I remember thinking those exact words. *Not again, damn it!* As if that little boy was Mark all over again.

I slipped the safety off, just as I had been taught back when I fired a few pellets into a rubber sheet in the back room of that shop in Queens. And I pulled the trigger. The pistol was set on automatic, so a dozen or more pellets thudded into the dry wood just above his shoulder. With the first pop, Jesse cringed and huddled up small and covered his face with his hands. But the volley lasted only a second or two, and when it ended he straightened up and looked at me with furious eyes—black, raging eyes. And, of course, that hard, crooked turn to his lips.

"It's just a BB gun," he said.

"You think it won't hurt if I actually shoot at you? Maybe next time I will."

"No you won't," he said. He startled me by striding forward. He knew me now, knew that the pistol and I were a couple of frauds. And he was such a brave little boy, so fearless. When I think now of all he must have endured in his twelve years to become that way, the painful life he must have lived . . . Even now, even as I write this, I can't stop the tears. I ache for him. I ache and ache and ache and ache.

70

GATESMAN could not catch his breath. He pushed off the swing and stood, closed the journal on his index finger, the finger marking the page, held the book in one hand as he turned and stared at the barn. *I looked in the barn!* he told himself. *I fucking looked!* He lurched forward but then stopped himself, thought, *Wait!* and stood there blowing out his breath, panting as if he had run a couple of miles.

"This can't be true," he said to the barn. "Dear God, please make it not be true."

He felt momentarily as if he might pass out, and leaned one shoulder against a support post, felt the sharp corner bite into his skin. It hurt but he did not move, he needed the pain to keep him alert. He remained in that position for thirty seconds or more, eyes closed as he fought the vertigo and struggled to fill his lungs with air.

Finally he stood upright again, and with watery eyes,

considered the yard, the road, the field of scrub grass. "Goddamn it, Charlotte," he said.

He stood there breathing, trying to do nothing but breathe, trying to hold everything else in check. Finally he was ready to return to the swing. He crossed to it and sat, but even then held the journal closed atop his lap, one hand flat atop the cover.

Most of the crows were silent now. Two still calling to each other. *A couple of slackers,* he thought, though he did not turn to look toward the woods now, he preferred the mountains in the distance, found they helped him catch his breath. No matter how things changed, the mountains were always there. Through everything he had seen and heard and experienced in his life, the mountains never moved. They changed in color, perhaps, looked more rounded in full-leaf than when the limbs were bare, and there were a couple of towers poking out of them now that had not been there five years earlier, but the mountains themselves did not move or diminish, and the road that wound through them was the same road he had driven a hundred times, and though there were more houses along the lakeshore now, a couple more houses every summer, the lake was the same and so was the way the sunlight shimmered on the water, and there was a trout stream deep in the woods that he kept for just himself. It would all be there when he needed it.

He opened the journal again. Ran his finger down the page. And found his place.

71

HE probably intended to simply pick up his shotgun and walk away from me, smirking to himself the whole way home. I know that now. I know that's what he would have done.

But at the moment all this happened, I saw everything through my own self-righteous anger. There was only me and Jesse, standing a few feet apart in a dim and dusty barn, and the rest of the world had gone dark around the edges. I had threatened him, tried to scare him, but he wasn't the least bit afraid or intimidated by me. In the dark shine of his eyes I saw myself as he saw me—a fraud. And I hated him for showing me that.

He came forward and reached for the shotgun and I made a grab for it too. There was no thought behind my action—not then, anyway—though I know now what unthought intention made me go for the shotgun. I would not let it happen again—that look Mark had fired at me across the lobby, that flippant disregard with which he had reduced me to insignificance. I reached for the shotgun low on the barrel this time. Jesse grabbed it near the end of the barrel. He seized it with both hands and yanked hard, pulling it through my hands, through my stupid, clutching, blind, indecent hands.

The boom of the shotgun hit me full in the face. It knocked the breath out of me, and the sudden sight of Jesse blasted into the corner of the stall nearly knocked me unconscious. He had pulled the barrel straight toward his chest and now he lay there in a tiny dark heap in the dark corner of the stall. The air stank of gun smoke, and it burned my nostrils and eyes, and the boom just kept echoing and echoing inside my head. All the strength just went out of me then, and I fell down onto my knees, just dropped down and flopped sideways against the wall and sat there on that cold, sour ground and gasped and gasped and gasped for breath.

I recall how excruciatingly hard it was to drag myself up onto my feet again that morning, up off that shit-permeated floor. I remember the effort it took not to look into the stall as I half-stumbled, half-crawled down that stinking dirt hallway, that cow-run or whatever it is called, to the wide opening at the rear of the barn. The pasture was all weedy and overgrown by then; no cow had grazed or shat or mooed there since long before I moved in.

I made it just outside the door before my body collapsed. Still gasping and wheezing, still struggling to inhale just one fucking lungful of air, I dropped down onto all fours with my face in the grass, and I just kept gasping and moaning for I don't know how long. It was all just too impossible to comprehend. Both my mind and my body were reeling, as if Earth itself was spinning and lurching and bucking through space like a kicked ball. One second, the universe was black and swirling, and then I would have what seemed a lucid thought, the realization that I was only dreaming, and I would lift up my head and see an impossibly bright world, then I would think, *No, you are not dreaming*, and the awful pain would smash through me again, a vicious, hot, smashing swell of pain, and I would bury my face in the grass again and rip out clumps of grass and cram them against my eyes, wanting only to black out my consciousness.

Then, out of this black swirl of disbelief, a thought came to me: I hadn't even checked on Jesse to see if he was alive! Maybe he was still alive!

I jumped up and flew, and I mean I *flew* back to the stall. At the stall door, though, I slammed into the sight of him again and could go no farther. He looked so tiny there in that shadowy corner, a baby of a boy in a man's hunting coat. In the dimness, the front of the coat was black with blood, though there was not as much blood as I expected. I expected to have to wade through the blood to get to him. And I knew then that he was dead and had been dead within a millisecond of the blast. His heart had stopped pumping.

The shotgun was right where we had dropped it, only a few feet from Jesse's boots. I stared at it awhile. I envisioned myself picking it up and standing the butt on the ground, slipping my mouth over the barrel, sliding a hand down the barrel to the trigger housing. In my mind, I saw myself flying backward out of the stall, dead and free before my body hit the ground.

So many times since then I've wished I'd had the courage. As many times as there have been days and nights since then.

What I actually did was turn away and head outside again. At some point I started running, running blindly into the pasture and then toward the far fence, running and falling. I came up against the fence and then ran alongside it for a while, searching for the gate, then gave up and turned around and ran in the other direction. At least I think that's what I did. Maybe that's just one of the nightmares I've had since then. If so, it's the one that seems the most real to me, the most vivid. In any case, it's fair to say that I was in all ways incoherent and had no idea what I was doing or why. Maybe I was hoping to plow into something and bash my brains out. All I know for a fact is that I eventually got my wish and fainted dead away out there in the weeds.

When I came to, the air was warm, and at first I felt better, refreshed, and I lay there in a state of near mindlessness as I watched a beetle climbing up a stalk of weed. It was Queen Anne's lace, I think, but my nose was only three or four inches from the stem, so close that I could see the little hairs on it. And there was a tiny black bug, shaped like a beetle but not much bigger than a tick, climbing up the stalk, weaving its way around the hairs as it climbed. Sometimes it got sort of impaled on one of the hairs, then had to wiggle its way off before climbing again. I had one arm under my head, as if I had simply chosen to lie down and take a nap. And the grass tickling my nose smelled so sweet, so earthy and clean. For a few delicious moments my mind was blank, except for what I took in through my senses.

And then I sat up, I guess, and looked at the sky, and my God, it was eggshell blue and beautiful. A few long, thin clouds stretched out above me like islands on the calmest of seas. And the only sound was that of a single crow somewhere out in the stubbly cornfield. It cawed twice, fell silent for fifteen seconds or so, then cawed again. The air was warm and clean, and I felt light and airy myself. I just lay there listening to the crow and smiling and breathing in that salubrious air.

But then what I had done came rushing back to me, the full and terrible knowledge of it. When that happened, every detail of the day became offensive and ugly, everything I had loved just moments earlier. The scent of grass and air, the stillness, the once-beautiful sound of a caw echoing from the trees. The heaviness in me was crushing, but I wanted to be crushed. I wanted nothing more or less than total obliteration.

I got up finally and dragged back through the field and into the barn and looked at him. It is impossible to describe how I felt at that moment. But I now understand what compels a father or mother who witnesses their child's death to immediately take his or her own life. The pain is just too great. It permeates every thought and feeling, it poisons and leadens every breath. I again contemplated picking up Jesse's shotgun and propping it against my chin. My head felt ready to explode anyway, so why not?

I don't know why not. I don't know why I did what I did. And I don't excuse my reasoning, if such fragmented, convoluted thought can be called reasoning. But I convinced myself that I would be blamed for what had happened—blamed and punished for what was in fact an accident. I was an outsider in this place, I didn't fit in, and nobody was likely to show an ounce of compassion for me. If this horror were discovered, I would be made to repeat over and over how I had forced Jesse into that stall. The police would dig copper pellets out of the dry wood. First I had frightened the little boy, then tortured him with the pellet gun, then finally I had shot him with his own gun. This would be the accepted truth, and I knew it with absolute certainty. There would be no more lemon sunshine on a meadow for me. No more covered bridges or Amish buggies. No more shows at Margo's gallery or dinners in the city with June, no more browsing the book tables in Washington Square, no more mugs of tea or work at the easel in the dewy mornings. No more crows calling from the woods. This life I had made for myself, this life I had fought for, tooth and claw, would be over. Because of an accident. A stupid stupid stupid stupid stupid stupid accident.

Breaking into that dirt floor with its compacted layers of old manure and straw was like digging into concrete. I'm sure there were more efficient tools for the job upstairs in the barn, but those were Mike's tools, so I went for my garden tools instead, tools I knew as old friends, tools that fit my hands. I managed to break through the hardened dirt with my garden weevil, a tool like a corkscrew on a long metal shaft. It works very well at twisting dandelion clumps out of soft sod, but the tines strained hard against the earthen floor of the stall. I used the long-handled spade for scraping and scooping dirt out of the widening hole. I worked breathlessly, frantically, as insentient as a beast.

By the time I finished, every muscle and bone in my body was burning. My shoulders felt as if they had been beaten with a board. Two blisters had sprouted on my hands, and I had worked them bloody. The ground, after I lay Jesse and the two guns in it and covered everything with dirt, had a noticeable rise to it, so I carried the extra dirt out to my garden a shovelful at a time, flung it and scattered it, then worked it all into the topsoil. I hated myself every step of the way, loathed what I was doing. But I kept telling myself, *You have to do this, Charlotte. You've no choice but to do this.*

Afterward I pried two boards off the stall wall, the ones with copper pellets embedded in them. These were all from my air pistol. Jesse had taken the shotgun blast full in his chest. There was no exit wound, maybe because of the heaviness of his hunting coat, or just the nature of shotgun pellets, I don't know. There was almost no blood on the ground—anyway, none that I could discern in the adumbrated light.

My actions, when I look back on them now, appear so calculating and cold. But they were not. I was capable of seizing on to only one thought at a time, of pulling a thought out of a black swirl of panic and acting upon it. *Bury him*—that's as complex as my thinking was at the moment. My body was in overdrive but my mind was barely even conscious. Because all the while I ached with an ache of unfathomable regret, a scalding, red throb of shame and terror and recrimination.

When the hole was covered and smoothed out and, to my eyes, the stall looked in no way odd, would call no attention to itself, I carried the boards outside to the fifty-gallon metal drum I burn my trash in. Then I went back inside the house and removed every stitch of clothing I had on and crammed it all into a plastic garbage bag. I put on an old house dress, and, using one of those sawdust bricks I use to start fires in the fireplace, I set the boards and my bagful of clothes ablaze in the trash barrel. I stood there for several minutes, alternately peering anxiously toward the road (nobody slowed down or showed any interest in me) and watching the fire eat up the evidence of my guilt.

Afterward I went inside and scrubbed myself raw in the shower. I worked quickly, knowing I had to get through this before I let myself fall apart. I then put on jeans and a pullover shirt and took the old house dress outside and tossed it onto the embers too. Then I went inside again and sat by the window and watched the road and waited for it to come alive with police cars.

72

GATESMAN stood up then and, carrying the journal, made his way to his vehicle. He opened the door, reached inside for his flashlight. The long, thick-handled light felt especially heavy in his left hand, the journal in his right hand peculiarly light. What felt heaviest were his footsteps, his breath, the slope and drag of his shoulders. To keep himself from becoming short of breath, more exhausted by his thoughts than the much-less-demanding exertion of walking, he turned his mind elsewhere. *On a morning like this,* he thought, *Deer Creek will be clear and fast. The trout will glitter in the sunlight.* In his mind's eye he could see a fat one moving in on the fly as he twitched it through the water, the trout's rainbow scales glittering red and orange as it swam.

He crossed close behind the barn then, came to the corner of the fenced-in pasture. He unlatched the gate and stood for a moment, considering the weeds. Even now there was a vague hint of a sinuous path. *You thought it was made by some animal,* he told himself, and shook his head, stood still for half a minute, then turned and continued on.

In the barn he switched on his flashlight and aimed the powerful beam into the corner stall. In the center of the stall was the same stack of twelve bags of fertilizer he had glanced at a month earlier, four courses of three bags each, crosshatched atop one another, the top bag split open, its contents spilled onto the floor—everything exactly as he remembered it. But now he had to wonder why Charlotte failed to mention the bags in her journal entry. Not a single mention of them.

He pictured the little boy crowded up against the wall, the too-large hunting jacket, the boy's face split by shadow and light. It was then he noticed the missing boards. He moved into the corner of the stall, played the light over them. *Yes, there, right along the edges. This wood hasn't been exposed to the weather as long. Lighter in color. This is where she pulled off the boards. Why didn't I see that before?*

Because you were looking for the boy, that's all, he reminded himself. *That's all you were looking for then.*

Still . . . he thought, and regretted the oversight. *Not that it would have changed anything,* he told himself. *But still . . .*

Next, he played his light around the bottom of the bags. *Twelve bags at forty pounds each,* he thought. *Four hundred and eighty pounds.* The thought took the last of his strength away, sucked him dry.

He went back out to the pasture as quickly as he could, stood for a while leaning against the top rail. He could hear the intermittent squawks of crows squabbling in the trees. Normally they would be out scavenging at this time of day. Either rain was on its way or else they had found a meal out there in the woods.

This realization made Gatesman think of an old riddle: If a tree falls in the woods, does it make a sound?

And he answered it, *Yes.* At the very least, other trees hear it. The animals hear it. The bugs and ants and snakes hear it. The woods, he knew, all woods and other secluded places, hear accidents daily, accidents no human eye ever sees, no human ear ever hears. Squirrels fall off branches and break their necks. Birds collide in midair and tumble to the ground. A running doe can step into a chipmunk hole, break a leg, then lie on the ground for days and days before it dies. And before long, all traces of that deer will be gone. The crows and vultures and other animals clean up the meat, then bacteria cleans up the hide and bones. The teeth are the last thing to go. Eventually they get scattered too, little seeds that never sprout. In this way the forest cleans itself, as does the desert, the ocean, all the natural places.

Nature does its job, he told himself. *Now you do yours.* When he thought he was ready to return to the journal, but still in no condition to return to the house, he sat against a fence post with his face to the sun. The light glared off the parchment and stung his eyes as he read.

73

With every passing minute I grew more apprehensive. I don't think it's an exaggeration to say that I was literally out of my mind with fear. I kept trying to think logically, but what an irrational mind sees as logical is just the opposite. All I knew was that the police would have to show up here sooner or later, and before they did, I had better cover my tracks.

I got the push broom from the basement and took it out to the barn and swept the entire plank floor clean of any trace of my footsteps. But then the floor looked too clean, suspiciously clean. So I climbed up into the hayloft, yanked a couple handfuls of hay out of a bale, and sprinkled it down onto the floor, tossing it out in all directions. Then I had to get back out the front door without leaving any footprints in the new dust, so I literally tiptoed along the wall until I was outside again.

Then I took the broom down to the stall and swept the stall, not neatly this time, but as messily as I could, just trying to cover up the shovel marks. But this time, a rise in the center of the floor was noticeable to me. I knew I had to do more.

I chose the Walmart in Lewistown for two reasons. First, I had never shopped at that one, only the closer one in Carlisle. So I was less likely to be recognized there. Second, Walmart keeps their gardening supplies outside, so I had a smaller possibility there than at my favorite nursery of being noticed when I loaded up the Jeep.

Along the way I passed a dead deer along the side of the road, and the sight of it gave me another idea. I felt sure that the police would use dogs when they conducted a search, probably the kind that can detect cadavers. But could the dog distinguish between species? I pulled over to the shoulder and thought about trying to load that deer into the Jeep but then realized that it didn't make any sense. Why would a deer jump the pasture fence, go into a stall and lie down and die?

So something smaller maybe. But what kind of animal? Of course I thought of the raccoons then, the ones who raided my garbage every month. So I got back on the road but kept my eyes open for the right piece of roadkill.

I wasn't even sure what the opossum was when I spotted it. It was white and mangled, and that long, ratlike tail, that ugly snout—just the sight of it made me sick to my stomach. But I was already thoroughly sick to my stomach with even worse, more indelible images in my head. So I pulled over just behind the flattened opossum, and when the road was clear in both directions, I jumped out. The only thing I had in the Jeep to pick the animal up with were the baby wipes I keep in the glove box, so, with one in each hand, I grabbed the thing by its tail and one paw and dumped it on the floor mat on the passenger side. I gagged the whole way to Walmart.

There were three registers in the garden supply area. One was tended by a young man with a wispy beard, maybe midtwenties but no older. But he looked too bright-eyed and sharp, I could see his intelligence even from twenty feet away, where I was pretending to appraise the display of solar patio lights. Then there was a sullen, emaciated teenage girl who was more interested in her conversation with the adjacent cashier, a weary-looking woman old enough to be the girl's grandmother, than in her customers, whom she rang up without even looking at them. Most of the time she kept stealing glances at the young man.

I waited until her line was empty, then hurried to fill it. "I need ten bags of that fertilizer mix outside," I told her. "No, make it a dozen. Twelve bags."

She reached for the laminated card with a lot of bar codes on it. "The Miracle-Gro?"

"No, the Earthscape, I think it's called."

"Twenty- or forty-pound bags?"

"Forty."

She ran the bar code over the scanner but still didn't lift her eyes to me. "Twelve, you said?"

"Yes. Please."

I paid with cash. The only time she met my eyes was when she handed me the receipt. "I'll ring for somebody to load them for you. You have a truck, right?"

"Right," I said. "But I don't need any help, thanks."

Her gaze had already wandered back to the young man. "Just show the receipt if anybody asks."

Nobody asked. I heaved all twelve bags into the back of my Jeep, then slammed down the tailgate. And that's when it hit me. The clarity. The full, sudden acknowledgment of what I was doing and why I was doing it. I swear to God, it hit me like a searing, blinding blast of heat. As if the sun had exploded right before my eyes. I couldn't breathe. I couldn't see anything but a throbbing brightness. I stood there gasping and half collapsed against the tailgate. The brightness was inside my head as well as outside and all around me, and I thought to myself that maybe this is what a stroke feels like, maybe this is what Daddy feels every time he has one of those little explosions in his brain. And I *hoped* that I was having a stroke. I hoped that it would kill me right then and there. Because I understood with a sudden damning clarity that now my life was forever changed. That nothing I could do could ever change what I had done.

Eventually I climbed back into the Jeep and drove home. That dead opossum on the floor stank to high heaven. The stink stuck in my nose and throat, so I kept the window down in case I vomited. The only way I could hold down the nausea was to stare at that mangled little body with all the hatred I could summon and think, *That's you there, Charlotte. That's you from this day on.*

74

OKAY, I'm back. Sometimes I have to take a break from this, have to go crawl into a corner and sob my eyes out. But I'm trying to get this written as quickly as possible. I need to.

So back to that day, that endless, excruciating day. I pulled the Jeep down around to the pasture but not into the pasture. I knew that I would leave tracks if I went off the lane that Mike's tractor and wagon had worn through the grass. So I had to haul those bags one at a time into the stall. But first I laid down the opossum. Then stacked the bags on top. But then it all looked too neat and new. So I ripped open the top bag and spilled some of the fertilizer around.

What more can you do? I kept asking myself. *What more can you do?* Nobody who has never experienced this kind of senseless panic can understand what it is like. I felt like I was overdosing on speed, like my head and my heart and my lungs were literally going to explode at any second. I wanted to scream and scream and scream and scream. I still want to. I guess, though, that what I'm doing now is a kind of scream. I do feel a lessening of pressure the more I write. But I am not doing this for me. In fact, this is the first time all month, and probably well before that, that I am doing something not for myself.

So I burned the floor mat and sprayed air freshener through the Jeep. Went back inside and waited for the shit storm to hit.

In the afternoon I heard the rumbling of Mike Verner's old red Farmall. I hadn't looked outside in a couple of hours by then, so I was surprised to see that the sky had darkened off to the west and that a massive dark cloud was slowly moving in. Then I just stood by the window in my numbed state of shock and watched Dylan spreading lime over the cornfield. I wondered if he had gotten that tattoo yet, and, if so, if he had tried yet to scratch it off.

After a while, and I really have no idea how long, Dylan brought the tractor to a halt. He wasn't far from where Jesse and I had exited the woods that morning, so when Dylan hopped down off his seat, my heart seized. I felt another panic attack coming on. I kept thinking, *Get back on your tractor, get back on your tractor.*

But Dylan reached in behind the tractor's seat and pulled something out. At first I couldn't see what it was, but then I saw that it was white. A roll of toilet paper. He glanced back toward the house, just a quick look over his shoulder. I ducked away from the window for a few seconds, and when I peeked out again, he was nowhere to be seen.

I sat breathless at the corner of the window, and Jesus, how my chest ached. I can feel it again right now, that crushing, airless fear. I felt like I was holding my breath the whole time he was in the woods. But it wasn't long before he came trotting back out, shoved the toilet paper behind the seat again, climbed up, yanked at a couple of levers, and the tractor rolled forward once more.

The surge of relief that hit me when he went back to spreading lime, how strange that seems to me now. But no stranger than the fact that a minute or two later, the relief turned into uncontrollable, convulsive sobbing again. I just wanted to give up, that's how I remember it. I just wanted to pass out and never wake up.

I slid down to the floor, curled up into a tight little ball. My body felt so sore and beaten, and I kept sobbing because I didn't know how to quit, didn't know how to sob myself back to something better. Eventually I must have sobbed myself to sleep.

When I woke up, Dylan and the tractor were gone and the massive cloud was so close that I could see the charcoal squall lines reaching down to the ground. Plus the wind had picked up and there was a chill in the air. Most chilling of all, though, was the fear that maybe Dylan had noticed something out there in the woods, something that meant nothing to him at the time, but later when the police questioned everybody would take on new meaning. Had either Jesse or I left something out there? Had I dropped anything? Had Jesse? At that moment, in the state I was in, everything was significant, everything was incriminating. So I hurried back outside, coatless this time, and into the woods.

The only thing I could find was the little pile Dylan had left behind and the dirty wad of toilet paper. Did it matter? I wondered. *Think, Charlotte, think! Should it be there or not?*

I couldn't think straight, obviously. So I just scooped it all up in my hands, kicked some leaves over where it had been, and ran back home. I dropped it in my garden plot, then thought twice about burying the toilet paper. Picked it out, carried it inside and flushed three times. Then I raced back outside and with my hands mixed Dylan's scat in with the soil. I was too exhausted, too numb, too fucking delirious to even wash my hands right away. Because I stood there in the yard staring across the field at the woods, and there were my footprints in the lime. One set going into the woods, another set coming back. I stood there utterly breathless. *I can't do it,* I thought. *I can't erase all those footprints.*

It was done, it was over, I was going to be caught. And the only thing I felt was relief. And with that relief, a little of my strength returned. Enough that I was able to go back inside, take a shower, and get myself ready.

I was seated at the vanity, brushing my hair, when the rain hit the windows. I looked out and could see nothing but the wall of rain slanting hard toward the house.

An hour or so later, the rain stopped. The black cloud was grinding its way to the east, leaving only a filmy layer of gray for the sun to shine through. I went back upstairs to the window and looked out at the field. Nearly all of the lime, and my footprints with it, had been washed into earth.

Strangely, this time I felt no relief. Because nothing was over. In fact, that was the only thought I was capable of for the rest of the afternoon and evening, the one that kept playing on a loop in my brain until I finally silenced it with wine and pills, *It's not over, it's not over, it's not over, it's not over . . .*

75

AND you know the rest, Marcus. Most of it, anyway. You showed up the next morning. I told you I'd had a migraine, which was only partially true. Everything I told you from that day on was only partially true. I am very, very sorry.

It's taken me most of two days to write this, and now the rest is up to you. I don't know anybody else who has the shoulders for this kind of work. Only you. I'm sorry for this as well.

One last bit of information: I talked to Dylan's father this past Friday, the same day I mailed my note to you. I drove out to the house to ask if they had had any news from the boy. He looked so old, Marcus, though he is younger than me, I think. But there was a slackness to his posture, dark moons beneath his eyes. His complexion was pale, face drawn, none of that hard, muscled, sinewy look I imagine he sported just a few months ago. He was doing something in his garage when I pulled into the driveway, turned and saw me behind the windshield, then eventually came up to my door. I could feel his exhaustion.

"I'm Charlotte Dunleavy?" I told him. "I live out on the old Simmons' place?"

He blinked. Gave me a little nod.

"I was just wondering . . . I mean I think about Dylan all the time."

He blinked again, though this one looked more like a wince.

"I used to talk to him sometimes when he was out in the field for Mike Verner. Sometimes he'd stop by the house for a glass of lemonade."

Something sparked in his eyes then. I thought surely he must remember me from the night I had visited Dylan in the hospital; surely he would say something now, accuse me, whip me bloody with his words. Maybe that was what I wanted. But all he said was, "Is that right?"

"Sometimes he'd just get a drink from my garden hose. On really hot days he used to wash himself down with it."

I have no idea where this fiction came from. But even as I spewed it out, I could see Dylan drenching himself, could see him gasping when the first gush of cold water hit his shoulders and back. I could see that broad big-toothed grin. I could see the spray from the hose making a rainbow in the air.

His father smiled. "I think he might have mentioned you to his mother and me."

"We had some pleasant conversations," I told him. "About his music. His girlfriend. And I was just wondering. How is Dylan doing these days? Do you know . . . I mean . . . Where is he living now? Is he still playing music?"

Maybe fifteen seconds passed. "Last time we heard anything was a couple days after he left here."

It was what I expected, what I already knew in my heart. I asked, "Was he in Tennessee by any chance? He always used to talk about going to Muscle Shoals to become a musician."

"He didn't talk long. Said he was using a friend's phone. We called the number back, but it just kept ringing. A week later there was a recording said the line had been disconnected."

"Did he say where he was?"

"Missouri," he said.

"Branson?"

He shook his head. "It wasn't the right area code for Missouri. I looked it up."

"He might have been using a cell phone."

"His mother said he sounded like he'd been drinking or something. He hung up before I got a chance to talk to him."

I have sent a letter to Margo, the woman who sells my paintings in Manhattan, instructing her to send to you all profits from the sale of the paintings still in her gallery—and by the time you read this, my paintings will have more than tripled in value! Please distribute the money equally between Livvie and Dylan's parents. I hope that Dylan's mother and father will use the money to track him down, hire a good investigator, get the boy home again. I hope they can salvage his life better than I was able to.

In my studio you will find a new painting on the easel. This goes to Livvie. When you see it, you will know why. Tell Livvie that I painted Jesse as I see him now, not those other times but now, with my eyes wide open.

The Jeep is hers too. The house and everything in it. The necessary papers are all in the safe in my closet. The door to the safe is open. Maybe she won't want any of these things after you tell her what I did. Maybe she couldn't stand to live here. In that case, she can sell everything and keep the money, I don't care.

Or maybe you don't have to tell her, Marcus. I don't know what's best. I'm leaving all that to you. You are my clean-up man.

As for this journal, you decide. If you think Livvie should have it, give it to her. I trust to your expertise and your compassion. If you want to give it to the newspaper, show it to the world, so be it. I do not care. My reputation, my work, it is all behind me now. Now there is only the something else. The next something else.

There's a word I would like you to look up, if you will. It's important, Marcus, so please, after you've finished reading this journal, please do this before you do anything else. I need for you to know this word. *Jhator*.

I went back into the woods this morning, Marcus, just to see how it might feel. And you know what? It felt fine. So I will be returning there this evening, in the hour of magic light. I think that if anybody can understand why I have made this choice, you can. You cared about me when no one else did, not even myself, and that has meant so very much. Please forgive all I have done. And please understand why I must go now. There are no answers here, but I have to believe that there are answers to be found. And I am anxious to discover them. I love you and I love Livvie, but I love Jesse more. And the boy who shoots crows is waiting.

76

THERE were more pages in the journal but no more writing. Gatesman sat there turning page after empty page until he had turned the final one.

He closed the back cover and sat there awhile. Then he used his cell phone to call his office. He spelled *jhator* for Tina and asked her to call back as soon as she had found a good definition. She pretended to be irritated with him, said, "Do you think that's all I have to do? Help you improve your very limited vocabulary?" And he knew that she would make him wait fifteen, maybe twenty minutes or more, only because he had refused to tell her why he wanted the information, refused to satisfy her curiosity. This made him smile. And the sound of her voice brought him back to his own world again, back to where he needed to be in order to get his work done.

During the past hour he had been aware in a distant way of the few cars passing out on the asphalt, those lives in hurried movement, those purposeful lives. His own car had surely been noticed parked there in Charlotte's driveway. *What's the sheriff doing out here this morning?* people must have wondered.

He went to his vehicle then and popped open the trunk, zipped open a black canvas duffle bag in which he always kept a change of clothes—khaki trousers and a navy blue sweatshirt with a white Nittany Lions logo across the chest. He lifted the clothes out, laid the journal inside, laid the clothes on top, and zipped the bag shut. He closed the trunk lid. Then he stood there in the driveway and tried to slow his breath. The air was clean and light, but his limbs still felt heavy. Maybe one matter had been resolved, but there was still work to be done. There was still, as always, unpleasant duty to attend to.

He had some calls to make, but he would wait for Tina's call first. Charlotte had asked him to wait. And he was in no hurry now.

The air was so clear and the sunlight so sharp that it stung his eyes. He thought the scent of the air unusually light and clean, in a way it can be only in spring—not the sad, still cleanness of autumn nor the sharp, stinging cleanness of winter; not the heavier, clean quiet before a summer thunderstorm, but the almost-cool, trembling cleanness of fields and trees greening, and he felt this cleanness deep in his chest, an ache that felt as deep as the sky.

"Jhator," he repeated to himself, and wondered what it meant, though he had his suspicions. He turned to face the woods then. From where he stood, it all looked so quiet.